SUZANNAH ROWNTREE

Dark Clouds

Miss Dark's Apparitions, Volume II.

To my $25 Kmart "mum" jeans -
No man could ever hold me like you do.

Chapter I.

It is a truth insufficiently acknowledged that even beautiful, delicately nurtured, lofty-principled young ladies must eat *somehow*.

I myself am an excellent example of this. Here am I, Molly Dark (of the Saltoun Road, Brixton Darks), with a mother and three younger sisters to support on the slender means afforded by my own employment as a governess. This is due to my father—whose ghost continues to haunt me every evening at sunset with a punctuality which, had he shown it at all during his lifetime, might have saved me all this trouble—having gone away and ruined us somehow in Hong Kong; so that it is a mercy, as Sir Humphrey Seton often reminds us, that he impoverished only his family, and not also his friends.

Here I am, I say, caught in this predicament and wholly incapable of supporting my sisters in the manner to which they ought to become accustomed. Really, I don't think it *entirely* my own fault that I sought to remedy the situation in the ways I have. Nor have I done anyone a bit of harm.

It's true that I don't *really* connect people with the spirits of their departed dead. When people die, their spirits tend to move on fairly quickly to a different—and, one hopes, a better—world. Most of the ghosts I have seen are what I refer to as imprints—little more than memories going silently through the habitual motions of life. My own belief is that these apparitions persist largely because the people—or sometimes places, or things—left behind have not been able to give them up. In short: when I have held séances, they were intended to lay not so much the dead, as the living, to rest.

Then, of course, there was that other business—what my accomplice, Miss Nijam, referred to with her customary brevity as *the melusine job.* Yes, I suppose one *could* say that the two of us insinuated ourselves into the house of the last Bourbon queen, claiming that I was the lost heiress to the French throne. I am afraid that was not strictly truthful of us. Even so, I flatter myself I came out of that business creditably; for despite our first, imperfectly honest intentions, Nijam and I solved the mystery of the princess' disappearance and installed her husband in his rightful inheritance.

All of which is to say that there's a right and a wrong way to do anything. Take marriage, for instance. I have always known that I must marry money, and the more there is of it the better I shall like it. The world uses such hard words for people like me! I shudder to be thought an *adventuress,* or a *fortune-hunter,* or even *that sly minx Molly Dark, who has got Sir So-and-So into her clutches*—and yet a young lady must eat, and so must her ailing mother, and so must her three gifted young sisters.

So I shall marry money. But I shall make the money so happy it will never know the difference. The money may dictate; I shall yield. The money may come home at the end of some long, hard day in the arena of masculine endeavour, and I shall fetch the money its slippers, and kiss it, and caress it, and tell it with melting looks how much more splendid a sum it is than

2

any other. I shall handle the money so wisely that it will never for a moment regret the moment of weakness in which it was induced to make me an offer. I do not know, of course, if I shall be able to *love* the money, or whether it may someday be inattentive or inclined to stray. But every good thing comes at a price; and no price is too high, if it may shield me and mine from the workhouse or the gutter. I have always hoped for love, of course; but at the very least I shall be able to find it in my children.

This was, in any case, the plan. But how, I asked myself that sunny spring morning, as the Orient Express left Budapest by the bridge over the Danube and gathered steam for the next leg of its journey towards Vienna—*how* was I to arrange the matter? It was true that my financial straits were at present not as pressing as they once had been. Franz Haber—the commoner who had espoused the Bourbon princess, Marie-Caroline, and inherited her fortune—had proposed a scheme by which I and a disreputable gang of confederates were to resolve the injustices committed by people so rich and monstrous, they were able to silence all witnesses but the wronged dead. Criminal investigations are not commonly left to languish without some eminent person wishing to suppress them; and thus we were obliged to operate outside the law. However, a recent expedition to Jerusalem, from which we were at present returning, had left me in a state of some doubt about this venture. How *were* we to know that moving that old ladder would so nearly start a war? The success of the enterprise, I thought, was unlikely. A more permanent income was desirable; I must fall back upon my first plans.

Yet I was no longer as young as I once had been, and my matrimonial prospects practically nil. As a governess, a succession of watchful employers had kept me firmly out of the way of moneyed young men; while as an imposter in the noble Schloss Frohsdorf that winter, the gentleman with whom I had been on the terms of greatest intimacy had been Vasily Nikolaevich Romanov—a disgraced Russian grand duke, a practiced *roué,* and an imposter in his own right. Even had he been in the possession of his lost fortune, rather than a wanted fugitive, there was surely no proposal he could make to which a plain gentleman's daughter, or a woman of sound principles, could listen. I except, of course, the proposal he *had* made to me, whereby I should marry him under an assumed identity, as the melusine Princess Marie-Caroline. But that would have been preposterous. I did not intend to spend the rest of my life impersonating a melusine, in the knowledge that should my masquerade be discovered, certain death was the least horrifying of the fates that awaited me.

Around us, the green plains of Hungary stretched out to a horizon faintly edged with distant mountains. I sighed and closed the book on my lap—I was scarcely one volume into *Can You Forgive Her?* and unlikely to make greater progress today. Beside me, one of the disreputable confederates I have mentioned—Mimi Laine, whose gifts as a ballet-dancer were almost entirely eclipsed by those of a circus-acrobat and cat-burglar—shifted beneath the voluminous coat that covered her dainty figure, murmured "You kiss him, *I'll* go through his pockets," and drifted back to sleep.

I beg to assure the gentle reader that she was certainly not speaking to *me.*

The silence was short-lived. Presently an imperious knock sounded on the door and Mimi sat up with what I can only describe as a snort. "What is it, Vasya?" she called.

Mimi's senses were finely-tuned—but then, like so many of the young dancers at the St Petersburg ballet, she had once served as a dainty to the vampire princes of Russia. The bite, she said, made one fleeter, faster, and stronger. It did not, of course, transform one into a vampire; royal blood was required for that.

The door opened, admitting a whiff of pleasant pine scent; and the Grand Duke himself slid into the compartment, casting a shadow over its gleaming dark wooden panels and brocaded seat. His valet-bodyguard and the fourth member of our party, Alphonse Schmidt, was visible keeping watch in the corridor. As so often happened in Vasily's presence, I found myself a little short of breath, as though he had absorbed all light and air into himself. Vasily was not himself a vampire, but he once had been, and his former habits lingered: I had once seen him use his teeth to tear out the throat of an enemy. Now he fixed me with those hypnotic grey-green eyes and said in that velvet-dark voice, "Do me a favour, Miss Dark?"

It should have been impossible to refuse such a plea; but circumstances had conspired to give me iron self-command and a deeply ingrained distrust of handsome reprobates. "That depends," I said primly, "entirely upon the favour in question."

"Someone boarded the train at Bucharest," he informed me. "An American with a black glove on his right hand. He's in the dining-car now. Be a dear and charm him into telling you where he's going, where he's been, and what his business was in Roumania?"

"Another of Vasya's old friends, no doubt," Mimi observed drily. "Don't do it for free, Dark. You're a professional now."

"I should be forever in your debt," Vasily said with persuasive inexactitude.

5

Privately, I thought he had a nerve asking me to act as a sort of intelligencer on his behalf; but curiosity proved too much for me. I, too, had noticed that Vasily had a great number of former acquaintances whose company he was anxious to avoid. If I did as he asked, I might possibly learn something about him; and knowledge, in my precarious situation, was power.

Besides, the thing would break up the monotony of the train journey. Whether at home in the happy old days when my sisters and I used to put on Christmas pantomimes with our friends, or more recently when masquerading as a melusine in the Schloss Frohsdorf, I had always enjoyed the challenge of playing a part. As a gently reared young woman, I had all too few opportunities to do so.

"I'll do it," I conceded, rising from my seat. "You had better come along, Mimi, to make me look respectable."

Mimi stuck out an expectant hand. I looked at Vasily. Sighing, he planted a handful of silver francs within. This transaction concluded, I led the way to the dining-car.

A few passengers were scattered around the car—chatting, sipping coffee and passing the time as they chose. I spotted my quarry at once: a gentleman sitting with his back to me, holding a newspaper open with a black-gloved right hand. "Tea, please," I said to the waiter, before approaching the reading gentleman. Stopping half a step behind him, I sank to my knees with a whisper of white skirts, and then said winningly, "I beg your pardon, sir; is this yours?"

The newspaper sank, the gentleman turned, and a pair of pale blue eyes creased a little at the sight of the clean handkerchief I was offering him. "No, it isn't," he said briefly.

"How strange! I found it just now beneath your chair. Mimi,

6

perhaps *you* can find the owner." My chaperone thus disposed of, I laid a gloved hand on the chair facing the American. "May I? You have an accent I've never heard before," I added, as the silence threatened to lengthen.

This was not strictly true, either. But just as I expected, he proved susceptible to the flattery. Folding the newspaper away and proffering his left, ungloved hand, he said: "Warren H. Vandergriff, of New York."

I kept my countenance at the initial, pressed the hand, and sat. Mr Vandergriff was very typical of his countrymen, I thought: grey, desiccated, and *perfectly smooth,* with a dry white hand and a face that had never known wind, or sun, or beer. He might be anywhere between five and thirty or forty, and I suppose that in his lean and hungry way he was even handsome; although there was something indefinably wrong with his face.

"Mary Dark, of London," I replied. "And what brings you to Europe, Mr Vandergriff?"

He leaned back, taking a sip of coffee through thin, smiling lips. "I'm afraid the real answer will shock you, Miss Dark."

"Oh! Well, *now* you had better tell me, or I shall be imagining any number of dreadful things."

That flattered him. "Well, then: I was buying a Roumanian castle; and it cost me a cool two million of your British pounds."

I *was* shocked, though it is hard to say whether it was by the sum, which was fabulous beyond the dreams of avarice, or by the ill-breeding that led the man to boast of it to a chance acquaintance. "You look like a man who could do anything he sets his mind to," I said, recovering my breath, "so perhaps I ought not to be surprised."

I hoped this was not laying it on too thick.

"Ah! But it's what I'm going to *do* with the castle," he replied. "I'm going to have it dismantled from the gables to the foundation, labelled, packed up with all its furnishings, and shipped to Rhode Island. I want a nice summer home, and I'm determined to have one with a bit of history to it."

This was even worse. What a *ghastly* idea! Mere filthy lucre could never buy a history. I resisted the urge to ask whether he also meant, like the Major-General in Gilbert and Sullivan's operetta, to adopt the deceased ancestors in the family chapel.

"Dear me!" I said. "That seems a great deal of trouble to go to, for an old house that will probably be terribly dark and draughty, and expensive to keep up."

His thin mouth stretched across his teeth in a smile. "Expense means nothing to me. You said I looked like a man who could have anything he wanted—but forgive me. I know the British think it's bad taste to talk about money."

Naturally, I must demur. "I've done without it too often to think so."

"Well, then," he said, taking this as an invitation. "You're used to a society where the division is between the lords and the misters. Except that the lords can survive a close brush with the misters, because in the end the lord will still be a lord, and the mister will still be a mister. In New York, we have no lords. It's all between old money and new money; and the old money misters won't hob-nob with the new money misters, for fear that someone might mistake one of the second for one of the first." He gave a grim smile. "My money may be new, but it's every bit as good as the old—and better. I defy Mrs Astor to afford a Roumanian castle."

"Indeed?" Now that the first shock had passed, I was partly

fascinated, partly repelled, by this man—as any young woman in my place might be. Wealth such as this could not be the meed of hard work and perseverance. It could only be the spoils of conquest and rapacity; and yet, what comfort it might promise! and what security!

"I'm afraid I don't know Mrs Astor," I added, as the waiter brought my tea.

"Lucky you. London society isn't such a bunch of stiffs."

"You're familiar with London, then?"

"I've got a family connection with the city. My aunt is Lady Seton."

I nearly dropped my teacup in surprise. The name was as familiar to me as my own. *Dark & Seton* had been the firm in which my father had been the senior partner—the firm he ruined before he died. And Sir Humphrey, some twenty years previous to *that*, had made headlines by marrying a wealthy young American heiress.

"I say! Is Lady Seton really your aunt?"

"Do you know her?"

"Not terribly well," I confessed. She had spent a great deal of time with her husband in Hong Kong; and in any case, since my father's death, we had fallen rather beneath the notice of the society we had once enjoyed. Invitations had dwindled and, in time, ceased. In a way it had been a mercy. We could no longer afford the clothing, or the conveyance, necessary for participation in the society we had once kept. All the same, Sir Humphrey had always stood ready to assist us in times of pecuniary emergency; it was mainly due to him that I had attended St Alphege's, and become qualified to earn my meagre bread as a governess. "My father was once a business partner of Sir Humphrey's, and he has stood a benefactor to

9

us since."

"Dark," Mr Vandergriff mused. "I remember hearing that name about fifteen years ago. Dreadful business. I'm told the firm nearly went bankrupt. My grandfather had to put up the cash to keep Seton afloat."

I felt a blush of shame warming my cheeks. "Sir Humphrey has been very kind to us."

"Yes, he's been lucky." And he launched into a long and detailed explanation of how Sir Humphrey had rescued the firm—now *Seton & Associates*—and had established himself as one of the most successful import-export men in Hong Kong. "My grandfather," he added, tapping the fingers of his black-gloved hand on the table with a curiously heavy sound, "made his fortune in transcontinental shipping, New York to San Francisco—by rail, you understand. The next step is San Francisco to Hong Kong. And Seton's just the man for the job."

I renewed the sounds of appreciation I had been making for the past fifteen minutes. I need scarcely conceal from the gentle reader with what rapt attention I had been listening to tonnage, poundage, and such sums of money as I had scarcely dared to dream of, even in my gilt bed in the Schloss Frohsdorf.

"So you are going to London," I conjectured, "to put the matter to him?"

"And to see my aunt, before she and Seton return to Hong Kong for good."

"What! altogether?"

"They remained in England only as long as the old baronet was alive. He died nearly a year ago—as I'm sure you know."

"And what then for you? Your family in New York must be missing you."

"Not particularly. My father has the business well in hand. I haven't got a wife. It's time I enjoyed myself before I settle down." He smiled at me, revealing a row of even, white teeth.

He had no wife? I could scarcely believe my luck. Mr Warren H. Vandergriff was by every indication spectacularly wealthy, matrimonially unfettered, and best of all, not entirely beyond my social reach. And to think that barely an hour ago, I had been drooping in my compartment bemoaning my unhappy lot! I ought to show more trust in Providence.

"And how *do* you mean to enjoy yourself?" I asked, concealing my satisfaction.

"By hunting."

He so utterly lacked the reddened, beefy, beery countenance of your fox-hunting squire that I should have found it difficult to believe him, had it not been for a certain grim relish in the way he spoke the words. Quite possibly his idea of hunting consisted of sitting in a tent drinking gin and tonic while the beaters scared up tigers and elephants. "And what will you hunt?"

He leaned forward, his eyes alight with excitement. "The *most* dangerous game: Man."

"Man!" I responded in a whisper, perhaps to outweigh the loud volume of his voice, or to avert the curious glances being sent our way by our fellow-travellers. Where was Mimi? Ah—there she was, seated at the table beyond Mr Vandergriff, watching us with a look of intent concentration. "Aren't there *rules* about that, Mr Vandergriff?"

He smiled and sat back, evidently pleased with the shock he had elicited. "I mean, of course, *criminal* man. I'm what you might call an amateur sleuth, Miss Dark. I match my wits against some cunning brute, and I put him in the dock…and if I'm lucky, a noose."

It was at this moment that a change came over the dining-car. Until now, the place had been populated only by the living, except for a lady who had shared her table with another in black crepe. I felt almost certain that this was the imprint of a departed sister, since I could sense the quiet companionable mood that hung around them.

Now, no doubt summoned by his reminiscences, ghostly imprints congregated around Mr Vandergriff too: a pair of men in overalls and flat caps; a coloured newspaper boy; and even a middle-aged lady in a white dress trimmed with lace, like my own. Their eyes were fixed upon the man who had described them as game, and I was nearly overwhelmed with conflicting emotions. I felt fear, dread, resignation, and—from one of them—a terrible, scalding malevolence so overwhelming that for a moment I was compelled to grip the edge of the table to keep myself from flying at Mr Vandergriff's throat with hooked nails and snapping teeth.

Some cunning brute, he had said; and while I did not think that this described the newspaper boy, it certainly suited at least one of the others.

Mr Vandergriff was still talking; I scarcely heard him. "Miss Laine," I gasped, and the next moment the imprints parted and Mimi was at my side. "Excuse me," I said to my interlocutor, only half aware of what I was saying. "I had better collect my things for the next stop."

"Your stop's Munich, not Vienna," Mimi put in.

Rather officious of her, I thought. Couldn't she see I was nearly suffocating? "I don't feel well," I said faintly. "I beg your pardon, Mr Vandergriff."

He got hastily to his feet and took my hand. Instead of

shaking it as he had done when I first sat down, he stooped gallantly to kiss the air above my glove. Such was my hurry to get away from the man and his shades that I scarcely noticed; but in the Calais coach my head cleared, and I could have cheerfully kicked myself for my folly. Americans did not kiss a lady's hand without meaning something by it. To cap it off, Mimi had quite clearly announced that I would be getting off the train at Munich. How could I follow this tempting bachelor to London *now?*—for, despite the imprints that gathered around Mr Vandergriff, it was plainly my duty to seek a better acquaintance with him.

No sooner did the question present itself, that any number of answers came to mind. I might suddenly be called home; or perhaps my mother, whom I was going to meet, should come down with cholera and beg me not to expose myself to danger.

Really, any excuse would do. Mr Vandergriff had not once asked me about myself. I could tell him almost anything I pleased—why, I could tell him I was fleeing the dishonourable advances of a wicked grand duke; I might beg him for his protection. Reluctantly, for the romance of the thing appealed to me, I discarded this idea. Miss Nijam—if she were here—would lecture me on the importance of simplicity. And she would, of course, be correct. It was one of the really intolerable things about Nijam that she *was* invariably correct.

I tapped on the door of Vasily's compartment, and Mimi followed me into the narrow space. Vasily sat within, absorbed in his newspaper. Alphonse Schmidt stood by the window brushing the Grand Duke's winter coat; in the morning light he resembled nothing so much as a young warrior angel. It was these fair, chiselled good looks, as far as I could tell, which

13

had driven Miss Nijam away from us; and I wondered, not for the first time, whether she was quite right in the head.

"Miss Dark," Vasily cried, rising from his seat, and gesturing me to take it. "What have you learned?"

I tucked myself primly onto the damask cushion. "I really don't know," I said. "Why is Mr Vandergriff of such interest to you?"

Mimi plumped herself down beside me. "Very good," she said approvingly. "Never give something for nothing."

"He *told* me he would owe me a favour," I agreed. I had not forgotten what Vasily had told me himself when he consented to join Franz Haber's crew of larcenous philanthropists: that he considered me his enemy and meant to have his revenge for the way I had cheated him out of the Bourbon fortune. The more favours I accumulated, the better. "But I'm not asking for a favour; it's only that I cannot answer his question until I know more."

Mimi gazed upon me with a whole new respect. *"Konstit on monet, sano mummo kun kissalla pöytää pyyhki!* Well, Vasya?"

Vasily looked confused. *"Whose* grandmother is wiping the table with a cat?"

"It's a saying we have. That there are many ways to achieve a thing." Mimi frowned. "Dark, do not allow this evasion. He is arguing only because he does not like to answer."

Vasily bowed slightly. "I should know better," he said ruefully, "than to try it on *you,* Mimi! My dear Miss Dark, the answer to your question is simple. All the world knows that Vandergriff fancies himself as a detective. You understand how that might pose a difficulty for *me.*"

I opened my eyes very wide. "Indeed, your grace, I don't."

He cleared his throat. "The truth is, as I'm sure I've

14

mentioned before, that I have from time to time taken into my protection a number of unattended diamonds, emeralds, and the like…"

Schmidt looked pained. Mimi, beside me, was laughing. I felt my angelic expression tremble—a weakness which made Vasily throw up his hands.

"You know very well why I'm anxious to avoid Vandergriff's acquaintance, you minx!"

"I beg your pardon," I said, "only you seemed suddenly so very nice about it! What did you want diamonds for, in any case? To bestow on a mistress?"

"His mistress was *me,* and I never saw a single diamond!" Mimi said, aggrieved.

Vasily frowned. "The diamonds were a wedding gift; for a *friend.*"

"If you think we will believe that you are a greater fool than I took you for," Mimi declared. I said nothing. I had disbelieved Vasily once before, when he had claimed to be a grand duke; and I had been wrong. In this moment I did not think he was deceiving us.

"The other takings," Vasily added in the same forbidding tone, "I have been selling one by one, to support myself in the manner appropriate to my station. And now, Miss Dark, your intelligence."

"Well then: Mr Vandergriff told me of his pastime as a detective," I said, unable to repress a shudder at the memory. "But as to why he's aboard this train, he was buying a Roumanian castle, which he means to dismantle stone by stone and send to some American island as his summer house. He is travelling to London."

My intelligence was so negligible (apart from the size of

Mr Vandergriff's fortune) that I almost felt sorry for having used it to extort information from Vasily in return. I was not prepared for the look of relief that crossed his face at the news. Ought I to have squeezed harder? Some fine day when I was least expecting it, Vasily would betray me; and I meant to be ready for it when the day came. Forewarned is forearmed; and the more I knew about Vasily, the better I should be prepared.

"Then Vandergriff is not here for *us*," said Nijam's Alphonse, in a tone of some relief.

"Indeed." Vasily fixed his hypnotic eyes upon me. "Still, let us keep an eye on him. If you learn more about our fellow-traveller on your way to Munich, my dear, telegraph to Schloss Frohsdorf at once."

"Of course." I swallowed. "As a matter of fact, I've decided not to stop at Munich. I'll go to London instead."

Vasily's eyes narrowed. "This is a sudden decision."

I *had* been about to travel to Munich; from there a train would have taken me north to Carlsbad, where my mother was at present undergoing a course of treatment at the sanatorium in the company of old Mrs Haber. I had meant to visit her before returning to Vienna, the Schloss Frohsdorf, and whatever new task Franz Haber might find for us. But really, there was no hurry. Franz had suggested I spend a week or two at Carlsbad; we had gone through a rather harrowing experience in Jerusalem, and he had encouraged us to recruit ourselves at leisure. There was no reason I should not recruit myself in London instead. As for my mother, who was expecting me—why, I should have to telegraph to explain my absence, but I did not feel that I was being an undutiful daughter. Since my father's death, my first duty had always been to leave my family, to go out into the cold world and provide for them.

I knew that if I went to Carlsbad now, I would always be haunted by the spectre of this lost opportunity; that I would find no more peace in the company of this ghost than I did in that of any other.

"It *was* a sudden decision, but my young sisters are living in London virtually alone," I explained. "My mother would prefer I visited them."

This was not strictly the truth, but of course I could not tell him I planned to ensnare and marry a detective. It was not strictly an untruth, either. I felt sure that, put into similar words in the telegraph I was even now mentally composing, the reasoning would appear compelling to Mother as well.

Vasily, however, proved a harder nut to crack. "My dear! I was under the impression that you were very eager to return to the Schloss Frohsdorf. There are matters we should discuss, to prevent any repeat of the unfortunate occurrences at Jerusalem."

"And we *will* discuss them," said I. "All in the fulness of time."

He paid no attention to these sage words. "I do believe this is about the American," he said, in a terrifyingly silky voice. "He's rich and unattached, is he? And now you mean to drop everything and run to London after him?"

For a moment I had no idea what to say. Then I lifted my chin defiantly. "I don't know why you should be so shocked. You say yourself that you are only interested in women for their money."

"In my case it's fair, because women are only interested in *me* for my money. Isn't that right, Mimi?"

"Ha! I don't know what else you would have to offer them."

This took my breath away. "Mimi! What an *extremely*

unkind thing to say."

"But not entirely incorrect," Vasily said, grinning almost savagely.

I was ready to give up trying to improve their manners—an impulse I think every governess will sympathise with, but one which was quickly proving itself hopeless. "There's another excellent reason for going to London," I added, although in truth I had thought of it only at that moment. "I believe Miss Nijam is there, and I think we can all agree that we might have fared better had she been with us at Jerusalem."

Vasily only laughed at me. "Very well, my dear: run to London after Warren Vandergriff, if you must—and marry him, if you can. Had I not been born a man I should attempt to bag him myself."

Schmidt, by the window, had held his customary peace during this conversation; but now his brows were knit in a frown. "Marry whom?" he said now. "Not Vandergriff? Surely you're already married to sir?"

Mimi whooped, and Vasily turned his eyes to the heavens. I choked: "I beg your pardon?"

"You *said*—"

"My poor Schmidt!" Vasily broke in. "Ladies, you had better depart. I have evidently neglected Schmidt's upbringing. It's a judgement on my wicked life, that I should be obliged to explain such things in such detail to such an innocent. You see, my dear fellow, it's like this: when a man and a woman wish very much to cheat a third party out of an inheritance…"

The door closed, and Mimi and I were alone in the corridor.

"Has Schmidt always been like that, I wonder?" said I to Mimi. "Me married to Vasily! The thought!"

"*I* think that if you and Vasily don't want to be mistaken for an old married couple," Mimi said, with much too satisfied an expression, "then you had better stop acting like one."

And with that manifestly unjust observation, she vanished within our own compartment.

Chapter II.

Mature consideration convinced me that at that first meeting, I had not done too badly in rushing from Mr Vandergriff's presence. I wished to fascinate, but not to cloy. From then on I arranged matters in such a way that I did not see the American gentleman at all until three days later in London, when the Dover train was panting into Victoria Station. When Mr Vandergriff emerged from his compartment, he was startled to collide with a familiar-looking young woman, who uttered a genteel exclamation and dropped her book and ticket.

"Mr Vandergriff, I *do* beg your pardon—I wasn't looking where I was going," I cried. "I do hope you aren't hurt."

Having knelt to retrieve my things, he returned them with a smile. "Miss Dark, wasn't it? This is a surprise."

I searched his pale eyes for any hint of raillery—such as I would certainly have found in those of the wicked Grand Duke—but there was none. I cast my eyes down and pretended to be very busy brushing a speck from his arm with my gloved fingers. "Oh, well! I was coming to London to see my sisters; I didn't want you to think I was *pursuing* you."

"I wouldn't think such hard things of any girl."

"But I'm sure a lot of them must consider it," I said, casting an audacious glance up at him from beneath my lashes.

"Is that so?" he observed wryly, almost to himself. No doubt he thought me quite transparent. I intended him to. Much good it would do me, if he failed to grasp the nature of my interest in him.

He did not speak again until he had assisted me to alight from the train and ordered his valet to carry my carpet-bag beneath the great grey arches to the busy street beyond. "Is this all your luggage? May I call you a cab?—and since we are both in London, I hope to have the honour of calling upon you."

Victory was mine! I suppressed my triumph: having once shown my hand, I would now play a little nearer the chest. "Nothing would give me greater pleasure. But I'm not sure that would be proper, Mr Vandergriff."

"My friends call me Griff. I promise I'll be good—whatever that means in London."

"And mine call me Molly," I said, showing my dimples. "But I'm afraid it's not a matter of your behaviour. You see, my mother is at present from home undergoing a cure, and I am obliged to chaperone my sisters. I'm afraid it would be out of the question for me to host callers of my own."

He frowned. "Then I'm not to see you again?"

"I didn't say *that,*" I said archly. Just then a cab answered his hail from amidst the busy traffic in Terminus Place, and I stepped into the brougham and made certain that he heard me give the address—Number 45, Saltoun Road, Brixton.

I sat back, trying to think what it was about the American's bland features that was so unsettling. They were not at all ir-regular or deformed; only there was something slightly wrong with them. Just before Westminster Bridge, recollecting that I did not in fact mean to go home at once, I rapped on the roof of the cab and gave the driver an address in Bloomsbury. This proved to be a grimy tenement full of stale food smells, tired university students and the ghastly imprint of somebody who had hanged himself on the stairs not so very long ago. I wanted to see Nijam, but I had all that weary journey for nothing, because she was not at home. I slid my card beneath the door of the microscopic flat from which she had most recently written to me; and then I went gratefully out into the fresh air and set out for home, going down Gower Street past the British Museum. Little did I think—but no. I must not anticipate my story.

* * *

I arrived home to find two pale faces staring intently into the street from the grimy window-panes of the downstairs bow window. As I alighted from the cab, two hands waved energetically; I heard the thump of running footsteps, and a muffled cry of "Katie! Katie! It's Molly at last!" Evidently, the telegraph I had sent from Calais had been received.

I suppose I should give a description of the house at Saltoun Road: but indeed it hardly seems worthwhile. Imagine a long tunnel-like row of semi-detached houses, each one built of a peculiarly anaemic and colourless brick, each one being outfitted with a small area; upstairs and downstairs bow windows bracketed with white Corinthian pillars; and a doorway outfitted with more of the same, the pediment being ornamented with acanthus leaves and the stern, noble, mass-produced plaster face of a pagan god. Ours was one of these, indistinguishable from the rest except for the spectacles which my sister Emily had pencilled in protest upon the face of the

22

assembly-line god; and even this touch of festivity had been rendered dull and smudged by the rain.

To me the house had only two virtues: first, it housed the people I loved best in the world; and second, it was so new that no one had yet died there, and as a result there were no imprints attached to the place.

The door burst open as I approached, and my sisters threw themselves on my neck, smothered me with kisses, and bombarded me with questions—how had I been? and what was Austria like? and how was Mummy? and had I had supper?—as they drew me through the narrow, dingy hallway into the kitchen, which was the only room in the house where a lamp was lit.

Old Hannah, who in better days had been our housekeeper and still claimed the title, held up her hands with exclamations and tottered to the cupboard for the remnant of a loaf of bread. It had been a good four years since I had been home, and when I saw how old and frail our housekeeper had become—we were all the family she had, and could not possibly have sent her away—I was glad that I had chosen to come home, if only to satisfy myself that my scapegrace sisters were not running wild in Mother's absence.

"Stop it, twins, you'll talk her to death!" Katie ordered, pushing her papers into a stack and shutting them between the leaves of a big folio of Shakespeare which she had scattered, together with pens and ink, over the kitchen table. My middle sister, although she had never been very strong, was beginning to make a name for herself as a poet: she had had several poems published in *Blackwood's* and other magazines, and there was talk of having her produce a volume.

She was thinner and paler than she used to be; I wondered

uneasily whether she, too, ought to be sent to Carlsbad for the good of her health.

"Sit down, Molly, and we'll get you some dinner," Katie added. "You don't mind eating in the kitchen, do you? We don't eat in the dining-room any more, except on special occasions."

"And we haven't had one of *those* in ages," said Emily.

"Except for birthdays," Lilias reminded her. "You *will* be here for our birthday, won't you, Molly?"

Emily and Lilias, who were fraternal twins, were the youngest. In four years they had grown nearly as tall as myself, although they were thin and gangling as colts. How odd it was to see them with their hair pinned up and their skirts let down! They had quite become young ladies.

"I should very much like to be," I said, recalling in amazement that the anniversary would occur within the fortnight. "How old will you be, again? Sixteen?"

"Seventeen! Molly, how could you forget?" Lilias said reproachfully. "I always said I wouldn't start writing down the chronicles of Selidore until I was sixteen, and I began *that* a year ago." She was the family novelist, and had been telling the tales of Selidore to her dolls, her family, and everyone else who would listen for nearly as long as she could talk.

"How is Mother?" Emily put in. "Has she been painting anything while she's been in Germany? She said she was dying to paint some mountains again." Emily herself liked to paint people—portraits or scenes—but it was Mother who had first put a brush in her hand, and for some years had been helping to keep the family solvent by painting what felt like endless country cottages, all of them glowing gently with light and domesticity, when what she really wanted was crags and ruins.

I bit my lip, knowing that I had better make a clean shirtfront of it. "I haven't been to Carlsbad, girls. I came here instead, to see you."

"Oh, Molly, you shouldn't have worried about us! Katie's been taking good care of us—haven't you, Kate?"

"Yes, against all odds," said the sister thus addressed, putting a plate down in front of me: bread-and-butter, and a little jug of gravy to go with it.

Hannah clicked her tongue and said, "I'm afraid it isn't much."

"If we'd known you were coming sooner," Katie said firmly, "I might have bought a larger Sunday joint."

"It's wonderful," I assured them, but privately I was beginning to worry. The house was dark; the fire was low; a cold draught came in from a broken window-pane, which had been stuffed with a rag, and I was nearly certain the dark patch high in the corner was mildew. And then the supper was so sparse! and Katie looked so pale!

A movement near the door caught my attention and I looked up to see the thin, stooped imprint of my father making its nightly visitation. At that moment I could have picked up my tea-cup and flung it straight at his gentle, sorrowful-looking face.

"Tell us about your new position, Molly," Lilias demanded, propping her chin on her hands. "Is it in Vienna? Are they nice children? Do you think it will last long?"

"I don't know," I told them, wrenching my attention back to the moment. "It pays well, and it means I can travel more than I used to."

"You never said precisely who the people were," Katie put in.

"They must be rich, to pay you so well," Hannah said.

I drew a deep breath. I could never tell them the truth—that I had been an imposter, a thief, a grave robber, a medium, and an adventuress—yet I was obliged to tell them something. "It's a widower, whose wife was a connection of some sort of royalty. His name is Franz Haber, and he has a castle outside of Wiener Neustadt."

The twins giggled. "A *castle*? What is it like?"—"Is the widower *handsome?*"

I shook my head. "Take pity on the poor man! It isn't so very long since he lost his wife."

"But you didn't answer our question, Molly! Is he a *handsome* widower, like Mr Rochester?"

"Who has been filling your head with this nonsense? I'll send you to bed early if you can't be sensible!"

Emily said plaintively, "You can't *possibly* send us to bed any earlier than Katie does. That would be *cruel.*"

Katie shook her head at them. "It isn't frugal to burn coal and gas late into the night."

All the laughter died on my lips and I put down my spoon, no longer feeling hungry. "Katie," I said gently, "is there not enough money to keep the lights burning?"

The kitchen was suddenly quiet. Katie looked at Hannah, and then at the twins. "Well," she said doubtfully, "I suppose there *was* enough, but…"

Awful visions roamed through my head. Mother was gone, Hannah was old, and they had never been left alone like this before. Had they fallen into the hands of usurers? Or had they frittered away everything I sent on new hats and trips to the pantomime?

"Please tell me what happened to it," I said faintly.

Lilias got up and marched over to the stove, from which she extracted a loose brick—knowing my sisters, they had prised it out on purpose, feeling that poetry demanded no less a hiding-place for the loot—and withdrew a darned old stocking stuffed with papers. "There," she said, putting it down on the table before me. "We've had to spend some of it, of course, but we managed to save some, too."

I opened the stocking and drew out, in horror, nearly all the money I had been sending home these past few months. There must have been pounds and pounds of it in big crumpled notes. Somehow, the truth was worse than I had imagined. They had not even spent the money on pleasure.

"Oh," I said weakly.

"I didn't want to fritter it away on things we didn't need," Katie said anxiously, "for we might want it later; if Mother didn't get well, or if you found yourself out of employment again. We haven't been going cold or hungry, I promise."

Perhaps not—but they had been diligently pinching as many corners as they might, and far more than they needed to. I said none of this: I only sat back in my chair and said, "Oh, girls! I'm so very glad I came."

We went to bed not long after, for I was very tired from my journey, and my homecoming had left me feeling more than a little shaken. Katie, after all, was more nearly right than she knew: there was no certainty in this venture of Franz Haber's. We had succeeded in Jerusalem more by luck than design, and I had not forgotten how Vasily had threatened me with betrayal. We could barely do our work at all without Nijam; and if Vasily abandoned us, he would take Schmidt with him, and possibly Mimi to boot. After that, Franz Haber and I would be obliged to part ways, for there was no possibility of my continuing the work alone.

Mr Vandergriff must be secured at once. If I did not hear from him within a day or two, I resolved that I would summon up my most brazen face and presume to call upon Lady Seton.

Happily, I did not need to. The next morning over breakfast (tea and cold toast, with a little jam) I was pleasantly surprised to find a letter beside my plate.

"Molly's handsome widower is missing her already," Lilias declared in a stage-whisper as I broke the seal. I paid no attention. The contents of the envelope were much too fascinating.

- Sir Humphrey and Lady Seton -
request the pleasure of your company
at a private exhibition of the Seton Bequest
- At the British Museum -
Great Russell Street,
on Thursday evening, 19 April 18—

Beneath Lady Seton's flowing hand was appended a message rather more bold and masculine: *Aunt Charlotte's carriage will call for you at nine. I hope this will satisfy the proprieties—Griff.*

"Oh, it will," I murmured.

"Who is Sir Humphrey?" Emily asked, breathing down my neck. "And who's Griff?"

"Manners, my dear! Don't read other people's mail! Sir Humphrey is Father's old business partner, who paid for my schooling; his father died and he inherited the title. I suppose the old Baronet Seton must have bequeathed some of his curios to the Museum when he died."

Katie's eyes gleamed. "You must go, Molly. Perhaps the

Noor-Jahan will be there."

"The Noor-Jahan? What's that?" Lilias asked, putting up a hand to conceal the sad fact that her mouth was full of toast.

"They say old Sir James Seton brought home from India a diamond worth *two million* pounds," Katie said with relish. "And they say it's *cursed.*"

"I'm sure that's just a story," I said. "If there was really a diamond, one of the Lady Setons would be wearing it about everywhere."

"Not if it was cursed," Lilias pointed out, and of course I could not argue with that.

I passed the bit of pasteboard to old Hannah, who put on her spectacles to peer at it. "An invitation!" she said in her quavery old voice. "We haven't had one of these in Lord knows how long. And it's tonight! What will you wear?"

"Don't you worry about that," I told her. "Girls, we've a busy day today. We're going to spend all that money on things we want."

"What! on new frocks?" Katie protested, getting the wrong idea at once.

One of the first things I had bought myself with Franz Haber's money *had* been a new white frock—but my old one had been in a sorry state, and at that time my future had seemed quite assured. "On new frocks, if they are needed," I said firmly. "But first on coal and beef and men to see about the windows and the roof. You've been very frugal, Katie dear, but I sent that money home to keep you all warm, and clothed, and fed. I like to think of you so; it keeps me going."

"There!" said Hannah. "Didn't I tell you, Miss Katie?"

Katie looked dubious, but held her peace. Emily clasped her hands. "Molly! May we have a *bicycle?*"

29

"Good heavens," I said blankly. "Whatever for?" I had never heard a good word about bicycles. They encouraged young ladies to clothe themselves in unfeminine garments and to roam about alone, at will. Moreover, physicians warned that the saddle endangered one's most delicate parts.

"It would save ever so much time and money," Emily said eagerly. The petulant, complaining tone I had noticed last night vanished on the tide of her enthusiasm. "I could pedal myself to my art classes, instead of needing Hannah or Katie to take me by cab."

"Any time one of us needed something urgently at the grocer's, she might dash out on the bicycle," Lilias added.

"Hannah is too old to ferry us about, and Katie has important work of her own to do!"

Both of them gazed at me imploringly. I could not help feeling how dingy and dark and lonely the house must be, and how much a little more freedom might mean to them.

"Bicycles are not respectable," I said feebly.

"Princess Duleep Singh is always being photographed on hers," Lilias answered at once. "And *she* is the Queen's own goddaughter."

I felt that I was trapped, but it was Katie who came to my rescue. "For shame, girls, to be speaking of bicycles when Mother is ill and there are broken windows to see to!"

The twins' faces fell, but they made no complaint. Emily took a dissatisfied bite of toast; and I vowed to myself that I would buy her a bicycle the moment Mr Vandergriff asked me to marry him.

No sooner had I made this splendidly reckless resolution, than the knocker on the front door went *rat-a-tat-tat*. The kitchen was electrified.

"First an invitation, and now a visitor!" Lilias said, jumping up from her chair. Before I could rein her in, she had stampeded down the hallway and thrown open the door. "Good morning," I heard her say to the person on the doorstep, "and who might *you* be?"

"P. Nijam, for Miss Mary Dark," came the answer, as neat and precise as a postal-address. I started up and flew into the corridor. On the doorstep was a young woman of Oriental descent and wonderful, aristocratic beauty, dressed in severe black.

"Thank you, Lilias. Go and help Hannah put the breakfast things away, and then put on your hat; we shall be out all morning. Miss Nijam, do step into the sitting-room."

Having disentangled the most lively of my sisters from the dangerous society of Miss Nijam, I got my visitor alone in the sitting-room. I had written on my card yesterday to say that I would call again in a few days; I had meant her to understand that while she was not precisely *unwelcome* at my home, it might be wiser of us to meet elsewhere. But of course, I had forgotten that Nijam did not understand hints unless they were delivered with the concussive force of a rolling-pin.

"Nijam," I said warmly, offering my hand to my visitor, "how *good* to see you again. I trust you're doing well. What brings you to London? Do you have relatives in town?"

"No," Nijam said—with that single word disposing of all my questions. "I have a job for you."

It was just as I feared. "My dear Nijam, I can't join you in another job just now. I have sisters to look after." And, I did not add, whom I must keep in the straight and narrow. I did not want them knowing *anything* about my acquaintance with Nijam.

"I'm told," Nijam said, with a dismissive wave of her hand, "that you will be attending the opening of the Seton Exhibit at the British Museum tonight."

I managed to refrain from gaping. "How on *earth* did you know that?"

"I asked Sir Humphrey's valet."

"And he *told* you?" It was difficult—nigh impossible—to imagine Nijam successfully wheedling information out of anyone.

"He did—shortly before attempting a liberty upon my person."

I must have altogether lost the battle with my countenance. What an extremely courageous person! I hoped he was not now lying altogether in ruins. Still, it could not be denied that the impulse was an understandable one. If one managed to overlook *every* word that came from her mouth, Nijam was what could justly be described as a Stunner.

"Poor fellow! But really, Nijam, I must decline to take on this job of yours tonight. It's a social, not a professional occasion. Perhaps, if you had taken Herr Haber up on his most generous offer, we might have—"

"That would have been impossible," Alphonse's Nijam said forbiddingly. "Besides, I'm not asking you to do anything compromising. All you need to do is ascertain if there are any Vedic manuscripts among the artefacts bequeathed to the Museum by the late baronet. They may be on display, or they may be in the storerooms beneath the Museum, or they may still be in the possession of the Seton family. You know Sir Humphrey; ask him. That's all I ask."

It was such a simple little thing that I nearly laughed. "Then why don't you ask him yourself?"

"For the same reason I could not impersonate Marie-Caroline," Nijam said wearily. "How do you think it will look, a half-Indian nobody asking a baronet about Indian artefacts? When the manuscript vanishes, I am the first person he'll suspect."

To the feeling of being crushed, was added the consciousness of deserving it. "Do forgive me," I said. "Is the manuscript so very valuable?"

"All I know is that a Scottish mathematician has offered a fabulous price for a copy of the Halayudha Sutras, and I am the only one who knows that Sir Humphrey Seton likely has it. *He* probably thinks the manuscript is worthless, but *I* need the money. I've been to every university from Warsaw to Paris to London, and I can't find laboratory space at any of them. If I can't set up my own laboratory, I can't find out how to restore Alphonse Schmidt's memories. This is my last resort, Dark."

She refrained from pointing it out, but I knew that I was the one to blame for her predicament. Had I not unearthed Franz Haber and pushed him into claiming his dead wife's inheritance, Nijam would have had a fortune with which to set up as many laboratories as she liked.

Under such circumstances, how could I refuse?

"I'll do it," I told her. "But you know, don't you, that we all miss you terribly? We very nearly came to grief in Jerusalem without you."

"I don't doubt it." She bit her lip and hesitated. "You really ought to have someone like me to take care of you all."

"That's just what I thought," I confessed, hopefully. "I'm doing my best to keep Alphonse Schmidt safe, but I don't think of everything."

"I'll give it some thought," Nijam said, "but I cannot promise

I'll be able to find anyone as cautious and efficient as myself."

This, of course, was not *precisely* what I had hoped to hear. But I swallowed my disappointment and politely thanked her.

Chapter III.

Who among us has not marvelled at the noble proportions of the great British Museum, or the vast collections of artefacts, curios and books housed within? One enters beneath the great pillars of the entrance, with its pediment depicting an allegory of *The Progress of Civilisation,* and finds oneself in a veritable wonderland.

That memorable evening, however, was my first visit to the noble pile since I was a schoolgirl, and I found it a far more unsettling experience than I had at first expected. Electric lighting had recently been installed, illuminating the facade with golden light across which the pillars supporting the pediment ran like purple bars. From the downstairs vestibule a massive staircase led to the upper floor, where Sir Humphrey waited with his lady and the director of the Museum to welcome their fashionable guests. The season not yet having commenced, the party was a relatively small one, being largely composed of gentlemen whose business had not permitted them to leave the city for Rome, or Cannes, or another of those fashionable wintering spots.

In consequence, the living at the museum were nearly outnumbered by the dead. I passed an Ancient Egyptian person on the staircase, who startled me considerably with her transparent white gown and boldly painted eyes. She was quite crisp and clear, too; her imprint had scarcely faded in the long centuries since her death—unlike, say, the blurry gentleman in the curled beard, naked except for a kilt, whom I guessed to be an Assyrian. Imprints did not as a rule last thousands of years; but a memory of these people had been preserved in this place, linked to the items they had used during their lives: vases, knives, jewellery or strongest of all, human remains.

Upstairs, the imprints tended more towards Romans and Anglo-Saxons. Attempting to steer my course between a centurion in full regalia and a red-haired bog woman in gold arm-rings, I misjudged myself and jostled against one of the few other young women present—an enviably small and dainty person with jet-black hair, a rosebud mouth, and a magnificent pearl necklace with which Miss Laine would have fallen in love at once. She was holding a glass of punch, which I narrowly avoided spilling down her magnificent Worth gown.

"I beg your pardon," I said as she exclaimed over my clumsiness; but then, to my great surprise, I found that I knew her. "Miss Henry?" I ventured. "Do you remember me—Molly Dark?"

Miss Henry blinked at me; and two or three other girls, whom I might also have known in the years before my father's disgrace, moved towards us. I had never been particularly fond of Susan Henry, but her younger sister Millicent had been bosom friends with our Katie, and I knew how much it would mean to my sister to renew the acquaintance.

Miss Henry, after a moment's confusion, smiled at me. "Molly Dark?" she said. "What a surprise! But oh dear—perhaps you don't know that this party is by invitation only? It isn't open to the public, you know."

She might as well have slapped me; I found myself blinking, and a hot tide of shame crept across my face. It was exactly like being at school again.

"I *do* have an invitation." Even as I said the words, I was ashamed of how my voice quavered. "Mr Vandergriff sent it."

"Mr Vandergriff? The American millionaire?" one of the other girls said, and some of them put up fans to hide their smiles.

"I'll introduce you to him, if you like," I said; but the words sounded hollow. I saw myself through their eyes, badly dressed and intruding where I was unwelcome; and felt suddenly sure that Griff would see me the same way. I might have fascinated him on the train, but tonight I could not help but show at a disadvantage.

"That's very kind of you," Miss Henry said scornfully, "but I'm already acquainted with Mr Vandergriff. It's very odd that he should never have mentioned *you.*"

With this parting shot, she gave me a frosty bow and went away, taking her pack with her. Looking back on the affair from some years' distance, I am now inclined to think that having perceived herself outmatched, she had determined to withdraw in good order. This was not how it appeared to me at the time, however. Miss Henry's contempt was undisguised; and a part of me could not help but feel that I deserved it.

Sternly, I pulled myself together. Was I not Molly Dark, a mistress in the art of pretending to be what I was not? Did I not have sisters and a mother depending upon me for their support? And was I to be daunted by such a clumsy attack?

Sir Humphrey, who resembled someone's jovial old uncle in a Dickens novel, welcomed me with his customary ponderous humour. "Miss Dark! What a great pleasure it is to have you among us. I began to fear your mother no longer approved of me."

There was no good answer to this question. I could hardly accuse him of neglect, or my mother of hostility; and I did not mean to confess to poverty. That left only flattery. "It was extremely kind of you to think of me, Sir Humphrey."

"Oh, don't thank *him*," Lady Seton said with a laugh. A good ten years younger than her husband, she retained the slight beauty and forthright mode of expression that must have set London tongues clacking twenty years ago when she first crossed the Atlantic from New York. "It was my nephew who insisted on your coming. Griff! Come and get your little friend before somebody else does!"

The crowd parted, and Warren H. Vandergriff greeted me with his outstretched left hand. I shook it, which seemed to be his preferred mode of greeting—much more civilised, thought I, than the way Vasily had seized and kissed me without so much as a by-your-leave.

"You were very kind to come," Griff said earnestly. He had not spared my dress a glance. "Care to see the collection?"

We moved into the still more crowded room opposite the stairs. During the day it would have been illuminated by the glazed skylight above, but tonight an electric chandelier shed light into every corner. More electric lights had been installed in every one of the glass cases which lined the walls, so that the wonderful Oriental artefacts within blazed with light: jewelled daggers; swords with zig-zag blades; gilt idols with many arms; paintings of turbaned emperors and their dusky ladies; hookahs; tiger skins; inlaid furniture; and more. The crowd here was more varied, too. I felt a moment's surprise

38

and pleasure to see so many Indians. There was a man of something like Nijam's complexion but darker, in a rather splendid costume consisting of a sort of embroidered shawl or jacket thrown over his stiff white shirt-front; the hat on his head, and the belt at his waist, was alien to Picadilly, but his walking-stick and gloves might have come directly from some gentleman's outfitters in Bond Street. There was a lady in a snowy white blouse that might have come from my own mother's wardrobe, but to it she had added a length of brightly coloured silk, wrapped and pleated about her waist, the end of it being drawn over the shoulder and passed over her long black hair. A dozen others milled about in the room, in their own or European garments.

Nor did Griff, to his credit, seem to find their presence at all remarkable. "I suppose you know the provenance of the collection?" he asked, as we began to circle the display-cases at the room's outskirts.

"The old baronet collected most of these things in Bengal, I think?"

"Yes; when he was in the East India Company, during the great mutiny. It's rumoured to be one of the finest collections in England, but even I had not seen half these things until the old gentleman died and left them to the Museum. Or most of them; some of the more valuable items are here on loan."

"I *heard* that there were a number of very fine manuscripts in the collection."

"Yes, but none of them very interesting to look at, except for certain sutras a great deal *too* interesting for general public view; and so I believe the Museum declined them."

Apart from the mystery of how a manuscript could possibly be too interesting, this was most illuminating. Nijam's

Hallelujah Sutras, or whatever they were called, were almost certainly still in the Seton family's possession.

I paused to gaze at a helmet encrusted with rubies. Well could I imagine some maharajah wearing it into battle! Beneath it was a curious pair of items, each bearing five short curving iron blades affixed to a central bar, with a ring at each end.

"Tiger claws," Griff explained. "They can be concealed within the hand, or worn over the knuckles. I'm told they were particularly good for assassinations."

"Dear me!" I said with an unfeigned shudder.

"A savage weapon," he said, "for a savage people."

At one time I should not have thought twice about words like this; but hearing them now I could not help feeling how they might have struck Miss Nijam, had she been there to hear them—as so many of her compatriots were.

"Oh, fie! One of them might hear you!"

"That's unlikely," he said with a laugh. "We are all Anglo-Saxons here."

Releasing his arm, I turned to survey the room. It was still—to my eyes—full of Indians, some in Eastern clothing, some in Western, and some in a mixture of the two. Yet they moved through the room silently, making no sound at all: no voice, no footfall, no rustle of silk. As I watched, one of them brushed past a portly old gentleman who was very closely inspecting a case nearby; the young Indian drifted through him like a shadow.

The blood turned to ice in my veins. Dead! All of them, dead!—and so many of them wearing the fashions of thirty-five years ago, when the old baronet had lived in India! Certainly a great number of Indians, as well as English men and women, must have perished in the mutiny; but these people looked so *ordinary!*

"Is something wrong, Miss Molly?" Griff inquired, and I made a valiant effort to gather my wits. It was not always easy for me to distinguish between the dead and the living, but this was hardly likely to recommend me to Griff as a wife.

"I beg your pardon, I thought I caught sight of an acquaintance. What is over there, in the centre of the room?" I added, for there were a great many people gathered around some sort of steel cage that gleamed richly in the blazing electric lights.

"Ah, but that is quite literally the jewel of the whole collection," Griff said with a smile. "The great Noor-Jahan diamond, given by the Great Mogul, Aurangzeb himself to the Nawab of Bihar, who gave it to old Seton."

"So it is real?"

"As real as you or me. Come and look your fill; it will be on display only until Seton returns to Hong Kong."

The first crush of onlookers had lessened, allowing us to approach the cage; but two familiar-looking gentlemen stood before it.

"Everyone is asking," said one of the men—as a matter of fact it was my old friend, Sir Humphrey—"whether your grace means to hold another of your famous entertainments, now that you've returned from the Continent?"

"I'm afraid I've come on a matter of business, not pleasure," came the answer, in honeyed tones I knew only too well. I must have made a sound of amazement, for they both turned to look down at me.

"I don't believe you've been introduced to my young friend," Sir Humphrey said to the other gentleman.

Grand Duke Vasily Nikolaevich Romanov—whose eyes

41

were obscured, for some reason that escaped me, behind dark glasses—smiled thinly. "Not—*introduced*, no," he conceded, with an infinitesimal but infinitely meaningful pause. Then he bowed over my hand, and I felt my entire face burning with the memory of the moment he had greeted me with the most thorough—indeed the only—kissing of my life. That had not been a proper introduction at all; and now, as I felt the warmth of his breath and the brush of his lips through my glove, I asked myself whether *this* could be called a proper introduction, either.

"I brought Miss Molly to see the Noor-Jahan," Griff said at my side. The gentlemen stood aside with apologies, and while Griff introduced himself to Vasily (*how* I hoped the latter would behave!) I approached the illuminated cage.

This surmounted a marble plinth, upon which, displayed on a bolt of red velvet and covered by a glass shade, reposed the largest jewel I have ever seen, whether before that day or since. For a moment I was absolutely entranced. Large enough to fill my palm, the great ovular jewel winked like a fire from within its setting—surrounded by a ring of smaller diamonds, and clasping together five strands of pearls, the whole forming a collar that could have purchased a small kingdom.

"How do you like it?" asked Sir Humphrey.

"It's beautiful," I said sincerely. "I don't believe I ever heard the true story behind it, Sir Humphrey."

"My father saved the life of the Nawab and his family during the Mutiny," he said readily. "This jewel was given him in gratitude, but it came with a terrible warning. Anyone who touched the jewel with impious hands was destined to madness."

"I wonder if the old story is true," Vasily put in from behind

42

me—I could feel him burning like a fire at my shoulder, faintly scented with pine. "Perhaps it was put about to discourage thieves. A stone like that would be a great prize—for a great thief."

I was sorely tempted to tread on his toe. What *was* Vasily doing here? Did he consider himself a great thief in search of a great prize? But to ask the question was to answer it—of course he did!

"Curse or no, a thief would be very foolish to try his luck with the Noor-Jahan," Griff said from my other shoulder, startling me. I had almost forgotten he was there. "For one thing, the publicity of the display means the jewel would be missed at once."

"I don't know," Vasily said with a shrug. "An aunt of mine once had some diamonds stolen, and the thieves switched them with paste and sold them to an Antwerp merchant before anyone looked closely enough to see the difference. If I had not happened to be at the auction when they were sold, my aunt might never have seen the bauble again."

"Ah," said Sir Humphrey, "but how could anyone replicate the Noor-Jahan with the necessary precision? When my father brought the Noor-Jahan home to London from Calcutta, he had three identical necklaces in three identical chests—two of them done in glass, as decoys. It would have been a ticklish business for anyone to steal *three* necklaces; as they must have done, to be sure of getting the real thing. My father kept one of the decoys as a record; it precisely replicates the dimensions of the real stone and the real necklace, so that if any substitution was made the difference would be easily spotted."

"Not that that would be necessary," Griff added. "Any glass or paste substitute would scratch under a penknife, which would never be the fate of the real diamond. But even that measure would be superfluous, since the diamond can never be taken from the cage. Miss Molly, your hand is small; reach through the bars and touch the glass, if you are able."

I managed to wriggle my fingers through the grille of the cage just far enough to touch the glass box surrounding the stone. The moment I did so, a small trapdoor opened beneath the Noor-Jahan, depositing it—pearls and all—into a dark recess within the plinth.

"The diamond is now secure in a strong-box, of which only Sir Humphrey and myself know the combination." Griff spoke with an air of satisfaction as the trapdoor slid with a click back into place, leaving the glass shade empty. "An innovation of my own, which I spent a very pleasant afternoon devising. No, no!" he added, to Sir Humphrey's protests. "I took great pleasure in doing it, I assure you! I am always willing to assist a friend!"

"You're a white man, Griff," Sir Humphrey said with a chuckle, "but I suppose I shall now need to retrieve the diamond." And he turned, making a signal towards the door.

"Be careful it does not send you mad," Vasily said with a laugh, as a guard bustled his way from the door, drawing a key on a fine chain from his pocket.

"I am not in the least afraid," Sir Humphrey chuckled, as the guard unlocked the cage; but I noticed he drew on kid gloves, all the same. The guard removed a marble panel at the side of the plinth, and Sir Humphrey bent down to fiddle with the combination-lock; I noticed that Vasily turned away almost conspicuously, and made a show of tidying his hair in a small hand-mirror—something which the other gentlemen present would dismiss as a decadent Continental affectation, but which struck me as having an almost sinister significance. Indeed, I felt sorry I had not also kept an eye on Sir Humphrey—not that I intended to steal the Noor-Jahan, but that I had long been in the habit of collecting whatever useful stray bits of knowledge might benefit me under some unforeseen future circumstances. But I was too late. Within a moment, Sir Humphrey straightened, cradling the jewel and its strings of pearls gently in gloved hands.

"Perhaps you would like to try it on, my dear," he said to me, in an avuncular tone—"If you are brave."

My hands fluttered to my throat. I was wearing my new white afternoon dress, and the neckline was high and prim, which was no doubt why Sir Humphrey thought I would be brave enough. As for myself, I had a suspicion about the Noor-Jahan and its curse, and I would have liked nothing better to test whether I was correct. Also, for once in my life, I wished to wear something truly rich and rare.

"If I *may*," I whispered.

"Of course you may," Sir Humphrey said. "Why, you might have had any number of such baubles for your own if your father had been more circumspect in his dealings."

It was no more than the truth, so I did not know why Vasily gave a little hiss between his teeth. But he was all smiles a moment later as he cut neatly in front of Griff and collected the proffered necklace.

"Allow me, Miss Dark," he said.

I sent him a look which I hoped communicated my displeasure—how could I fascinate Griff with Vasily blundering into the way?—but the censure was wasted on him. Vasily drew his fingers across the delicate skin at the back of my neck as though he wished to move some of the short, curling tendrils out of the way; I hoped neither he nor Griff heard the shiver in my breath at his touch. Then the diamond descended like a weight on the lace at my bosom, and the collar cinched close around my neck.

So far, so good. I turned. "How do I look?"

"Like a grand duchess," Vasily murmured into my ear before stepping away.

Russia being full of grand duchesses in the most magnificent jewellery, that ought to have meant nothing. But Griff seemed to attribute far too much importance to the compliment. "Like a queen," he put in, as though this was an auction, and he was obliged to raise the bidding. Really, I was vexed! It was just as well that I had not visited the buffet-table in the antechamber, for at this juncture Vasily would certainly have found himself with a cupful of blancmange in his pocket.

"Well, I *feel* like a fraud," I said, perhaps a little tartly. With the words, I touched the weight at my throat with a gloved hand; and perhaps it was this that provoked what happened next.

My surroundings faded away. I saw a room in some oriental mansion, the door barred and jumping in its sockets with heavy, noiseless blows. Suddenly it burst open and a man entered wearing the scarlet tunic of the English army—a man whose resemblance to Sir Humphrey made it clear at once whose father he was. I hope never again to see such a countenance as this: streaked with black powder and perspiration, spattered with blood, and disfigured with rage. The men behind him were no better. Seton shouted soundlessly at the occupants of the room, a terrified huddle of gorgeously dressed women and their children and servants. One of them, a noble-looking woman whose skin shone like burnished bronze in the dying sunlight, tried to approach Sir James with outstretched, supplicating hands. He levelled a pistol at her breast and shot her dead—I clutched my heart, feeling her brief, violent agony. As she staggered to the ground I saw him shout again.

None of my visions of the dead ever made a sound; but I could see the shape of the words on his lips, and knew he was demanding the Noor-Jahan diamond.

But then the terrible scene changed. I saw other things, *felt* other things, with a breathtaking rapidity. At a small house in the jungle, an Indian potentate, decked in jewels or silks, was shot with a rifle by a pair of nobles; they then turned the weapon upon the young turbaned boy who watched in horror. Somewhere in a palace, a queen was beaten to death with bricks by her maids and left lying in a pool of her own blood. In a garden, a prince passed beneath an archway at the head of a procession and crumpled beneath a falling stone. I saw a venerable old man being held down, a lancet threatening his eyes, as fiercely bearded men made demands of him; I saw a broken warrior with blind and bleeding eyes, hiding a packet behind a brick in the wall of his cell, and then most horribly of all I saw a bloodied young man with a shaven head bound upon a chair. At a gesture from his aged, sallow-cheeked tormentor a ruffian came forward with a long-handled crucible, and poured molten lead upon the youth's head.

All these horrible things assailed my eyes one after the other with barely a pause in which to draw breath; and in those shattering moments of anguish and despair I felt what those unfortunate souls had felt, and knew that all of it had happened because of the diamond I wore at my throat. Then blessedly, a voice broke in upon the nightmare in which I was helplessly trapped. "Get it off her," Vasily snarled, and the strangling weight of the jewel was torn from my neck. In a trice I found myself back among the electric lights and black frock coats of the British Museum. The sense of relief, at war with the lingering agony and shock of the vision, proved too much for me. Dark veils descended over my sight, and I fell into oblivion.

Chapter IV.

I cannot have been insensible for very long; I came to myself just as a steely arm was lowering me onto a sofa in the antechamber. "You'll be sorry for this," I murmured.

"I should hope not, Miss Molly," answered an amused voice quite different to the one I had been expecting. I found myself blinking up at Griff.

"There," he said, withdrawing that uncomfortably hard arm from beneath my head. "Just you lie there and regain your breath; and I'll fetch Lady Seton. The diamond, if you please," he added, turning to Vasily, who had apparently trailed him to the antechamber and stood a little way off with both hands in his pockets, looking something between a magnificently gloomy bird of prey, and a schoolboy in a sulk.

"Oh yes—the Noor-Jahan," Vasily said with his most winning, and therefore most untrustworthy smile. He dug the bauble out of his pocket and handed it back; and Griff pushed his way back into the exhibition room, at the doorway of which a number of curious faces had gathered to watch.

Vasily moved closer, giving me a satirical look. "And what, precisely, am I to be sorry for, my dear Miss Molly?"

I sat up like a jack-in-a-box to confront him. "How should I know?" I hissed. "What *are* you doing? Why aren't you in

Vienna?"

He shrugged. "It is as I told you—I meant to keep an eye on you."

It wasn't his *eyes* I worried about, but I didn't know how to point out that tracing my neck with even his gloved fingers was well beyond the bounds of propriety. Since I was too well-brought-up to allude to such intimacies, I took the offensive, sinking my voice to a whisper. "Are you sure it's not the Noor-Jahan you're keeping an eye on?"

At the mention of the diamond, his eyes lit with fire. "It's haunted, isn't it? All that nonsense about Seton's father saving the family. Tell me you mean to steal it."

I felt suddenly very tired. *"No,"* I said, in as determined a whisper as I could muster. "I mean to do nothing of the sort! And what are you doing here in England using your proper name? I thought the Tsar had sent his secret police after you."

"By great good luck, the Tsar is not on the best of terms with the English; while I, as you have seen, am." Further opportunity for explanation or remonstrance was lost to us, for Griff now reappeared with his aunt, who proved to be the sensible sort of woman who always carried a bottle of smelling-salts about with her.

"Well, this is a pretty kettle of fish," Lady Seton said, depositing herself on the sofa and waving the bottle beneath my nose. "Why, I told Sir Humphrey I didn't mean to wear that bauble, and he had to go and put it on you. I just don't know why he doesn't sell the great bauble and get me something I can wear."

"You don't believe in the curse, surely, Aunt Charlotte?"

"Of course not! Only I don't like to take chances. The Orlov diamond must be at least as big as this one, and there was never any talk of *that* being cursed. Do you think that Russian fellow would know who to ask, if I wanted to buy it?"

"*I* think we are neglecting our guest," Griff said, planting a chair immediately opposite me. He sat, rested both his elbows on his knees, and looked keenly into my face. "Miss Molly, why don't you tell us what happened just now?"

Until this moment I had hardly an idea of who Griff was. He was less a man than the grey outline of one, a shimmer of dislodged air at my side. Now I suddenly felt acutely aware of him: his narrowed blue eyes, the complete stillness of his too-smooth face, the overwhelming attention of a formidable intellect.

All of a sudden, it struck me what was wrong with his face: the skin seemed drawn too tightly over the bones, so that there was a suggestion of the reptilian in his taut lips. No wonder he seemed so cold-blooded.

"I—I don't know," I stammered. I knew, of course, that imprints were able to attach themselves to a physical object; but the ghastly events the stone had forced me to witness were among the most vivid I had ever experienced, and if others had seen similar visions, it was no wonder the stone had a reputation for driving people mad. I could scarcely explain *that* to this steely, cold-blooded man, or to his cheerfully frivolous aunt. "The room was warm. I must have been taken ill."

"Does this happen often, Miss Molly?"

"I'm afraid it does, from time to time." I did not like admitting to anything that might lead him to think me in the grip of some mysterious illness, but the truth was that I never knew when some ghostly onslaught would leave me reeling with shock, and it was best to make an explanation at

51

once. "Please don't be worried on my behalf; it's nothing."

"I'm sure," he said, as though his mind was already on the next question. "What did the Grand Duke say to you while I was gone?"

My mind was wiped suddenly clean of thought. What did he know about Vasily? What did he suspect?

My speechless alarm may have been the best answer I could have made. "Griff!" his aunt scolded. "You can't ask a young lady a question like that!"

"The Grand Duke seemed very intent in whatever he was saying," Griff said doggedly—an observation which, although true, showed a heroic lack of self-awareness. "You know, Miss Molly, that you have friends who care for you."

"I don't understand," I said shakily. "Is the Grand Duke not quite respectable?"

Of course I knew the answer to this—of all the people with whom I was acquainted, only Mimi Laine could possibly be less respectable than Vasily—but I wanted to know why *Griff* wished to warn me about him. However, my question succeeded only in breaking the taut attention with which Griff had regarded me: he sat back and ran his left, ungloved hand through his mousy-brown hair. "Perhaps I am jealous," he told me with a laugh. "You may say I have no right to be."

"Oh, no," I whispered. It would have been nice to be able to summon a blush, but I had to make do by fluttering my lashes a little and looking down at my hands. "You are only trying to help me; I know that. Please, Lady Seton," I added, "I *am* sorry to bother you, but I feel tired, and—"

"Of course," Lady Seton declared. "I'll have my carriage sent for at once, and Tombs shall accompany you home."

She was as good as her word, and within ten minutes Griff

was helping me into her ladyship's carriage, with her ladyship's maid sitting inside ready to see me home. A number of other carriages were waiting in the Museum forecourt to carry their masters home, and as Lady Seton's rolled out the gate I was quite sure I saw Alphonse Schmidt huddled into his greatcoat atop one of them. Of course if Vasily was here, Schmidt could not be far away; nor was I particularly surprised some time later at home, when I let myself into my bedroom to find Mimi sitting on the bed with her stockinged feet stuck under the coverlet. It was late, and the fire in the stove downstairs was long out by now.

"I do hope you haven't let yourself catch a chill," I said, with a pointed look at Mimi's feet.

"Not at all; your quilt is sufficiently warm. Vasily sent me to tell you he's staying at the Savoy Hotel, and when do you want him to come and see you about that diamond?"

I didn't want Vasily to come and see me about anything. I was trying to catch myself a wealthy husband, and with my chief quarry actively concerning himself with the safety of the diamond, there was nothing I wished less than to join a conspiracy against it. Still, every time I closed my eyes I saw the poor Indian lady being shot down like a dog by Sir James Seton. There was no doubt that the jewel was stolen property; that the blood spilled on its behalf was crying out for justice, and that I had been appointed to right just such wrongs.

Had Vasily not witnessed my fainting-spell, I should have been sorely tempted to forget what I had seen—if such sights could ever be forgotten. But he *had* seen it—and moreover had evidently interested himself in the jewel long before *my* intrusion.

"The stories are true," I said pessimistically. "That jewel is cursed, and I for one want no more to do with it."

Mimi took me at my word. "Splendid! Then you won't mind if we take it ourselves." Unearthing her toes, she wriggled them into her soft climbing shoes.

I threw up my hands. "Wait, wait! You mean that if I help him steal the Noor-Jahan, Vasily will see it returned to its rightful owners?"

Mimi shrugged. "There are ghosts attached to it, are there not? Vasily said you were quite overwhelmed by them. Are you afraid?"

I could scarcely repress a shudder. I had always expected my gift one day to overset my reason; yet, as violent as the evening's visions had been, I seemed little the worse for wear. They were no worse than the other horrible things, of which I had already seen a great number. The visions had a nasty habit of haunting my dreams, but *they* were not what frightened me just then.

No; it was Vasily who gave me pause. If I *did* help Vasily to steal the Noor-Jahan, who was to say he would not seize the opportunity to double-cross me? The wicked Grand Duke had not forgotten what happened in Vienna, when I tricked him out of the Bourbon fortune. And he had undeniably been interested in the Noor-Jahan well before I discovered the imprints attached to it.

It was not that I thought Vasily might harm me, or hand me over to the authorities. A scoundrel he might be, but he still thought himself a gentleman. It was only that I knew well how precarious was my position in the world. Griff was by no means secured. Should any hint of scandal attach to me, or even should I lose my employment with Franz Haber and be unable quickly to find a new position—as was all too

54

likely given that I had been dismissed from my most recent employment without a character—all of us might in one rush descend as far as the gutter. There had been a schoolfellow of mine at Saint Alphege's, like myself without friends or protectors in the world, who in her very first position was unlucky enough to attract the attentions of the gentleman of the house. I am inclined to think that she was not at fault herself, for who can say what threats or persuasions were used upon her? but the damage was irrevocable, and it was whispered that she had then been forced to go into the demi-monde to earn her bread, and that was nearly the last any of us heard of her. One of our number, who had become a Radical and a suffragette, attempted diligently to find her; she concluded that poor Mary-Kate had fallen as low as a Spitalfields hovel before being murdered in her bed by a maniac. I did not, I say, think that Vasily might intentionally harm me: but nevertheless the risk of harm was great.

I could not risk allowing Vasily to surprise me; I must make sure that he did it under my watchful eye, where I might have some say in the result.

"Whoever takes the diamond," I said slowly, "must return it to the people it was taken from; that's the only way to lay the imprints." I did not voice the doubt I felt: how were *all those ghosts* to be satisfied? Even before Sir James Seton had made himself the stone's last, rapacious master, the Noor-Jahan had been part of a long and bloody history of extortion, death, and torment.

Mimi was smiling—a startlingly rare occurrence. "I knew you would be in it," she said. "This will be a theft worth talking about!"

If I was to have any success, I wanted at least one trustworthy ally.

"I'll be in it," I told Mimi, "on two conditions. First, no one will pocket the diamond for themselves; and second, we can't do it without Nijam; not with someone like Mr Vandergriff taking an interest in the stone. Nijam is coming here in the morning. Perhaps I can persuade her to join us."

"Good," Mimi crossed to my window and threw it open, leaning out to scan the street. No doubt this was the way she had entered. "I'll tell the others to be here."

With that she vanished into the night. "Mimi, wait," I hissed, not daring to shout for fear of waking my sisters. By the time I had followed her to the window and leaned out, she had already faded into the night.

I closed the shutters and leaned my hot forehead against the glass, hardly sure whether to laugh or cry. Vasily was about to steal the second most famous diamond in England out from under the nose of the man I meant to marry—and he wished to use my house as his headquarters.

* * *

"Girls," I told my sisters the next morning, at the breakfast-table, "I shall be receiving some visitors this morning."

"Oh, whom?" Lilias demanded, in her excitement nearly pouring milk onto the table rather than into her tea. When *I* was that age I was much more carefully raised. Young people should be seen and not tolerated. Evidently Mother had been letting the youngest ones get away with *murder.*

I restrained the reproof which rose to my lips. "Well—Miss Nijam is one."

"And the others?"

56

Perhaps I was weak, but I really did worry what would happen if I failed to tell them *anything.* The twins at least were capable of taking matters into their own hands, with disastrous consequences. "Well, one of them is some sort of Russian nobleman, I believe—"

"What sort of Russian nobleman *exactly?*" Katie wanted to know.

"Do you think your mother would approve?" Although age had rendered Hannah feeble, her wits were evidently as sharp as ever.

"Oh *Molly!*" Emily broke in. "Don't listen to Hannah! Say we can meet him!"

After the way he had persecuted me last night, it would serve Vasily right if I *did* let the twins near him. What was there, after all, so difficult to understand in *I am going to London to catch myself a wealthy husband; pray do not interfere?* "I don't approve of it myself," I said with feeling, "for he's astonishingly hard of hearing for a man of his age! and one must speak so very clearly to make oneself understood! Besides, we shan't be meeting for pleasure, but on business, and I don't—"

"What sort of business?" Katie wondered.

"We're a sort of charitable society," I said, which was strictly true, though so imprecise as to be practically mendacious, "and I *don't* want to distract you all from your very important work, so I do beg you all—"

The knocker went, and Lilias got up so fast I expected her chair to go over, *bang,* behind her. "I'll let them in!" she sang out, and before I could say or do anything, she had giggled her way to the front door and thrown it open. Emily was not far behind her.

"Katie," I appealed to my second sister. *"Will* you look after

57

them while I'm busy?"

"I'll do my best," she promised me, getting up to snatch the kettle off the stove, where it had begun whistling energetically. "Another cup of tea, Hannah?"

The newcomer proved to be Mimi. By the time I reached the front of the house the twins had ushered her into the sitting-room, taken her coat and her name, and asked if she wanted tea. "I'll take some milk, if there's any," she said, throwing herself towards an armchair in an improper but elegant sprawl.

"Ask Hannah to bring the milk," I said, catching Lilias by the ear and giving it a gentle tweak. "And then upstairs with both of you; you know Mother expects you to do your lessons while she's away."

They went down the hall with dragging feet, until Emily whispered something to Lilias and I heard them both hurry upstairs—no doubt to plant themselves in Mother's room, behind the big bow window that overlooked the street, where they might have a chance of peering at the arrival of the other guests.

"Are those your sisters?" Mimi asked, and when I wearily assented, she shook her head with what seemed like genuine envy. "You are lucky. My sister died when I was small."

I did not quite know what to say to this, so instead I tried to make small talk. Mimi, however, was already consumed by thoughts of our task. Before she had outlined more than three different lines of possible attack upon the Museum and the jewel, another knock came at the door. It was Vasily; I ushered the wicked Grand Duke and his valet from the front door to the sitting-room without any events more untoward than the appearance of two cherubic faces over the banisters above, and a quantity of whispering.

I felt curiously vulnerable as Vasily sauntered into my mother's sitting-room. He was of course too well-mannered to openly stare at the apartment: at its faded wallpaper, with the patch of mildew in one damp corner; or at the threadbare carpet, the furniture of which had seen better days; or at the darker patches on the walls, where the paintings Mother once wanted to keep had been taken down and sold. Still, I knew better than to hope that he missed a single detail of this refined poverty, any more than he could have overlooked the fact that it was I, and not some smart parlourmaid, who took his coat and hat.

Vasily had taken more than one liberty with my person, but it was now that I felt the most humiliated. Once he had been convinced I was a princess; and now he saw that I was scarcely even a lady. Perhaps he was marvelling that I should have refused to become his duchess.—Well. No doubt from this date I could mark the end of his troublesome attentions.

No one had spoken as I hung his and Schmidt's coats in the hall cupboard. That was to be expected of Schmidt, who never spoke if he could help it, and of Mimi, who had extracted a notepad and a stub of pencil from her pocket, and was now drawing diagrams of the Museum as seen from the outside. Vasily, however, was the sort of person who spoke nonsense merely to fill up the silence—and at present he was failing this social duty.

Having hung his coat, I re-entered the room to find him arrested before one of the few pictures that remained on the wall above the empty fireplace. "Is this your mother?" he asked. It was a portrait by Emily, painted earlier this year when Mother was ailing and all of us guessed, even if we did not then know for certain, that it was consumption. It was the best thing Emily had yet done, and her painting-master wanted it displayed at the Royal Academy this season. In it Mother looked like a lamp of pale and translucent glass set in the darkness: fragile and pallid but glowing with her own inner light.

"Yes," I said. "My sister Emily painted it before we learned what was wrong with her."

"Your sister has a rare gift," was all Vasily said, before seating himself where he could go on looking at the painting. For a moment I did not quite know what to make of this. Vasily sincere was somehow more unsettling even than Vasily satirical and calculating. Wild suspicions fleeted through my head. Vasily did nothing without an eye to his own profit. What did he want with my sister's painting? Or what if he took an interest in my sisters themselves? I shuddered to think of the effect he might have on them. Perhaps I ought to forbid him the house at once!

Before I could resolve these anxious thoughts, Mimi said, "I thought we were going to meet Miss Nijam here?"

"I thought *I* was going to meet Miss Nijam here," I murmured. But then the knocker went again, and Schmidt, who had been standing by the window looking out into the street, recoiled into a corner where he did a rather creditable job of hiding behind the aspidistra. That made it quite clear who had just arrived. I had witnessed Schmidt single-handedly thrashing a small platoon of Okhrana men and hurling himself bodily between his master and a ravening melusine. Thus far, Nijam was the only living creature of whom he seemed to be afraid.

I opened the front door. "Morning, Dark," Nijam said, brushing past me into the hall before I could stop her or find

60

the words with which to delicately explain that we would not, in fact, be alone. "I take it you attended the Museum—"

She stopped on the sitting-room threshold, and of course she immediately spotted Schmidt, for the aspidistra was but a scanty hiding-place.

"Dark," she said frostily, "I believe I have already made my views on this subject *more* than clear."

"I know," I assured her, getting her into the room and closing the door tightly behind us, for I was conscious that the house was full of attentive ears. "As I was about to say, your grace, it might be better if I spoke to Miss Nijam in private. Perhaps we might reconvene later, at your hotel?"

Vasily raised an eyebrow. "At the Savoy? My dear, you've no notion how public that would be. In our line of work we cannot afford to attract attention."

"Then why the dickens did you choose to stay at London's most fashionable hotel?" Nijam demanded. She did not approve of Schmidt being in harm's way. "You'll bring down vampires and secret policemen on your heads again, the way you did in Vienna!"

"My dear Miss Nijam," Vasily said, "a fashionable hotel is a discreet hotel. As for my brother's little intrusion in Vienna, that was on the Continent; this is England. I am protected here. For one thing, I have many powerful friends; and for another, the English regard my countrymen as barbarians and my family as bloodthirsty autocrats who are bent upon relieving them of their Indian dominions. There is nowhere in the world where we might be so safe—so long," he added, with a bow towards me, "as I am seen to abide by the law of the land!"

"Humph!" Nijam said.

I could not give up so easily. Gathering up my courage in both hands, I said, "Your grace, I don't mean to make you feel unwelcome in this house, but my sisters are very young and, at present, they are under my care. I do not mean that they should be exposed to any but the most unexceptionable society. Moreover, I must insist that they be left in peace to pursue their various studies and work, which as you have seen is of a very high order indeed. In short—"

A knock on the sitting-room door interrupted me. I caught my breath, afraid that my speech might have been overheard. "What is it?"

The door opened and my three sisters entered, as prim as you like and laden with tea-trays—a steaming teapot, a plate of seed-cake, sugar and lemon and even a glass of milk for Mimi. "The tea's ready," Katie told me, just as though butterflies wouldn't melt in her stomach. And after she had *promised* to keep the twins out of trouble! The traitor!

I swallowed what seemed like a very large lump of indigna-tion and said, "Thank you, girls. Please—"

"Here's your glass of milk," Lilias said, handing the item in question to Mimi. Then she turned to Vasily and added, in a strong young voice that made the windowpanes rattle, "HOW DO YOU LIKE YOUR TEA, SIR?"

Schmidt startled violently and came very close to overturn-ing the aspidistra. Vasily's polite smile did not falter, but he did blink rapidly once or twice and then send me a faintly narrowed look of suspicion before replying: "Black, if you please."

I will not deceive the gentle reader: in telling my sisters that the Grand Duke was hard of hearing, I *had* contemplated the likelihood that they might take me at my word. And hadn't it paid off beautifully? With great resolve I crushed the laughter that threatened to burst forth. "That's quite enough, Lilias! *I* will serve the tea; *you* have lessons to attend to."

Katie shooed them out, but at the threshold she turned, dropped a curtsey, and in a voice that, while not quite as strident as Lilias', might still have been heard in Tottenham, informed the company that it had been very pleasant to meet them. The door closed. I handed Vasily a cup of tea. "Well," I said into the echoing silence, "to business, shall we?"

"Not so fast," Nijam said with a frown. "Am I to understand we are *all* hunting this manuscript?"

Evidently she had arrived at the very reasonable worry that she would be obliged to divide the proceeds amongst the whole party, after which there would likely be too little for her to set up her laboratory. "Nothing like it," I soothed her. *"We* are after the Noor-Jahan diamond. The story about the curse is partly true: when I touched it last night I was visited by a number of the most shocking apparitions I have ever known. Sir Humphrey's father murdered at least one person to get his hands on the diamond; and anyone who takes the diamond for their own purposes will simply end up being haunted in turn. The only way to lay the ghosts is to give it back."

"Yes, but give it back *to whom?"* Nijam demanded, in a stubborn tone that suggested she hated everything about the idea.

Vasily seized on this at once. "That, Miss Nijam, is the question. To whom will you return the diamond, Miss Dark? To the Nawab of Bihar? *Is* there any such person?"

Trust Vasily to put his finger unerringly upon the problem! The gem's long history of bloodshed and terror unfolded in my mind's eye, the ghastly vision as fresh as it had been when I first beheld it last night. If Sir Humphrey's father had not come by the jewel honestly, few of its other owners had either. Giving it back to the Nawab would appease only the most recent of the ghosts attached to the Noor-Jahan—and surely the others deserved justice as much as they. Possibly the fairest end of the matter would be if the diamond was sold, and its proceeds put towards the welfare of the Indian people as a whole. But to whom should we sell it? To another Sir Humphrey, to be put on show in a museum—or to another Count Orlov, to be flaunted in some imperial sceptre?

"We'll give it back to the Nawab, or his closest heirs," I said, trying to sound sure of myself. "After all, I can't imagine that a jewel like that would be much good to a thief. Who would pay two million pounds for a stolen diamond that must be kept hidden in a vault forever?"

"I could name half a dozen," Vasily said promptly, "just from among my own family. Some of them have a very pure affection for jewels, stronger than either fame or fortune. Why else do you think I was at an Antwerp auction for stolen goods?" Schmidt made an uncomfortable noise into his tea. "How's this," Vasily went on persuasively. "I shall sell the diamond to my aunt, *sub rosa;* and you shall have two million pounds to distribute among the former owners; and as a commission I shall have whatever I can convince my aunt to pay, over and above the two million."

"I don't think so," said I, faintly. I did not know how to tell him, point-blank, that I could never entrust him with the sole custody of a diamond worth two million pounds. Was this how Vasily planned to double-cross me? "Herr Haber wouldn't approve of your taking a commission; that's why he is paying us so generously."

"Also we do not know whether you will take the diamond and disappear once you have it," put in Mimi, expressing my own fears with brutal force. "There are other ways to profit from the theft. Nothing is stopping us from taking the credit, even if we cannot take the jewel. People will come to me and beg. *Mimi, will you steal my grandmother's emeralds?* I shall be able to afford ballet lessons." Schmidt looked more pained than ever.

"But my dear Mimi, man shall not live by credit alone—as certain gentlemen of my acquaintance remind me daily; and how am I to maintain my mode of life without a large injection of money?"

Schmidt's teacup rattled as he set it down. "Forgive me, sir, but I agree with Miss Dark. I have no right to speak for others, but I for one cannot take such a thing with selfish motives; not when it has already been the subject of so much rapine and murder. I have done too much wrong in this world already, to add anything more to the balance."

That was Schmidt all over, of course: all he knew of his past was that he had been plucked out of a prison hulk named the *Akbar,* and as a result he believed—as firmly as Nijam believed the opposite—that he was some dreadful malefactor; when by comparison to the rest of the people who were at present inhabiting my mother's sitting-room, he was practically a saint.

Vasily spread his hands in a very Frenchified shrug. "I haven't the faintest idea why he does it; I'm sure it's only to flatter me. Very well, Schmidt! you have conquered. We return the diamond to some Indian punkah-wallah, who claims to be the last Nawab of Bihar, and wash our hands of the thing."

Of course he capitulated much too quickly to be trusted, but I was glad to have Schmidt and Mimi on my side. "Nijam?"

She had gone as pale as was possible for one of her rich complexion. "Absolutely not," she said. "Ghosts and curses? I've told you already: this is *precisely* the sort of thing I cannot afford to be mixed up in. It's difficult enough to be taken seriously as it is. I won't become the subject of a *Blackwood's* serial—*The Idol's Eye, Or, Pursued by Thugs!* No, thank you."

"But think of your people, Nijam."

"Who said they were my people? If they weren't such savages they'd take better care of their property; and since they are, I don't see why *I* should put myself out for them. If you won't help me with the manuscript, I have better things to do with my time."

I had seen Nijam angry before, but never so passionately: I had evidently touched a nerve. "I beg your pardon; I shouldn't have presumed. But I do mean to help you with the manuscript. Mr Vandergriff said the Museum didn't take any of them; the one you want is almost certainly still somewhere in Sir Humphrey's collection."

Nijam swallowed her anger with an effort. "Just my luck," she said bitterly.

She referred, of course, to the suspicion that would certainly be aroused should a young person of Indian descent suddenly disappear simultaneously with an Indian manuscript after which she had been inquiring. It was the old problem; the one that had first forced her to ask my help in infiltrating the Schloss Frohsdorf.

"My help is yours, Nijam, whatever you say to the Noor-Jahan," I promised her. "I'll call on Lady Seton tomorrow and ask about the manuscripts."

Nijam went to the window and looked out, broodingly, into the street. "Will this be before or during your attempt on the Noor-Jahan? Because the same people trying to steal two different things from the same person is hardly a foundation for success."

She was, of course, correct. I reflected with equal gloom upon my own private ambitions of marrying Mr Vandergriff. While I was silent, Vasily spoke.

"We mean to steal the diamond in any case," he drawled. "*Your* choice is whether to help us do it properly and get away with it, thereby improving your own chances of getting what *you* want. Or you might try it alone and leave us to our own devices. It's your choice."

This consideration operated upon Miss Nijam as powerfully as it had last night, upon myself. "How very generous of you," she said acidly. "Very well: I accept."

Chapter V.

Since we were all—at last—more or less agreed, Vasily and I sat down and shared everything we had learned about the Noor-Jahan: its history, its guards and safe at the British Museum, and—last but not least—the glass decoy kept by Sir Humphrey Seton as a precaution.

"The obvious place to begin is by stealing the decoy," Vasily announced. "We could then make a substitution for the original, as I said last night, and be far away from England before the hue and cry even went up."

Nijam sniffed. "In this line of work the obvious beginning is the worst beginning, surely. Seton will be expecting something of the sort."

"Naturally we won't do as he suspects," Vasily said with laughing eyes. "Once we find the decoy, we shall make a wax casting and return the original to its place. Sir Humphrey will never know, and we'll have everything we need to make our own decoy."

"And if we snatch the manuscript while we're at it, we'll cover our tracks," Mimi suggested.

"Then we make the decoy out of glass, I suppose," I put in. "But we should need to carry out the theft itself flawlessly, for the moment Griff suspects that the diamond has been meddled with, he'll test it with a penknife."

Nijam bit her lip. "They'll be expecting glass," she said, slowly. "What if we replaced the diamond with something harder?"

"Harder than glass?" Vasily frowned. "My dear Nijam, the whole point of diamond is that there *is* no substitute. There is white sapphire, of course, but a specimen of the correct size would be nearly as costly as the Noor-Jahan."

"Thanks; I'm aware." Nijam turned to me. "I was of course proposing a synthetic substitute. If I only had access to a laboratory, I could perhaps create something."

"What does one need in order to set up that sort of laboratory?" I asked.

"Quite a lot, actually."

"Make a list," Vasily put in, ignoring the cold shoulder that had been so resolutely proffered him. "Doubtless something can be done about it. Give her your notebook, Mimi.—Now, here's my plan. I shall visit Sir Humphrey, discover the whereabouts of the decoy and the manuscript, and invite him and his lady to dinner when next the servants have an evening out. Mimi and Schmidt, you two will break into the house—Schmidt to stand watch, Mimi to take a wax casting of the necklace and collect the manuscript. Miss Nijam will arrange our decoy, whether in glass or something better."

One person was missing from this list. I frowned. "I should go with Mimi and Schmidt."

"My dear, you aren't a professional of that nature. You should continue to fascinate Mr Vandergriff."

The very last thing I intended was to let Vasily shunt me to one side while *he* arranged the theft to his liking. Besides, he hadn't even stopped to ask what I might offer the enterprise.

"You can't very well walk into Sir Humphrey's house and say *By the way, my good fellow, where do you keep your valuables?*"

"I shall invent a pretext. The decoy will be in his safe, of course."

"Of course; and *I know precisely where the safe is hidden*," said I triumphantly. "My father several times took me with him when he went to discuss business with Sir Humphrey, and I can lead Mimi directly to the spot. Besides, while she is opening the safe and taking the castings, I can be finding the manuscript, since Schmidt must keep watch. There's no need to take any longer to complete the task than we must."

"I vote she comes," Mimi declared. "What do you say, Schmidt?"

Schmidt looked nervously at his master. "I think it might be best—"

"Oh, very well, very well! Have your own way, Miss Dark," Vasily said, but the twinkle in his eye was not reassuring at all. "Miss Nijam, have you that list of the things you'll need for a laboratory?"

Nijam had not even touched the notebook; but her mouth twisted as though tasting something unutterably sour. "I don't need a list," she said. "To gain access to the best chemistry laboratory in London, there's only one thing I need, and it's right here in this very room."

"Then name it, for heaven's sake."

Nijam pointed at the aspidistra.

"Alphonse Schmidt," she said. "Seton's servants have their evening off tomorrow night, so we haven't much time. Send Schmidt to meet me in the morning at this address." She handed her card to Vasily, as though poor Schmidt was not standing right there in the corner, staring into his teacup as

70

though he wished there was something stronger inside it.

"And now," Nijam added, "I must be going. Show me out, will you, Dark?"

I ushered her into the hall, where she shut the sitting-room door firmly behind us and began buttoning up her coat with swift, precise movements.

"Schmidt?" I asked, low and incredulous. I did not *think* my sisters were eavesdropping, but I spoke softly to be certain. "Are you sure about this, Nijam?"

She had never shared with me the precise details—but I gathered that some years previously, before he had lost his memories and been extracted from prison under parole as Vasily's manservant, Schmidt and Nijam had been much nearer than mere friends. Schmidt had no notion that this was the case; and Nijam, who was plainly still quite potty about him, refused to enlighten him. She professed to abhor all such forms of manipulation—and so, rather than winning back the man she loved, she by turns cold-shouldered and snapped at him, even while every fibre of her being was directed towards the restoration, not only of his lost memories, but also the love they had once shared.

"I can handle myself," Nijam said now, scowling furiously. Before I could mention the fact that she had not even been able to look Schmidt in the face long enough to give him her card, she jabbed a finger towards me. "The question is, can *you* handle the Grand Duke? It won't be the first jewel to attract him, and it's evident that he wants the bauble for himself."

That she had arrived at the same conclusion as myself made me still less inclined to doubt it; only I was not prepared for the thought to go through me with such a mortal pang. I had *liked* working for Herr Haber; the thought of marrying Griff was curiously unappealing by comparison.

"I know he means to have it," I said in a low voice. "But we can still circumvent him; and you've given me an idea of how. I'll explain it later; only are you sure that you can make a substitute?"

For the first time that day, genuine enthusiasm overcame Nijam's customary air of irritation. "It's been done before," she assured me. "The trick will be working out *how.*"

"And Schmidt will help?"

Nijam nodded. "Alphonse Schmidt," she said with determination, "is about to secure me a laboratory."

* * *

Nijam tells me that Schmidt did, in fact, keep the appointment she had made with Vasily; and arrived on her doorstep the following morning, no doubt with gritted teeth and the unconquerable determination to be as polite as ever.

"Ah, you're here," Nijam greeted him, with one or two gritted teeth of her own. "Just let me put on my hat, and we'll step down to the University College."

University College London is—as everyone knows—barely four streets away from the British Museum. Nijam's flat was on Gower Street, in a cramped tenement bursting with students from all over the Empire; and as she and Alphonse walked north towards the imposing grey university, with its neoclassical pillars and pediment, she almost felt unremarkable. The street was populated with a great many Indians, Abyssinians, Caribbeans, Africans and Chinese from around the Empire, who had come here to be educated by their rulers in the hope of being allowed to enter the Civil Service; I am afraid many of them also whispered forbidden things about Home Rule for their colonies. Nijam of course did not understand their chatter, for she had been raised in England by an English mother and had never learned the tongue of her fathers. She did not really fit in here, any more than she did elsewhere; but she *looked* as though she might.

If she or Alphonse spoke on the journey, Nijam did not describe it; but she did describe, with great pleasure, the eagerness with which they were received at the University when she spoke the wonderful words, *Alphonse Schmidt.*

"Not *the* Alphonse Schmidt—the bionic chemist?" a fawning scientist cried, capturing the bemused Schmidt's hand and pressing it warmly. "Not the brother of the late Professor Schmidt? A sad loss, my dear fellow, a terribly sad loss. His advancements in the field of revivification have never been equalled or even approached. Or—perhaps the reports of his death, like your own, have been exaggerated?"

Schmidt cast a look of mute inquiry at Nijam: evidently this was the first he had heard of his having had a brother. Nijam perceived her mistake at once. She really ought to have prepared him for his own celebrity. Had I been in her confidence, I might have warned her; but as it was, having been caught off guard, she could only scowl at the fawning scientist and say, "Herr Schmidt has received a terrible shock, from which he is still recovering. He would prefer not to discuss the matter."

"Of course—forgive me. What can we do for you today, Herr Schmidt?"

Alphonse cleared his throat, no doubt recalling that discretion favours the brave. "Miss Nijam will explain."

Nijam did explain—and to such purpose, that within a

73

breathtakingly short time the two of them were ensconced together in a laboratory dedicated to chemistry and wonderfully well-appointed. "Let us know if there's anything else you need, Herr Schmidt," one of the fawning scientists said as he bowed himself out.

It was, Nijam reflected, wonderful how *much* one could achieve in the company of a pair of trousers. Rubbing her hands briskly, she began rifling through the collection of minerals in the cupboard.

Alphonse broke his perplexed silence to ask, "What are you looking for?"

"Baddeleyite," Nijam said briskly, "also known as zirconium. Your part is done; sit down and don't touch anything."

Alphonse found himself a stool next to one of the high benches running beneath a long window through which the sun shone brightly; London was enjoying rare weather that April. "Did I really have a brother?" he asked her after another moment.

"So I hear," Nijam said. She had found her baddeleyite—quite an amount of it, in white powder—and put it on the bench, but then she went back into the cupboard and more slowly began to pick through the minerals within, reading every label. I will not venture to say whether this was really necessary, or whether the bent of the conversation made it expedient to conceal her face.

"How did he die?"

"Not having been present when it happened, I really can't say."

"Forgive me," he said humbly, and Nijam's heart smote her. She turned from the cupboard with a few likely additives, setting their little glass jars on the bench with a series of precise clacks.

"What I *can* tell you," she said between clacks, "is that you, Alphonse Schmidt, were once the most brilliant chemist in Europe, and if you had all your memories we would probably already be cooking up a Noor-Jahan decoy that would defy any number of gemologists."

He reddened. Perhaps the sudden warmth in her voice had done little to put him at ease. "Was I really?"

Nijam could not help a tight little smile. "Well. I *have* heard that your assistant did the best part of the work. But, of course, never had any of the credit."

"Oh. And why was that?"

"It's a mystery," she said. "I suppose we will never know. Ah! this must be the furnace."

* * *

I retreated to my bedchamber that afternoon with one of Nijam's little radio-transmitters to test whether the range would reach as far as Bloomsbury. "Nijam, are you there? Can you hear me?"

"You needn't shout," she said, in a voice that was only slightly muffled with distance. "It distorts your voice."

"You've improved the range? How convenient!"

"I was *hoping* to *sell* the invention," she said severely. "What is it?"

"Nothing in particular. Is Schmidt there? Did you find a laboratory you could use?"

"Yes, and I already have my first batch of samples cooking. What do you want with Alphonse?"

"Tell him to be at Brixton at nine." I paused, intrigued by

the slip of the tongue that had led her to refer to Schmidt by his Christian name. "Is Schmidt remembering anything?"

"No."

"I thought that perhaps being in a laboratory…"

Nijam sighed and her voice dipped. "When I said I wanted the strontium, he pulled it out of the cupboard without even reading the label. But it's only instinct, Dark; nothing more."

"You'll have your own laboratory soon," I reassured her, "and you'll find a way to restore all his memories in time, I'm sure. Do you have everything you need?"

"I've no way of knowing that," she said testily. "The baddeleyite forms diamond-like crystals, but only when it's superheated. What I need to find is something to bind the baddeleyite in its crystal form even after it cools. If Schmidt had his memories he could possibly guide me. As it is, the best he can do is look ornamental and shake hands with the other scientists."

"And I'm sure he does it wonderfully well." With a crackle, a new voice joined the conversation—Vasily, of course, with a third transmitter. "I've just come away from the Seton place. Sir Humphrey, Lady Seton, and Mr Vandergriff will be joining me tonight for dinner and some musical nonsense they call *The Gondoliers,* and you'll find the Halayudha sutras lying open in a glass case in the library."

"Griff didn't propose inviting me, too?" I asked, unsure whether to feel snubbed.

"Oh-ho! *Griff,* is it?" Vasily said with a shimmer of laughter in his voice. "No. I pressed him *very* warmly to do so, but he assured me you were indisposed. Perhaps he considers himself my rival."

"I beg your pardon?"

"My dear, I must go; but I'll speak to you again when I have the Setons and Vandergriff safely in my toils." With a click the transmission went dead.

"What does he mean, that he is a rival to Griff?" I protested. "Is he trying to sabotage me in this as well?"

"If you ask me, *he only does it to annoy, because he knows it teases,*" Nijam quoted; and with that self-evident truth I must content myself.

Had the reader been abroad in London that evening, he might at about half-past nine have seen a hired carriage waiting in Portland Place opposite the Seton townhouse, which is very large and grand. From within the carriage Schmidt, Mimi, and I watched the street. It was very quiet, being the off-season; and many of the houses were shut up and darkened, whether because the families who owned them were still sight-seeing in Europe or rusticating in their great country homes, or because like the Setons, they had gone out to dinner and given the servants the night off. From time to time a carriage or pedestrian went by; and a small group of Indian street-musicians—a piper, a drummer, and a man with a sitar—were playing some lilting tune up around Park Crescent.

"The house looks empty," I said doubtfully. Schmidt and Mimi—who was very daringly wearing a pair of trousers—both had piratical bandanas around their necks, ready to be pulled up over their noses to conceal their faces. I, however, being unwilling to expose my nether limbs to the scrutiny of anyone but myself, had availed myself of the one costume in which a lady might conceal herself without being marked down as someone who ought not to be trusted with the silver spoons. I was, in fact, wearing one of my mother's black mourning-dresses, and the thick, musty old veil that went with it quite concealed my face. All the same, I felt more than a little nervous, and the longer we sat here, the likelier it seemed that we would be discovered and arrested. "They aren't at home; perhaps we should go in at once."

Mimi touched her transmitter. "Vasily, the house is clear. We might as well go in."

"Stay where you are," Vasily replied, *sotto voce.* I heard a low hum of conversation and strains of music in the background when he spoke; I could imagine him in impeccable evening dress, waiting at a table at the Savoy for his guests. "Wait for my signal."

"Wait for *your* signal?" Mimi snorted. "Who made you the boss, Vasya?"

"Mimi, my love, I'm clearly the leader."

Another click heralded the arrival of a new participant in the debate. From the laboratory not far off in Bloomsbury where she was still observing her baddeleyite, Nijam said: "Excuse me, but that's not clear to *me* at all."

"Why not? I came up with the plan, and I am the one directing it."

"For now, perhaps, but that doesn't make you the leader," Nijam said stubbornly. Mimi rolled her eyes. Nodding to me, she slipped out of the carriage against Schmidt's silent protests.

"I suppose you want to hold an *election*." Vasily spoke the word with heavy disdain. "Very well, we can do that. Schmidt, who do *you* say is the leader?"

Nijam's Alphonse blinked. "Sir, I beg your pardon, but under the circumstances we should perhaps adjourn this—"

"Don't dodge the question, Schmidt," Nijam snapped. "It's

quite clear that our leader is Miss Dark."

"Nijam!" I objected. Vasily already viewed me as his rival; the last thing I wanted was to see the competition extend to other areas. "Each of us is equally important."

"What nonsense! This isn't about who's important. It's about who's the *leader*."

"They're here," Vasily said abruptly. "Sir Humphrey, Lady Seton, and Vandergriff. Tell Mimi to go ahead now."

"Oh, I'm afraid she's already gone," I informed him, and I wished I had been there, just to see the look on his face.

"There's Mimi's signal," Schmidt added, as a dim light flashed from across the street. He helped me out of the carriage and less than a minute later Mimi was admitting us by the front door. While Nijam and Vasily argued about leaders, she had been worming her way in at an upstairs window. Now, she and Schmidt covered their faces with their kerchiefs, as I did with my veil; whereupon Mimi gave me her dark-lantern, and I led the way to Sir Humphrey's study at the back of the house.

The great oil-painting of Lady Seton behind the desk had been removed, being replaced with a painting of Sir Humphrey himself in the regalia of his new title. But a push in the place I remembered, and the painting swung smoothly away from the wall, revealing the safe behind.

Mimi was all business. Responding only with a nod to the flourish with which I indicated the opening, she bent down to lay an ear against the safe, delicately working the lock. Schmidt remained in the front hall, keeping an eye on the street. I lit another dark-lantern and crossed into the library, where the manuscript awaited me—just as Vasily had said—in a case of dark wood panelled with glass. It was locked, but the key stood in the latch. The manuscript itself consisted of long rectangular leaves bound between painted wooden boards. It lay open for display, while others were stacked on the shelves above and below. Hoping that these were indeed the sutras Nijam required, I closed the boards on the long lines of incomprehensible writing and wedged them into the large pocket I wore beneath my black skirt.

So far, so good. I opened another of the ancient manuscripts in the case and laid it out in the same place as the one I had taken, hoping this meant the theft would go unnoticed. This done, I was in the act of locking the case when there came, like the crack of doom, a ghastly blare of sound—an alarm bell!

From the study I heard Mimi cry out, and after a moment or two the sound of a body falling. Twisting the key in the cabinet lock, I hastened in that direction. Schmidt, who reached the room half a yard ahead of me, threw out an arm to hold me back. In the same moment, a sickly-sweet scent wafted to my nostrils.

"Gas," Schmidt said. "Stay back."

Pulling his kerchief more tightly over his nose, he dashed into the smoky dimness. Mimi's unshuttered lamp stood on the desk, illuminating Mimi herself lying upon the carpet. "Schmidt!" I called over the din of the alarm as he bent to pick her up. "Don't forget the decoy!"

At that moment, the transmitter in my ear crackled to life. "Vandergriff," Vasily was saying at the other end, "what's the matter? Wake up, my friend. Seton, do you see his eyes? They're *glowing.*"

Through the transmitter, I heard a few indistinct words from Sir Humphrey—and then Vasily spoke again, more sharply. "What's that? He's a *prosthete*? Why isn't he moving, then? Is something wrong?"

Another click, and Nijam entered the conversation. Her voice was utterly devoid of any expression but urgency. "It means you must all leave the house at *once*. Dark—do you hear me?"

"I hear, I hear. Believe me, we're leaving."

"Good Lord, Dark, what is going on there?" Only when I switched on the transmitter to speak had she heard the shrill of the bell.

"I'll explain later," I gasped. Schmidt reappeared through the gloom carrying Mimi slung over his shoulders. The moment he was through the study door I clapped it shut behind him, hoping in this way to slow the spread of the gas. Schmidt slumped against the wall, taking a great heaving lungful of clean air. Mimi lay slack and unmoving about his neck, for all the world like a dowager's furs.

I employed the moment in reconsidering our plans. We could scarcely leave by the front door; anyone who heard the alarm would come running from that direction. A dark space beside the great staircase showed where a narrower corridor led towards the rear of the house, and the mews beyond—a much more likely escape.

Schmidt pushed himself away from the wall. "Someone rigged a gas canister inside the safe, as well as the alarm," he told me. "It must have caught Mimi in the face the moment she opened it. Chloroform."

"Chloroform?" I started towards our escape. "How can you tell?"

"From the smell," he said, as though this was the most natural thing in the world. "It's very distinctive."

"And the necklace?"

He handed me a jewel-case. Glancing within, I was rewarded by a glimmer of glass and imitation pearls. I touched my transmitter. "We have the decoy!"

"Stop talking and *go!*" Nijam screeched.

I did not dignify this untrustful comment with an answer—for something was waiting for us in the broom-closet.

That is, I presume it was a broom-closet, for our first warning was a loud clattering from within. Schmidt and I came to an immediate halt. The import of the sound became clearer almost immediately: the doors flew open, and with a whirring sound, a massive shape emerged from the darkness within, filling the hallway and cutting off our escape to the mews.

In the light of my dark-lantern I caught sight of something approximately the shape of a coffee-pot but many times larger, gleaming with brass and filling the corridor with a metallic groan and a waft of heated air. It swivelled to face us. The next instant the great black porthole at its apex illuminated with a cold, glaring blue light.

I staggered backwards, blinded. "SURVEYING," announced a mechanical voice. The best way I can describe it is that it was like a parrot's: it produced sound, but there was no intelligence or emotion behind the word. A moment later, in the same loud persistent tones, it announced, "INTRUDERS DETECTED."

"Front door," Schmidt gasped, seizing my shoulder in an attempt to put himself between me and the automaton. It was as well that he did not, for *he* was not wearing voluminous skirts and a sturdy whalebone corset. The infernal device spat what appeared to be a pair of fine needles at us, each of them drawing a thin copper wire behind it. They sank into my bodice just above the waist and buzzed viciously. Failing to penetrate the skin, they nevertheless rendered an unpleasant electrical shock; and because Schmidt was touching me, he felt it too.

"Miss Nijam," he called into his transmitter, scooping a hand about my waist, and with one motion both yanking me free of the horrible little pins, and sweeping me ahead of him towards the entrance hall, "there's an automaton here shooting at us with live electrodes."

Nijam snapped a word in reply. It *sounded* like "Water" but the word held no significance for me. "What?" I asked blankly, still scarcely recovered from the shock of having nearly been electrocuted by my own underthings.

Schmidt, however, needed no explanation. In the grand entrance hall, he dashed at the credenza, extracted an enormous spray of hothouse flowers from the massive Sèvres vase that stood there, and doused the pursuing automaton with the contents. There followed a flash so intense, and a bang so loud, that I thought for a moment we had both been struck by lightning. When my vision cleared, the automaton stood motionless, dark and smoking in the light of its own dying sparks.

The alarm bell, which had been going this whole time, stopped ringing. It left a no less ringing silence behind it. For a moment, Schmidt and I were half blinded and utterly disoriented.

"Water!" Nijam shouted over the transmitter. "Short it out! Confound it, are you still there?"

"Yes, and never mind," I told Nijam breathlessly. "Schmidt has taken care of it."

There was a clang, and I flashed my dark-lantern towards

the dying automaton. A hatch in its front had fallen open; and a canister rolled out and tumbled towards us, spraying gas as it went.

I did not wait to try whether this substance also smelled distinctively of chloroform. Nor did Schmidt. Hampered as he was by the dead weight of Mimi, whom he still bore upon his shoulders, he nevertheless moved nearly as quickly as I did. The door was still unlocked; and we collapsed on the front steps dizzy and coughing from such of the gas as had found its way into our lungs.

In the street, hasty footsteps sounded upon the pavement, converging upon our position. The police, thought I—no doubt summoned by that awful alarm! A shudder of fear went through me. All in a moment the future unfolded itself before my eyes—the arrest, the questioning, and the noting down of my name and address; the headlines in the papers; the ignominy, the trial, the sentence; and meanwhile the bitter shock and disappointment at home—my mother's untimely death of shame—my sisters cast out into a friendless world where they must sink to the very bottom! Unbearable thought! Desperation propelled me to my feet; I threw myself down the stairs and landed heavily in the arms of a turbaned gentleman smelling faintly of incense and spices.

The shock of collision, in my already half-addled state, loosened my grip on the jewellery case which I had carried thus far in safety. It fell open, spilling its precious cargo at the feet of a dark-complexioned young man who carried an elongated stringed instrument slung across his back. Kneeling to gather it up, he rose inspecting the contents of the box almost with reverence.

"Madam," said he in the purest English—so pure that I

84

thought at once he must have learned it abroad, by the book—"I owe you my thanks. You have saved me a great deal of trouble."

My thoughts were in an uproar; I could make no reply. Instead, the man who had seized upon me began to speak in a language as thick as honey and as resonant as a drum. He ended with an emphatic gesture of his head towards Schmidt, who had let Mimi down onto the doorstep and now sat limply beside her with his head between his knees. Two other men moved cautiously towards him; but Schmidt had now had two doses of the gas, and was evidently in no shape to do anything. One of them sniffed his clothes and then poked his nose in at the front door; he shut it again at once and spoke sharply to the others.

All this passed in a moment. I had by now gathered my wits sufficiently to conclude that I had fallen, not into the hands of the police, but of what appeared—from their clothing, and their language, and the instruments they carried—to be the same Indian street performers whose music we had heard up around Park Crescent not half an hour ago.

"Unhand me," I said frostily. "I am *not* accustomed to being embraced by strangers!"

My words seemed to fall on deaf ears. "Mirza Dara," my captor said. This seemed to be the name of the young man with the stringed instrument, for he turned away from the fainting Schmidt and the two of them exchanged words in their own language. As he spoke, the young Mirza, who appeared to be in command, indicated first myself and then the house.

"No, no, no," I cried out, perceiving at once what was intended. Had either of my hands been free I might have switched on my transmitter to call for help. "There's no need

85

for that! Perhaps we can help you!"

"You already have," the Mirza Dara said. Then the door opened just long enough for the Indians to thrust me inside the smoky hall alongside Mimi and Schmidt. The moment the door slammed behind us and I had the use of my hands, I switched on my transmitter and cried, "Nijam! Your grace!"

"Miss Dark." Vasily sounded breathless. "Tell me you're well away from that house. Vandergriff recovered his wits half a minute ago and told Sir Humphrey there were three burglars in his house. They've just driven away, and Lady Seton is sending for the police."

"No! You must stop them! We're trapped inside!" Coughing, I threw myself against the front door, rattling the doorknob. It would not budge; and in the darkness and the stifling clouds of smoke, I could find no way to open it.

"Miss Dark! Calm yourself and tell me—"

"I c-can't," I rasped. My tongue felt thick, as though it would not obey me. The last thing I knew was Vasily shouting my name. Then the door slid sideways beneath my fingertips, and for the second time in this volume of my memoirs, I fainted dead away.

Chapter VI.

Since I wish not unduly to distress my gentle readers, I might as well say at once that Sir Humphrey did *not* find the three of us insensible in his entrance-hall, and neither did the constabulary. This was entirely thanks to Nijam, who upon hearing that the lot of us had fallen foul of a prosthete, hired a hansom cab and was in Portland Place within half a minute of the crisis. The Indians were gone; the wedge with which they had sealed the front door from without was easily knocked aside; and the brougham which had brought us thither still waited patiently on the street opposite. Fresh air and some determined application of shouts and slaps did the rest. Within two minutes of the door closing upon us, we were in the carriage; and within fifteen, the three of us staggered into Nijam's laboratory at the University College and were deposited in a shadowed corner to recover. This was not particularly comfortable, the floorboards being cold and hard, and the entire laboratory being more or less overrun by mice.

"I have them safe at the laboratory," Nijam said into her transmitter. While Nijam had implanted her own transmitter beneath her skin, mine was not so permanently attached; it had been knocked awry during the course of our escape and

I had put it into my pocket for safekeeping. I did not, in consequence, hear Vasily's reply. "Yes! Of *course* I brought them to the laboratory; I can barely fit *myself* into my flat. You had better come at once." She turned on us, her lips thinned and disapproving beneath the electric lights. "Why did *no one* inform me there was an American involved? Don't you know what those people are like? If I had known the house was likely to be protected by a prosthete—"

I blinked at her. "You don't sound as though you like Americans."

"I don't," Nijam said. "My father married an American."

That piqued my interest despite her forbidding tone; Nijam had told me very little about her Indian parent. "Was that after his marriage to your mother?"

"No, it was before. They deported him for bigamy, and I never saw him again."

This was very shocking, but I reflected that my family also had bigamy in its closet; my great-grandmother had been obliged to flee to London from Belfast to hide her shame after being served much as the second Mrs Nijam had been.

"More to the point," Nijam added severely, "you *know* that Americans pride themselves on their prosthetic enhancements. Self-made men, they call themselves. *Everyone* knows that one cannot be anyone in America without a few millions, a chateau on Fifth Avenue, a duke for a son-in-law and half a dozen mechanical appendages, up to and including *automata!*"

"Well," I said feebly, "*I* didn't. Don't you, see, Nijam? This is why I wanted you with us. What would have become of us tonight without you? What would happen to Schmidt if the police took him up a second time?"

Nijam bit her lip. For a moment there was silence, until an

officious voice spoke from the doorway. "Miss? I beg your pardon, but are you supposed to be here at this hour?"

Schmidt, who had been tidied away like the rest of us behind one of the long workbenches, tried to get up; but Nijam forestalled him. "Why don't you let Dr Schmidt decide what his assistant is supposed to be doing?" she hissed, with energetic venom. The intruder retreated in disarray; and Nijam, thus revived, took a deep breath and smoothed back her already glassy-smooth hair.

One of the mice came near me. I waved a hand to frighten it away, but it took no notice and a moment later vanished—literally vanished—within the folds of my skirt. An imprint mouse! That was reassuring, but hardly relaxing. I shuddered to think how many of them must have met their ends in this place. One of these days I would ask Nijam what scientists had against the creatures.

Climbing to my feet, I perched on one of the stools at the workbench. "I don't understand how Griff knew there were three burglars."

"Well, isn't it obvious? His automaton was transmitting the sights, as well as the sounds."

"I didn't even know that was possible," I said shakily.

Vasily, who had evidently been following the conversation via Nijam's transmitter, now entered the laboratory and spoke without greeting: "That, I imagine, explains his peculiar behaviour at dinner. At first I thought he was having an apoplexy, for he ceased to move or speak; only stared into the distance. Do you think he was controlling the automaton from a distance? I take it you smashed the thing somehow; that was when he got up and ran for his carriage. Miss Dark, I hope you're not too shaken."

"I blame myself entirely," he went on after I, and Schmidt and Mimi from their positions on the floor, had assured him we were well. "I ought to have foreseen he'd be a prosthete."

"No use crying over spilt milk," Nijam said shortly. "Is there the slightest chance he might have seen your faces? No? Then the worst is averted, and mostly thanks to Schmidt. But you should all ask yourselves if this job is worth pursuing. This Vandergriff may have transmitters installed in other places; he might have other automata, and he very likely has offensive weaponry installed." She sent a severe look towards Vasily and myself. "You are, in sum, attempting to steal the Noor-Jahan out from under the nose of a person who sees everything and hears everything, and who will mash you to a paste if he catches up with you."

"We understand that the American is a monster," Mimi said dismissively. "I want to know who the Indians were."

I cannot say with any certainty that Nijam *did* grow three inches in stature, or developed a coating of ice, but she certainly gave that impression. "Indians? I *beg* your pardon?"

Mimi had been whispering with Schmidt; evidently this was how she knew of them. There was no hope for it: I must confess.

"We got out of the house, but there were four or five Indians waiting for us outside," I said weakly. "They took the decoy and shut us inside again."

"They *took* the decoy," Nijam repeated. She threw up her hands. "That does it. There's no point in going on now."

"But we can't give up," I protested.

I might have said more, but Vasily gave his most untrustworthy smile and said, "Indeed. It's out of the question that anyone should reach the diamond before Miss Dark."

"I didn't mean it like that," I said, reddening—although I did take his point; that if I gave up, the race would be on between Vasily and the Indians, and may the worse man win. "What I meant is that *I saw the ghosts.* I *saw* all the people who have been killed and tortured for the sake of that stone, and now I have a duty to help right those wrongs."

"Ghosts!" Nijam sniffed. "Not this again."

Schmidt, who had levered himself to his feet, now cleared his throat diffidently. "Pardon me for changing the subject, but—I believe Miss Dark has something for you, Miss Nijam."

Nijam blinked, and the ice thawed slightly as she grasped his meaning. "The manuscript—do you have it?"

"I do," I said, grateful to Schmidt for the reminder—and the obvious attempt to make peace. Once the thing had been extracted from my pocket, Nijam lit a lamp by which to examine the relic. "Is this the one you wanted?"

"How should I know? I'm not a mathematician, and I don't read Sanskrit," she said witheringly. But then she closed it with a sigh, running a hand lovingly across the worn cover. "We had an agreement," she conceded. "You've held up your end of the bargain; and if you mean to go on and steal the Noor-Jahan, then I'll hold up mine. But I do advise against it. A prosthete is no laughing matter."

"We won't go on with the job unless everyone is willing," said I. "I'm worried myself, but I can't back down; not now. We've already survived the melusines, after all." Personally, I had been a great deal more afraid of the Infanta Blanca than I was of Griff; who, after all, was a gentleman. "I vote we continue."

"As do I," Vasily agreed. "As our dear Miss Dark would say, *forewarned is four-legged.*"—I wished the mice had been real, so that I could have popped one under his hat.

Schmidt cleared his throat. "We knew when we entered Herr Haber's employment that we would be facing monsters, whether they be the sort with titles or without them. What would we be if we turned back now?"

"Rational," Nijam burst out. She threw up her hands and walked away, so that for a moment I thought she was about to storm out of the room altogether. But she turned at the door and paced back. "All *right,*" she said fiercely. "I agree. It's worth fighting monsters, simply for the sake of fighting monsters. I hope you're happy."

In the silence that followed, Mimi uttered a short, triumphant laugh. "Oh yes," she said. "It's very clear who our leader is."

Everyone looked at her in surprise.

She crossed her arms, gleeful. "All of you are wrong. It isn't Vasily, and it isn't Miss Dark. Nor is it Miss Nijam. It's Alphonse Schmidt."

To do him credit, Schmidt seemed at least twice as horrified by this as anyone else. *"Me?"*

Vasily laughed. "My dear Mimi! Really!"

"I am not *your dear Mimi,*" she said, prodding him in the chest with a finger. "And all of you know I am right. Whatever Schmidt decides, you and Miss Nijam fall in with it at once. Since there are five of us, Schmidt has a majority of three to two. Therefore, Schmidt is the leader."

There was a brief, blank silence in which I beheld something truly wonderful. It cannot be given to everyone to see, crossing the face of a hardened reprobate who has been a vampire and a thief and a renegade and goodness knows what else, a real, bright, honest-to-goodness blush.

"I—I—I am a Grand Duke!" Vasily sputtered. "My grandfather was Tsar Nicholas the First! I do *not* follow the leadership of my *valet!*"

I did not embarrass him by pointing out that *this* Grand Duke very much did. It was perfectly true. Nijam followed where Schmidt led because she was, as previously noted, potty about him. Vasily did so because he plainly could not bear the thought of losing the one last person he really trusted. It was really rather touching.

"Now," Mimi said, very pleased with the effect she had created, "what about that decoy?"

"We'll have to steal it back," Nijam said briskly. But even she was not immune to the general embarrassment: "And the Grand Duke is right. Don't give Schmidt a fat head. It's not good for him."

* * *

Nijam had described Griff as one who saw everything, heard everything, and could mash us to a paste if he chose. Certainly he had, via his automaton, seen a great deal more than any of us had bargained for. Yet I felt almost certain that the three of us had been well concealed, I behind my veil, and Schmidt and Mimi beneath their masks. If the following day found me anxious to hear from Griff, it was largely because I fancied the notion of hearing all about my burglary from the person most likely to be investigating it.

It was Sunday morning, and of course my sisters and I attended church. I was fidgety throughout the service—although I do remember the text: it was *Inasmuch as ye have done it unto one of the least of these My brethren, ye have done it unto*

Me. The afternoon was no better; I tried to read aloud from *The Pilgrim's Progress,* but my mind reverted ceaselessly to the house at Portland Place and what might be happening there. By tea-time, unable to bear it any longer, I sat down and wrote Griff a little note, which I dropped into a red pillar-box since I did not have a footman to carry it directly. The next morning, which was Monday, I had a reply by my breakfast-plate: Griff begged me to forgive him for not calling on me sooner and asked whether I cared to take luncheon with him at Claridge's.

Of course I accepted, although my reasons were not purely selfish. It had been decided that while Nijam and Schmidt attempted to create her decoy and track down the Indians who had taken our rightfully stolen property, and while Vasily and Mimi devoted themselves to a study of the British Museum and its weaknesses, I must keep a close eye upon Griff. Thus, one o'clock found me taking my place opposite the American at one of the little round tables downstairs at the Claridge's restaurant—a sacred place I had heard of but never seen, all gilded arches and red carpet, potted palms and society ladies in extravagant furs and flighty hats.

"I do hope I'm not keeping you from important business," I told him with my widest-eyed look, when first greetings had been exchanged, and our food had been ordered. There was no wine, because Griff was a teetotaller; but the menu was splendid: lobster Newburg, asparagus with hollandaise, chicken with watercress, and cheese and dessert to follow. Perhaps I ought to have brought my sisters, for I was sure I would be unable to eat half so much. "You said you'd been busy lately?"

If he suspected me of being one of Sir Humphrey's larcenous guests, Griff made no sign of it. "I have been," he said rather grimly. "I'm not sure if you read the papers, Miss Molly."

"Almost never," I said. In fact I was rather fond of the society columns; but I was almost certain this frivolous pastime would only sink me in Griff's regard. "Why? Have *you* been in them?"

"Not myself; Sir Humphrey. But I don't want to alarm you."

"I believe I'm already alarmed. I hope nothing dreadful has happened to Sir Humphrey!"

"It's nothing very bad, but two nights ago his house at Portland Place was broken into by a gang of ruffians. There was a paragraph about it in the *Times*, and of course I've been assisting with the investigation. But don't worry yourself, Miss Molly—we shall catch the miscreants."

This was precisely what *did* worry me, though of course I did not say as much. Indeed, I felt a frisson of excitement. Really, this *was* a wonderful game: he the hunter, and I the quarry, and he knew nothing of it. "How thrilling! Was anything taken? Have you any clues?"

"The police are on the case, of course—fine-combing the house for clues, and the neighbourhood for anyone who might have seen something. There's a group of Indian street-musicians they are anxious to question, for instance. But I know for certain *they* aren't the culprits."

"How so?"

"Because," Griff said, lowering his voice, "they were all in men's clothing, and I have excellent reason to believe that one of the thieves was a woman." He drew back as the waiter arrived with our food, and took a pill with a mouthful of water to wash it down. A smile played on his lips as he added: "But as to your other question—yes. Something rather important *was* taken."

The words were calculated to put the listener into a fever

of anticipation at the very moment the waiter's presence enforced our silence. "Don't be a tease!" I reproached him the moment we were alone again. "Tell me at once what they took!"

"Well, then, I trust to your discretion: it was the glass decoy Sir Humphrey told us about some nights ago at the Museum."

I had my look of artless surprise ready to go, and clapped both my hands to my mouth. "Oh, Griff! Not really? Think of the look on their faces when they find that all they took was a bit of glass!"

This display of feminine silliness pleased Griff immensely. "Oh, I doubt they were labouring under any misconceptions. The whereabouts of the real diamond is no secret; half of London must have been in to gawk at the Seton Collection over the past two days. No—there's bigger game afoot, Miss Molly. The only reason to steal the decoy, would be to switch it for the real Noor-Jahan. And that's another reason why it couldn't be the Indians. This is a job that will require professionals."

"Mightn't Indians be professionals?" I asked, thinking of Nijam, and how near we had come to grief without her. Griff only laughed as though I had said something rather amusing. Since the question was not entirely relevant, however, I went on: "If the police are barking wide of the mark, then whom do *you* suspect?"

Before Griff was able to answer, a shadow fell over our table and we looked up to see—Vasily. "Vandergriff! Miss Dark!" he said winsomely. "What a pleasant surprise!"

I could have throttled the wretch. I had taken the precaution of telling Nijam via transmitter with whom I would be spending the midday hour. Evidently, Vasily had listened

96

in—and now once again took possession of my hand as though he thought it belonged to him.

"Vandergriff, you're just the man I wished to see," Vasily said, having kissed my fingers. "The other night at dinner you mentioned that an acquaintance of yours was collecting French art. Do you think he'd be interested in anything of Meissonier's?"

"For a Meissonier you could get any price you like," Griff said, "fifteen thousand francs or more. And if William Whitney won't pay it, then I will."

"What excellent news," Vasily said, in a thoughtful way that told me he was now adding French art to the list of fine things he was willing to steal. "I may have something of the sort at home in Russia. Miss Dark, I have a quarrel with you."

The sudden change of subject barely flustered me at all. A quarrel with me? That was nothing to the quarrel I had with him. "Oh? Do tell," I said in a tone nearly as frosty as Nijam's own.

"Yes," he said with a deep bow, "how dare you look so lovely taking luncheon with anyone but myself? I envy you, Vandergriff." He shook hands with Griff, and the depths of my embarrassment did not prevent me noticing something rather peculiar: I was almost certain I saw the American's hand steal out and dip into the pocket of Vasily's jacket. A moment later Vasily was gone, and Griff reached for his wineglass with the hand that had just been inside Vasily's pocket—now quite definitely empty.

"Something the matter?" Griff asked.

I must have been frowning at the wineglass as it was carried to his lips. "I beg your pardon," I said, to cover my suspicions. "I haven't the slightest notion why Grand Duke Vasily should say such outrageous things."

He leaned nearer, and once again I felt the overwhelming force of his narrowed gaze. For a moment I thought I knew how an ant feels as the bootheel descends... "You seem to be closely acquainted with the Grand Duke. That's mighty fine company for a humble governess to be keeping."

My throat went quite dry. "Grand Duke Vasily was one of the guests in a house where I was working once, in Europe. I think it amuses him to torment me."

"I don't doubt it." His attention never wavered from my face. "You asked whom I suspected, Miss Molly. The truth is, I suspect everyone."

I hoped my laugh did not sound too forced. "Not me, I hope?"

To my relief, he laughed too. "What, a neat, dainty little Englishwoman like you? No; it's as I said: this is a job for professionals." He sent a meaningful look towards the distant table where Vasily was settling in behind a newspaper. "The police can do the hard work, but I'm going on a hunch. The Grand Duke invited Seton and myself to dinner on the very night the house was burgled. And he was asking questions about the Noor-Jahan two nights previously."

I scarcely had to pretend my horror. "The *Grand Duke?* How can *he* be a jewel thief?"

"Maybe he's like me," Griff said softly, his eyes flickering once again towards the man across the room. "Maybe we both like to hunt the most dangerous game there is. And made no mistake, Miss Molly: the hunt is up."

He smiled at me and dug into his asparagus. I managed to follow suit. I had little appetite, but by dint of trencherwork I might avoid conversation and indulge myself in gloomy thoughts. It appalled me to admit it, but Griff was right. Vasily *was* a hunter. Once, he'd been a vampire, and his prey must have been men and women. He must miss the thrill of the hunt; he must have become a thief at least partly to satiate those predatory instincts. Like a horse that runs only because it cannot bear the thought of being outrun by another horse, Vasily likely could not help himself: I had tricked him once, and now he must trick me in turn.

But of course Vasily was a known quantity, and though I dreaded the moment when he would betray me, I was as ready for it as I ever could be. Griff, however, was wholly unknown. Not even Nijam could say for certain what he might or might not be capable of; it all depended upon his prosthetics. He might have eyes and ears everywhere—or he might not. Still, Griff had told me himself on two separate occasions that he was a hunter, for whom the thrill of the chase was all-engrossing. If there was any way for him to watch and listen, he would have and employ it.

With that thought, I knew precisely why Griff's hand had been in Vasily's pocket. And I knew, too, what must be done next. I asked Griff about his Hong-Kong-to-San-Francisco shipping plans, and forced myself to swallow a few more mouthfuls of food that tasted like dust. We were waiting for dessert when I excused myself.

The ladies' lavatories were small and cramped by comparison to the rest of the hotel, but they were, at that moment, quite empty. I shut myself within one of the stalls to search my own clothing and was gratified to find no foreign objects lurking within the folds of my skirt. This done, I opened my transmitter.

"Vasily, it's me," I said without preamble. "Not a word; but look in your right coat pocket. Drop what you find into your water-glass."

There was no reply, and for a moment I feared he had not heard me. But then the line crackled and Vasily murmured, "There's nothing here."

I *might* take him at his word—and then, too, I *might* see the whole lot of us taken up by the police for burglary, and then there would be the headlines, and the scandal, and Mother never able to hold up her head again. "No, really, I'm positive there is. Say nothing, but come to the lavatories at once."

I was almost sure I heard him sigh; and less than a minute later (although it felt like an hour) he strolled in at the corridor leading first to the ladies' room, and then to the gentlemen's. Without saying a word, I attached myself to the lapels of his coat and hurried him into the ladies'. You need not tell me how *very* improper this was, but I felt that it would have been even less proper to meet in the gentlemen's room.

"What a delightful surprise!" Vasily murmured.

I gestured impatiently for him to remain silent. With each passing moment I only felt more certain that Griff had planted some sort of listening-device, and I was frantic with haste, for heaven only knew how little time we had. Perhaps you will understand, then, that all feminine reserve abandoned me: I slipped my hands into the pockets of his coat, and upon finding them empty, I pulled his necktie loose. There was nothing lurking within his collar, and so I began feverishly to run my hands over his coat. My search was rewarded: I touched something on his back, in the hollow between spine and shoulder-blade, and stifled a cry of triumph. Having clapped my left hand over the tiny, squirming thing to trap it between his shirt and coat, I slipped my right beneath the coat to take hold of it; and so I had both my arms about a rumpled Vasily when someone at the door exclaimed "Sir!!!" in tones of outraged dowagerhood, and I perceived that we were discovered.

My first impulse was to spring away from him—and indeed I had already half turned to face the intruder when Vasily's arms closed about me like iron, and his hand forced my head against the snowy expanse of his shirt-front.

"Madam, I'm shocked!" he said, laughing—of *course* he would be laughing, the reprobate! "Is this any place for a lady?"

"I beg—cover your eyes, Mabel!—I *beg* your pardon?"

"I believe you've mistaken the sign on the door," Vasily told her, with unbridled cheek. "Don't you know this is the gentlemen's room? What will people think? A Peeping Tom is bad enough, but a Peeping Countess—!"

For a moment no sound was audible but a wheezing, impassioned breath and the absolute insurrection of my own thoughts. Then the Countess said, "Come away, Mabel! We shall depart this den of iniquity at once!"

They must have sailed away, for Vasily released my head and I, having withdrawn the little transmitter from his coat very gingerly between my thumb and forefinger, sent him an outraged look which was all I then had the opportunity to give him. I could not have said which was worse—Vasily's bad behaviour to a perfectly inoffensive old lady, or the fact that trapped as he was between the Charybdis of Griff's listening ears and the Scylla of the dowager's outrage, he had chosen to risk the latter, and sacrifice my fair fame to his own safety!

I was obliged to swallow my indignation, for there was no inaudible means of expressing it. I saw at a glance that Griff's

101

transmitter must be designed to transmit sound only and not images, for the thing was only about the size of Nijam's transmitters, or perhaps a little smaller—a gleaming metallic cartridge about the length of my little finger, all fitted with clicking and waving legs like a mad spider, with which it had evidently run beneath Vasily's coat to seek refuge. If you were fond of spiders it would have been beautiful. I was not. Shuddering, I took it to the nearest lavatory and was about to consign it to the depths when Vasily caught my wrist. Shaking his head, he took out his pocket-handkerchief, knotted the spider within, and tucked it into his pocket.

I could not let him go away without warning him, so I pulled the chain on the lavatory and under the sound of the cistern draining, leaned up to whisper in Vasily's ear. "Beware—Griff suspects you. Come to Brixton at five."

He assented with a nod. I reconnoitred the corridor to ensure that it was clear before sending him back to the restaurant. Some minutes later I myself followed; praying, as I resumed my seat opposite Griff, that the flush in my cheeks did not excite his suspicions.

Chapter VII.

While these exciting scenes were being witnessed at Claridge's, Nijam was inspecting her second batch of superheated baddeleyite for any signs of crystalline structure.

"How is it?" Alphonse Schmidt asked diffidently. He sat at a bench in the corner, filling a set of delicate glass bulbs with salt-water before tucking each of them with care into the specially-made pouches he wore on his belt.

Nijam only sent him a withering look. The question could not be a serious one. Had her efforts been crowned with success, she would even now be crowing loudly. As it was, all she had managed to produce was another bit of very unprepossessing burnt slag. Letting out a sigh, she swept the results into the garbage and buried her face in her hands. So far in her quest for a stabiliser she had tested six of Mendeleev's elements—which meant she yet had sixty left to try; and that was presuming she had mixed them with the baddeleyite in anything like the correct proportion.

A faint clink of glass dragged her from her musings to find Alphonse at the cupboard inspecting the minerals within. "Leave those alone," she snapped. "I don't want them mixed up."

"I only meant—"

"Kindly remember that *I'm* the one who does the work." Really, it was beyond bearing. Here she was in a chemistry lab., sweating blood over a chemical problem with none other than Alphonse Schmidt himself by her side—and all *he* was capable of making was a sodium-and-water solution!

"I meant to say—have you tried this?" he repeated doggedly, holding up a jar containing a lump of silvery metal in long, feathery strands.

Nijam frowned at the label. "Yttrium? Are you serious? Do you have any idea how rare this is—and how expensive?"

He flushed. "No—but I'd wager it's less rare than a diamond the size of a hen's egg."

"It may be, but put it back. At the rate I'm going through baddeleyite, I'll be lucky if they don't ask me to buy them several pounds of the stuff." She let out a sigh. "If you had your memories, we could solve this in half the time."

Schmidt frowned as though the thought was new to him; but he did as he was told, and put the yttrium back on the shelf. Nijam stared again at the cupboard, until she felt that she could stand it no longer. "We aren't getting anywhere," she declared, taking her coat and hat from the stand by the door. "Why don't we go out on that other business, and perhaps something will suggest itself by the time we get back."

They took the Euston Road west and presently passed Portland Place on the left before crossing into Marylebone. Halfway to Baker Street, Nijam said, "How did you come to lose your memories, anyway?"

"Well," he said with dogged patience, "I don't remember."

"Naturally; but it happened at about the time you were condemned to the *Akbar*, didn't it?"

"I suppose it must have."

"I've spoken about it to those who know," Nijam went on—without betraying the fact that she had done so specifically on Alphonse's behalf—"and I'm told that this sort of memory loss may be caused by siren attack, and that the *Akbar* is one of the customary places to immure the—er, the patient."

Schmidt was genuinely startled. "Good God! Do you mean to suggest that I might have assaulted a royal personage?"

Nijam took a deep, slow breath. Why should he presume any such thing? "I believe I *said* it might have happened the other way round—that a royalty might have assaulted *you.*"

He seemed not to hear her, so convinced was he that no royalty could possibly have done him an unprovoked wrong. "The Kings of Denmark are sirens, and so are the Kings of Greece. If you know something, Miss Nijam, tell me. Have I ever been to Copenhagen? Was I a person of criminal inclinations?—No," he added, as Nijam opened her mouth, "you did not know me except by repute; I was forgetting. Give me no false assurances."

Nijam ground her teeth, sorely tempted to speak anyway—to say that in her eyes he was a sort of present-day Sir Galahad, upon whose judgement she was even now ready to stake her life. But in doing so, she must also confess to having known him; and then she must confess to loving him; and then either he would turn away from her and break her heart, or else he would feel he owed her his troth as a matter of duty. And that would break her heart just the same.

"I say nothing as to who you *were,*" she said, almost gruffly, "but I do know who you *are,* Alphonse Schmidt, and it's no one to feel ashamed of."

After that they were silent until they reached the Hindustani Coffee House in George Street—*Estd. 1810, Prop. Mr Dean.*

The place looked just the same as it had twenty years ago, when as a girl she had hurried by on the other side of the street so as not to be mistaken for one of *them.* Now, Nijam hesitated outside the doors for such a long time that Alphonse sent her a doubtful look.

"Is this the place?"

She let out a sigh. "We're supposed to be finding Mirza Dara, but I've never had much time for my father's people, and now I don't know where to begin. Still, this ought to do as well as anywhere else."

She pushed open the door and led the way inside. Here they found a dark room, heated to an almost tropical warmth and full of hookahs, cane furniture, and sunburnt majors eating curry. One of them looked up when Nijam entered, and putting down his fork, called "Dean! Dean! Here's one of *your* sort."

The gentleman thus summoned proved to be a round, broadly-smiling, dark-complexioned man who descended upon Nijam with outstretched arms and a beaming smile. "Miss! Welcome!" he cried. Alarmed, Nijam took a step backward. Her skirts brushed against the solid presence of Alphonse behind her; but Mr Dean only pressed his palms together and bowed before breaking into a flood of Hindustani. He finished by flapping his white napkin at her in an inviting way. "Now, step this way, don't be shy! You and your friend are welcome here!"

Nijam followed him reluctantly to the service-door of the restaurant and through the busy kitchen beyond to a small, noisy room at the rear of the house, which must once have been the mews. The place was bare, with whitewashed walls, low wooden tables and only tattered cushions to sit upon—but it was filled with the metallic strum of a sitar, the chatter of a dozen or so Indians, and the scent of hot bread and spiced lentils, a far cry from the hothouse dignity of the front room.

Mr Dean said something to Nijam, again in Hindustani. "I'm sorry," she said, "I only speak English."

"Not to worry, not to worry," he said jovially in that language. "Go and sit down there—no, not that way—oh! I am so sorry, Mr Mukherjee, *so* sorry. Do come again." The gentleman thus addressed, who had seated himself in solitary grandeur near the open door, got up, levelled an offended look at Nijam, and stalked out into the street. "Your shadow fell over him," Dean explained. "He's a Brahmin and doesn't yet know our ways in England. What will you have to eat? We have bhaat, aloo bhaja, begun bhaja, dal, chingri machher malaikari, mutton, chatni, papad, and mishti."

The only word Nijam recognised amidst this rapid-fire menu was *mutton.* Already half overwhelmed by so much noise, such strong smells, and so many people, she could not bear the thought of adding spiced food to her overburdened senses. "Just tea, please. We came on business; we're looking for a man named Mirza Dara."

Afterwards, she could not quite remember whether the hush that fell over the room had begun before her inquiry, or because of it. Only suddenly there was no music and very little chatter, and more than one pair of eyes fixed her in place.

"Mirza Dara," Mr Dean said slowly. "Did I hear that correctly?"

"Yes," said Nijam, hoping devoutly that she was not making a mistake.

"I don't know anyone by that name," Mr Dean said with an uneasy laugh. "A mirza would not stoop to *my* house, I'm sure.

107

Tea for you, sir?"

Alphonse, who had always been fascinated by the strange and exotic, had already made himself comfortable at the table. "Yes, please; and I'll have some food as well, whatever you recommend."

The general chatter began again, but when Mr Dean departed, the sitar-player took his place. A handsome young man with a luxuriant drooping moustache, he was dressed in the picturesque clothing of a lascar: white trousers, an embroidered tunic fastened at the waist with a belt, and a turban-like headdress. "A mirza," he repeated with a smile. "Why are you seeking this man?"

Nijam scented a lead. "I thought he might be able to help me identify a Sanskrit manuscript. Do you know him?"

The lascar took a place, uninvited, at the table with them; and instead of answering the question, asked another. "Who told you this man could help you?"

"I heard the name somewhere; I can't precisely remember in what connection."

He laughed, evidently not for a moment taken in by her forgetfulness. "And what brings you *here* to find him?"

She must be honest where she could. Nijam straightened, looking the young lascar in the eye. "Before she died, my mother used to live three houses away from here, in Montagu Square. I came because I wanted to speak to Indians, and this was the first place I thought to come."

"I see. Will you show me the manuscript? My Sanskrit is not good, but if I am unable to help, I might perhaps know someone who can."

Nijam was carrying the manuscript in a heavy pocket beneath her petticoats; but it was no part of her plan to allow this youth so much as a glimpse of it. "It's a valuable relic," she said. "I will show it only to the Mirza. Will you lead me to him?"

The lascar watched her face for a moment, and there was a sharp edge to his smile when he asked, "What! do you think I will steal this thing from you, in broad daylight, in the house of Sake Din Mahomet?"

Words died on her lips as Nijam revisited her last speech and really *heard* what she had just said. This young man was a lascar—the lowest of ship-hands, acquainted with the roughest company; hired mainly because he would accept a third of the payment demanded by Englishmen, and take three times the brutality into the bargain. A moment ago it had only seemed rational to use caution with such a person. Now she began to feel her cheeks burn. The day stood at noon; Mr Dean's establishment was of unexceptionable reputation and his guests included at least one family with very pretty children; the lascar himself was well-spoken, neat, and gentlemanlike; and even had he not been, she was still here in the company of Alphonse Schmidt, who may have forgotten what he knew of chemistry but had gained a very broad scientific knowledge of the application of fists.

"What my friend *means*," Alphonse began, hurrying (as ever) into the awkward silence in an attempt to smooth over troubled waters, "is that—"

"I know what she means," the lascar said, raising his hand in an oddly imperious gesture that silenced Alphonse at once. Addressing Nijam, he went on: "Why should I lead you to the Mirza? You have done nothing but insult us since you walked into this room. If you want help, you must show the manuscript to me."

109

"Really, my good man, I must insist—" Alphonse began, bristling at the lascar's words.

But Nijam held up her own hand in a gesture that was the mirror of the lascar's. "I apologise," she said. "I have endured the prejudices of others too often to thoughtlessly repeat them."

She extracted the book from her pocket and took off the brown paper with which she had wrapped it to protect it. The lascar passed a hand over the age-darkened wooden boards of its cover almost reverently before opening it. "This is very old," he said. "And you are correct: the writing is Sanskrit."

"And the subject matter?" Nijam prompted.

"My Sanskrit is not good, as I told you," said the lascar, who was looking less and less like a shiphand with each passing moment. "But I recognise this name." He rested a long, tapered finger on one of the illegible words. "It's Halayudha's commentary on the Pingala Sutras. A poetry treatise."

A moment ago Nijam had been buoyed up on a swell of triumph. Now, she felt as though her barque had overturned, pitching her bodily into the cold waves.

"I beg your pardon? A treatise on *what?*"

"On poetry," the lascar replied.

"But are you sure?"

"Quite sure."

Poetry—and not mathematics at all! Nijam might have wept with vexation. She had gone to so much trouble—and all for nothing. Either I had fetched her the wrong manuscript; or the rumour which led her to seek the mathematical secrets of the Halayudha Sutras among Sir Humphrey Seton's inherited spoils had been altogether mistaken.

She snatched the book back. "Very well, but I want an

110

opinion from someone who *does* have good Sanskrit."

The lascar raised an eyebrow. "I assure you, the Mirza won't be of any greater assistance to you than I have been."

Unable any longer to tolerate the noise, and the smells, and the smiling young man who refused to tell her anything, Nijam erupted from her seat. Coming here had been a mistake. "Then I suppose there's no point in staying any longer. Come, Schmidt!"

Chapter VIII.

I, having survived the remainder of my luncheon with Griff, returned home to a round of tedious daily business—paying bills, answering letters, and escorting my sisters to painting lessons (Emily) and meetings at the *Blackwood's* offices (Katie). We were home by five o'clock; and I walked into the sitting-room to find it occupied by a perfectly monstrous bouquet of hothouse flowers. Pink roses and yellow peonies rose in a pyramid from a basket large enough to serve as a bed for an Irish wolfhound. It was as though the entire Hanging Gardens of Ancient Babylon had migrated to Brixton. My sisters' mouths fell open.

"Hannah!" I said feebly—the housekeeper had welcomed us home with an offer to put the kettle on. "Hannah—what on *earth?*"

She pushed her spectacles up her nose and squinted at the monstrosity. "A man brought them around this afternoon, Miss Molly. It seems hard to credit, but he insisted they were meant for you."

"It's the Eighth Wonder of the World!" Lilias burbled. She had been upstairs all afternoon scribbling sheet after sheet of paper, so engrossed that she had not seen the bouquet delivered.

"Peonies and pink roses signify happiness," Katie said wisely. "Look, there's a card with them."

Only one man of my acquaintance would send such an ostentatious gift, and the card confirmed my suspicions. Mr Warren H. Vandergriff thanked me for the pleasure of my company that day, and hoped that I liked flowers.

"Oh, it's that Vandergriff fellow!" Emily exclaimed. She eyed the arrangement critically. "Molly, his taste is *dreadful.*"

"Some people have more money than sense," Hannah sniffed.

It was at that moment that the clock struck five, and I recalled that this was the hour I had set for our next council of war. In another moment, Vasily and Nijam and the others would be knocking at the door. Just then, indeed, I heard a carriage halting in the street outside. I imagined the look on Vasily's face when he found the sitting-room occupied by a Great Giza Pyramid of roses. Then a horrible thought struck me. What if Griff suspected me after all? What if one of his little devices was hidden inside that basket, listening for every word I might say?

"They cannot stay here," I gasped, snatching at the flowery colossus. Hannah and the girls protested, but the basket was lighter than I had expected, and I managed to whisk the entire tottering edifice into the kitchen just as the knocker went at the front door. "I'll show them in," I said, depositing the basket upon the table.

"Can I put them in vases?" Emily asked.

I hesitated. Perhaps one of Griff's spiders was concealed within the basket; or perhaps it had already scuttled from its hiding-place and ensconced itself behind the curtains, but mature reflection persuaded me that the bouquet was probably harmless. Had Griff intended his gift to act as

113

a Roman Horse, he would have brought something small enough to be placed in a corner undisturbed; and he would have delivered it personally.

Nevertheless, I would not allow Vasily to make merry at my expense because of it. "Do so, and disperse them about the house, or it will look as though we're about to open a shop."

The door-knocker went again, and I fled up the hall to usher my first guests—Vasily and Mimi—into the sitting-room. There was a stray peony lying just inside the door, but I used my foot to nudge it behind an occasional-table.

"We can speak freely," were almost the first words out of Vasily's mouth. "I made sure to leave that infernal transmitter in my other coat, and I hope Vandergriff likes listening to the inside of a wardrobe."

"I thought you meant to carry it about with you; to put him off the scent."

"So I have done: all afternoon, while Mimi and I were wandering the British Museum in search of a likely way in. I flatter myself I put on a creditable performance; but it's over now, and I shall retire from the stage for an evening, at least."

"I think you ought to show more dedication to your craft. What did you find at the Museum?"

"Well, it's supposed to be haunted."

"I've no doubt of *that*," said I, with feeling. It was a mercy that so many of the imprints were so very old and faded; otherwise the place might have been as dreadful as a visit to a cemetery.

"Both the inner and outer courtyards are patrolled by night-watchmen," Vasily went on, "but we found an ingress by way of the basement beneath the Museum's ground floor."

"What he means," Mimi said, "is that *I* found a way in."

"My dear Mimi, that's because I was compelled to play

the blameless sight-seer for Mr Vandergriff's benefit. The basement, as I was saying, is a veritable warren of storerooms; but for our purposes, the main thing is the plant room, which houses the boiler. Beneath this room there's a tunnel built to accommodate a tidal stream, which provides water to cool the boiler. There's a ladder leading from the plant room into the tunnel, which connects to the London sewers through a locked gate; so that if we make our attempt at low tide, and if Mimi has lost none of her aptitude with lock-picking, we should find it quite easy to get in that way. So you see that we are only waiting now for a good decoy."

"And that depends on Nijam," said I, with a sigh. A knock sounded at the door. "That must be her now."

I saw at once that Nijam was in a mood. "You brought me the wrong manuscript," she said icily, sailing past me and into the sitting-room without taking off her coat or hat: the universal signal that a caller means not to stay a moment longer than she can help. "It's only a useless poetry treatise. The one I *needed* was the one holding the mathematical secret to a new calculating machine."

"Oh, Nijam, I *am* sorry."

Vasily frowned. "I certainly asked Sir Humphrey about the Halayudha Sutras."

"Well, it cannot be helped. On the other hand, I have not found the Mirza Dara—apparently *mirza* is some sort of honorific—but I found someone who claims to know him, and I am almost sure that he is in London still."

"That's very good," I said hopefully. "What's the name of the person you spoke to?"

"I didn't ask. He was very unhelpful, anyway. I ought to have stayed at the laboratory, Dark; I'm not cut out for this business. I'm an Englishwoman, and I don't pass as one of these people."

"But, Nijam, whether you pass mustard with them or not—"

"Where's Schmidt?" Mimi interrupted. I paused, seeing that she was right:. Nijam had entered the house alone.

"How should I know where Schmidt is? We went together to the Hindustani Coffee House in Marylebone, and he disappeared on the way home. I wasted the whole afternoon arguing with an officious professor who wanted to turn me out of my laboratory—and speaking of laboratories, no, I haven't produced a diamond, and I haven't the faintest clue when or how I will!"

With this she sank scowling into an armchair. Vasily touched the transmitter in his ear and said, "Schmidt, do you hear me?"

"Quite clearly, sir. If sir will wait just a moment, I'm coming down the Saltoun Road now."

If Nijam's mood had been palpable upon her arrival, so too was Schmidt's. He bounded through the door like a large and pleased golden retriever, announcing to the assembled company: "I've found them, sir: the Indians from the other evening."

"I *beg* your pardon?" Nijam said.

"I waited outside the Hindustani Coffee House until that young lascar left it," Schmidt explained. "Then I simply followed him all the way across London to a seedy establishment in Limehouse where, I was told, a lot of lascars board when they're in port. He's staying there with four others—I recognised the tall one's voice. I'll wager anything you like we've found them."

"Let us hope you are right," Nijam muttered, but her

pessimism was not shared by the rest of the company.

"The decoy is as good as ours," Vasily announced. "But we can scarcely go after it with Vandergriff breathing down our necks."

"Down *your* neck, Vasya; don't implicate *me* in this."

"Thank you, Mimi; with Vandergriff breathing down *my* neck. Indeed I'm almost certain he had me followed tonight; I shook off a shadow on my way here."

Nijam blinked. "The prosthete *suspects?*"

"Griff slipped a mechanical bug into Vasily's pocket at lunch," I told her. "He tells me he has a hunch Vasily is after the Noor-Jahan."

"Which is inconvenient, because it's true," she agreed. "The only thing to do is to fob him off somehow onto the Indians."

Vasily frowned. "But how? *I* can hardly alert him to their presence in London; he'd suspect me at once."

"Suppose we stole the decoy from the Indians," I suggested, "and then Nijam returned it to Sir Humphrey and said she had found it in Limehouse."

Nijam sent me an utterly withering look. "Yes, and suppose they put *me* away as the thief!"

"Oh. Yes, and then I suppose we shall be in the porridge anyway."

"We needn't be too clever," Nijam added. "Vandergriff wants to hunt thieves; I don't think he cares particularly which thieves he hunts. We needn't put ourselves in his power; all we need to do is muddle the scent. And it's *soup,*" she added, turning on me.

"Soup?" I blinked, utterly at a loss. Was she hungry? Come to think of it, it was practically tea-time. "Shall we adjourn so that you can eat your dinners?"

117

Nijam only looked more exasperated, but whatever she might have said was forestalled when a knock sounded at the sitting-room door. I opened it, admitting a comfortable mealtime sound, all crockery and clinking cutlery, which emanated from the dining-room. And here was Katie on the threshold looking ominously disingenuous.

"Dinner's ready," she announced.

Evidently Katie had joined the twins in scheming to fraternise with my disreputable friends. I determined that I should not fall for their tricks. Firmly, I said, "Go on and eat, then; just save a plate for me."

"If you say so," Katie said meekly; only to wriggle past me and say to the others, "What about the rest of you? I'm sure you must be hungry after coming all this way. Do come and eat; there's enough for everyone."

Nijam said, "I only stepped in for a moment; I'm going away directly."

"My dear Miss Nijam, you can't possibly think of going away!" Vasily protested. "We must plan our next—ah—steps."

"Schmidt says he hasn't had any lunch," Mimi declared. "Nijam wouldn't allow it."—"Miss *Laine*," Schmidt protested, flushing scarlet.

"Then it's settled," Katie said, and before I quite knew what was happening, we were all following her into the dining-room. Vasily had the gall to wink at me as he passed out the sitting-room door. Oh, the *wretch!* It was one thing to let him cheat *me,* but if he thought to do the same by my sisters, he was quite mistaken.

My father's ghost chose that moment to approach, but I brushed straight through him. "Remember what I told you," I warned Vasily as I followed him into the dining-room. Vasily raised an innocent eyebrow at me, and I placated myself with vivid daydreams of singeing it off with one of the dining-room candles.

A plentiful bouquet of yellow peonies brightened the credenza; I wondered how many other overflowing vases had been dotted about the house. As for the dinner, Hannah and Katie had prepared a hot joint, and gravy to go with it; fresh bread and butter, and green peas with mint sauce, so that I almost felt dizzy with the extravagance myself. Hannah, having laid out this spread, retreated ceremonially to the kitchen for her own dinner. I hurriedly presented my sisters to the guests, and then said grace.

Lilias, of course, was the first to address the Grand Duke; which she did very powerfully.

"WOULD YOU LIKE SOME ELDERFLOWER CORDIAL, YOUR GRACE?"

Nijam started, but Vasily sent me a sidelong glance beneath lowered lashes. Then, with malicious pleasure, he said: "You'll have to speak a little louder, my dear; I'm not quite sure I caught your meaning!"

I tightened my grip on my fork as Lilias repeated her question at a still greater volume. The nerve! How dare he turn my own practical joke upon me!

"Oh, thank you. I *will* have cordial, if you please. And call me Vasily."

This unleashed a torrent of ear-splitting questions.

"ARE YOU REALLY A GRAND DUKE?" Emily wanted to know.

"I beg your pardon?"

"A GRAND DUKE?"

"Oh, a Grand *Duke.* Yes, of course!"

119

"THEN WHY AREN'T YOU A VAMPIRE?"

Conflicting emotions had the rest of my guests in their grasp. Schmidt looked desperately confused. Mimi had her napkin against her mouth and had turned somewhat red; I had the uncomfortable notion that she, like Vasily, knew precisely what was going on. Even Katie had a look of dawning understanding. As for Nijam—well, I dared not look at Nijam.

I did not care. I had arranged for Vasily to be shouted at, as he so richly deserved; and he *was* being shouted at, and *I* would not be the one to make it stop.

"A *campfire?*" he said plaintively. "I do not understand."

All my sisters, I am afraid to say, were enjoying themselves hugely. Even Katie joined in the chorus: "A VAMPIRE."

"A what?"

Nijam slammed her fork on the table and said through gritted teeth, "Vasily Nikolaevich, how would you like to be murdered?"

"At as late a date as possible," he answered, abandoning his act at once. "My dear Miss Dark, have you been telling your sisters untruths?"

I attempted—and perhaps managed—an air of innocence. "Why, your grace, I only said that you were terribly hard of hearing and needed to be spoken to firmly."

Mimi burst into laughter. Lilias' mouth fell open. *"Molly! How could you?"*

"Indeed I find that terribly unjust," Vasily agreed plaintively.

"Molly looks like butter wouldn't melt in her mouth," Lilias said with a knowing sigh, "but she always does things like this. *Last* time she was home she made me an apple-pie bed."

Emily nodded. "Once she saved up a newspaper from April Fool's Day, and slipped it next to Papa's breakfast-plate the

120

following year. He was *terribly* puzzled by it."

"And once when we were *very* little she pulled the wings off flies and told me they were raisins," Katie said with a mournful shake of her head.

Happening to see the look of horror that fleeted across Schmidt's unguarded face, I felt my cheeks heating. Allowing Vasily near my sisters had rebounded upon me in ways I had never expected. He cast me a laughing glance, and I steeled myself for worse.

Instead, turning to Emily, he changed the subject. "I'm told you are the one who painted the portrait in the drawing-room, Miss Emily. It's very fine."

Emily blushed and mentioned her hopes of exhibiting at the Royal Academy this year; and before long Katie was telling him about her poems, and Lilias about her stories. Nijam and Mimi engaged themselves in a discussion of gemstones—Mimi having an acquisitive, Nijam a scientific, interest in the matter. Schmidt remained silent, listening gravely to Nijam and Mimi. I, too, remained silent but vigilant, ready to step in should Vasily's conversation with my sisters roam beyond the bounds of propriety. Yet, for all my sisterly anxiety, I began to feel a trifle mournful.

I had now spent a little time in Griff's company, and the only subject of our conversation had been Warren H. Vandergriff. Not once had he asked me anything about my sisters, and only very rarely about myself. It was difficult, in that moment, not to draw a comparison between him and Vasily, who seemed so openly aware of me and my affairs. Of course that was only Vasily's way—it was through his keen interest in others and their wishes that he was able to assess and exploit their weaknesses. But in that moment I gave way to a weakness of my own, and allowed myself to wish that things had been different—that I no longer had to be on my guard with Vasily, at every moment analysing his words and actions for the hidden blade; that I could be honest with my sisters, no longer bound to protect them from my confederates; in short, that I could have allowed the two separate halves of my life to meet together without fear.

But of course it was impossible.

"What an artistic family you are!" Vasily said admiringly, as Lilias and Katie informed him of their literary pursuits. "And what sort of artist are you, Miss Dark?"

"Confidence," Mimi muttered, her conversation with Nijam having reached a lull.—Schmidt seemed to have swallowed something the wrong way. My sisters, I am thankful to say, did not know what was meant by this.

"Molly is a wonderful actress," Katie said, eager to give me my due. "Not on the stage, of course; only at home. But you ought to see her do Lady Macbeth, or Richard III and Anne Neville."

"An actress! Really?" Those hypnotic eyes of his fastened with lazy humour upon me. "I should *never* have guessed."

"How did you come to be acquainted with Molly, anyway?" Lilias asked—conscious, no doubt, of how *very* few Russian grand dukes had been entertained beneath *any* of the roofs on Saltoun Road. This was dangerous ground, and I had at that moment taken a bite of mutton; I was silenced.

Vasily's lazy humour sharpened at the look of panic that must have flashed into my eyes. "How did I come to be acquainted with your sister, Miss Lilias? I entered the room where she was, and she fell into my arms with kisses."

That might as well have touched off a bomb in the room, for

only Nijam had been present at that meeting in the Schloss Frohsdorf. Lilias, for once in her life, looked utterly at a loss for words. "Who—*Molly?*"

Katie repeated, "Who, *Molly?*" this time in tones of complete scandal. Schmidt gasped "Miss *Dark!*" as though he imagined it had been my fault and not Vasily's; and Mimi clapped her hands and cried, "I knew it!"

"What do you think?" Vasily asked, evidently exulting in the sensation he had caused. "Shouldn't she make an honest man of me? Should I ask her now, Miss Lilias?"

But Lilias said not a word; for all her impertinence she had been carefully raised, and I think she had never been so shocked in her life. The silence dragged out, and then Vasily, whose laughter began to die a little, turned and saw me. I hardly knew what to think, and there was nothing I could say; I only knew that my cheeks burned, and I had the awful thought that while I had been ready for Vasily to betray me over the Noor-Jahan, it had not occurred to me that he would strike at me like *this.*

"Dear me," Vasily said at once, with hardly an alteration in his manner, "the looks on your faces! I do hope none of you will *believe* such an outrageous story. Forgive me, Miss Dark, for a jest in poor taste. Miss Nijam will bear me out; she was present on that occasion, and can vouch for it that Miss Dark conducted herself with perfect propriety throughout."

My sisters laughed with great relief, and the conversation went on, although Vasily took less part in it than he had formerly. By the time that interminable meal came to its end, the thing seemed to have been forgotten—forgotten, that is, by everyone except myself. I stood and directed Nijam, Schmidt, and Mimi to the sitting-room; but to Vasily I hissed, "I want a quiet word with you."

The front hall was dark—there was something the matter with the gaslight, which was for the moment left unrepaired and unused. I drew Vasily a short way up the stairs, so that we would be concealed from anyone going to and fro between kitchen and dining-room. The stairs also gave me the advantage of height—for if I meant to confront Vasily at all, I liked to have every possible advantage.

"Miss Dark," he whispered, even before I had turned to face him, "will you allow me to apologise? I misjudged the situation; I felt myself so much at home in this house."

"A nice home you must have!" I retorted.

Two steps below me, he barely came up to my shoulder. His face was a little gilded around the edges from the light that filtered from the dining-room below; but I quite clearly saw his look of distaste. "Believe me, such things are only jests with the people among whom I am accustomed to spend my time. I mistook myself."

Had I followed my own inclinations, I should have swallowed my fury and accepted his apology—not because it was good enough, but because it would have spared me the discomfort of saying all the things I had to say. Still, I forced myself to go on.

"Well: and did you forget yourself when you chose to follow me, first to the British Museum on Thursday, and then to Claridge's earlier today? Don't you see that I must marry money? My sisters are *gifted;* you said it yourself. They cannot be sacrificed, as I was sacrificed, to a life of drudgery just to keep the wolf above water. If I marry Griff I can support them—open doors for them. But how am I to secure him when you constantly thrust yourself between us?"

"I did it to *help* you."

"To help me! Do explain!"

He shrugged. "It's plain this arrangement with Haber will never last. Not without Miss Nijam; and as for me—well. At any rate I'll see you married to Vandergriff, if that's what you want. But you're going about it the wrong way. Vandergriff's a hunter, not prey. He won't like it if he thinks you're hunting him, but he'll do anything to avoid losing you to another hunter. For creatures like us, my little mouse, there's no spur like jealousy."

For a moment I was lost for words—and then I was furious again. "I never asked for your help!" I hissed. "This is *my* affair, and you're endangering both it *and* the Noor-Jahan job by your intrusion! And then, you harass me even when Griff *isn't* about! You can hardly be trying to make my *sisters* jealous!"

"My dear, I've already apologised for that foolish joke—"

"It was an *untruth*," I said. "You know very well that *you* inflicted that kiss upon *me*."

The reader may recall that I myself was not above a certain number of untruths. But *my* untruths exposed Vasily to a little harmless discomfort; *his* went directly to my reputation, than which no woman has a more precious—or a more fragile—possession.

This was his cue to apologise. Instead, his eyes narrowed and he stepped nearer, so that there was but one stair between us, and he was nearly on a level with myself. His voice was low and accusing. "Inflicted? You *enjoyed* it."

I had; but of course I could scarcely confess to having done so. "On the contrary: it was an ordeal, and the sooner we forget that it occurred, the better!"

"I *beg* your pardon!" For a moment, he sounded exactly like the outraged dowager Countess, earlier today at Claridge's. "An *ordeal?* To be kissed by *me?*"

"Do you find it so *very* difficult to believe?"

"Yes!" He was sharing the stair with me now. "No one has ever complained before! Quite the contrary, I assure you!"

The air between us felt charged, as if with electricity. This I did *not* like. It felt almost as though he might decide to prove his ridiculous point by force—and I recalled that first kiss *much* too well to rush headlong into another.

I retreated another stair, regaining my high ground both literally and figuratively. "Your skill or otherwise is hardly *apropos*—"

"It is!"

I was obliged to retreat upwards again. "A young lady in my position," I said severely, "must resign herself to being at the mercy of strange men, but my sisters are *not* in my position. My sisters are innocent girls for whom I have always striven to set a decent example, and I *will not* permit you to corrupt them!"

There was a silence. It occurred to me that this was the nearest thing I had ever seen to real anger in Vasily's eyes.

"How well you know me!" he said in a low voice that made my bones vibrate.

I summoned all my courage. "Do I not? Would *you* allow such a man near *your* young sisters?"

His lips pressed together. "Well you may know me," he said, "but I know you too, Molly Dark. God knows it has taken me long enough to peel back all your silks and laces, but I see you now. You are cunning and ambitious and you manipulate without mercy because you do it for what you think is right.

126

And—" again he advanced, and his voice changed— "you are beautiful when you're angry."

This time I held my ground. I was too angry to speak and much too angry to give way before him again. Above all, I was afraid. Something warned me that he told the plain and simple truth: that he had seen me through to the bone, all the dark and secret things I had kept hidden all my life—the wings peeled from the flies, the schoolmate reduced to madness; the ghosts, the appetites, the deceptions. He saw all this, and he held me in his hand, and would crush me at his pleasure.

"Don't be afraid," he said in a voice like the brush of a moth's wings in the darkness. "I've always been honest with you, my dear. I've always warned you not to trust me. You are only doing as you ought; I understand that. But—" his hands fastened upon my shoulders, and he bent down, so that his lips brushed my ear—"but you shouldn't be afraid for your sisters; it isn't them I wish to corrupt."

Whatever else I may be, I am still a gentleman's daughter from Brixton, and I have been properly brought up. And so, although I felt that strange electrical charge crackling in the air around us; although my head was full of blazing and audacious thoughts, although my knees felt weak and my breath came shallowly, at that supreme moment I held myself in the grip of the rigid self-control that had become the guiding principle of my life.

The next moment, I realised what his game was. Why, the cad! He wasn't trying to corrupt me—at any rate, not now. If he had meant to do so, he would already have kissed me again in an attempt to demonstrate his skill. No: he was trying to *frighten* me.

And this, in turn, meant that whatever the benefits of my

education, the present crisis required a quite different sort of behaviour than that to which I was accustomed.

"Oh, Vasily," I breathed, swaying towards him until little more than a breath separated our lips. My hands came to rest against his heart, which ticked fast and strong at my fingertips. "I'm not—I'm not afraid. Not of you."

His response was immediate—and dizzying. "Oh, *Gospodin,*" he snarled. In the blink of an eye, I found myself removed to arm's length. I remember that his hands trembled as he released me.

"Vasya?" Mimi's voice floated up from downstairs, and we both looked down to see her peering up at us from the hallway. "What are the two of you doing up there?"

The intrusion of a third party recalled me to my senses. How much had Mimi heard? How much had she seen? I pressed a hand to the lips that a moment ago had been so close to Vasily's own, feeling utterly scandalised with myself. What was I thinking, baiting him like that? I didn't *want* Vasily to kiss me; I had brought him here specifically to object to it! Why, I was fortunate it was only Mimi below, and not one of my sisters!

"I'm coming, Mimi," Vasily said harshly. He started down the stairs again, but then turned back to confront me—and I was glad that in the darkness he could not see how hot my face had become. "You are right," he told me in that same hash voice, apparently ill pleased with himself, "it appears that I do not corrupt ladies."

The next instant he brushed past Mimi and stalked in at the sitting-room door. I followed more slowly; and to my horror I found, at the bottom of the stairs, that Mimi was laughing.

"What is it?" I hissed at her.

She shook her head. "Nothing, nothing. Only, how the table turns!"

"Keep your secrets, then," I said acidly. There was a great deal too much talk of corruption around this house for my peace of mind. And I, evidently, was far too susceptible to it. The sooner we finished this job and went our separate ways, the better. I took a deep breath and followed Vasily into the sitting-room, where for the next hour, we all very seriously discussed our next steps.

* * *

Nijam went back to Bloomsbury that evening, but not to her flat. Instead, she had Alphonse escort her to the laboratory, where she started work on some items Mimi had requested. Having run a few preliminary tests to her own satisfaction, she was about to dismiss Alphonse and return to her own lodgings, when the cupboard with the minerals in it caught her eye.

"After all, why not?" she murmured; and added yttrium to her next batch of baddeleyite.

Chapter IX.

On the following afternoon, Nijam and her Alphonse called for me in the carriage and I told my sisters not to expect me home for dinner. In perfect silence, we collected Vasily in Covent Garden and drove along the Thames to Limehouse—which, as all the world knows, is the seedy quarter between Whitechapel and the West India Dock.

If Bloomsbury was where students and intellectuals gathered from across the Empire, Limehouse was the realm of sailors and lascars. Its narrow streets were lined with run-down old tenements converted into cramped boarding-houses, and colourfully-painted shops bearing names like Chong Chu or H. Doe Foon or Chee Kong Tong. Lascar Sally's, the establishment to which Schmidt had followed the young sitar-player, lay on the West India Dock Road beyond the Limehouse Cut, which was a canal, rather green and scummy.

Schmidt halted the carriage at the side of the road, switched on his transmitter, and called cheerfully, "This is the place, sir."

That was Mimi's signal; she had been watching the lodging-house most of the day from the window of the Chinese restaurant opposite, and now murmured through our transmitters, "Go ahead, Nijam. We have them where we want them."

Since Vasily carried Griff's little spider with him, each of us was careful to play his or her part. For Nijam and Schmidt, this meant absolute silence as they stepped from the carriage and crossed the road, which was noisy with trams and the chatter of voices speaking not only English but also dialects of Chinese, Arabic, and Hindustani. Nor did they say much as they entered the tenement and began to climb stairs. In time we heard Schmidt say in guarded tones, "Third floor; room eleven." Then he knocked. A moment later we heard the door open. A deep, accented voice spoke a wary greeting, and I heard Nijam apologising for yesterday's misbehaviour and asking to see the sitar-player.

"They're inside," Mimi announced through the transmitter.

Vasily nodded to me: the curtain had gone up on the next and most vital act of our play. I leaned over, opening the carriage door just in case Griff's transmitter should be sensitive enough to pick up the sound. "'Ullo, governor," I said in what I hoped was a creditable imitation of an East End accent, roughening my voice using a trick I had learned in my amateur-theatrics days. "Your man said you had a bit of business for me."

"I was told you could find me the Noor-Jahan decoy," Vasily responded crisply. "It was taken from my friend Sir Humphrey's house some nights ago; I am anxious to secure it. Tell me what you know."

"Yes; I've seen it," I said in the same hoarse accents. "An Indian fellow brought it in to the pawnbroker's up on the Commercial Road East, but the Jew there said it wasn't worth a brass razoo. So the Indian went away with it. But I saw him later at Lascar Sally's on the West India Dock Road."

"Thank you. There's a guinea for your information, and you

shall have another if you can give me the name of the Indian."

"Coo!" I said, hoping that this was not overdoing things. "Was that airy great bit of shine real, then?"

"No, it's made of glass," Vasily said off-handedly, pulling his handkerchief out of his pocket and placing it, with its little clockwork captive, on the cushions beside him. "Only it's in my interests to see the miscreants brought to justice, because someone appears to have got the idea that *I* am the one responsible. Sir Humphrey practically accused me point-blank." This was true; Vasily had very skillfully elicited the accusation that very morning. "Mind you remember what I've promised you, and don't go telling this to anyone else. Schmidt! Drive to Portland Place!"

With that both of us got out of the carriage to find Mimi, once again outfitted as a boy, leaning against a wall nearby. Climbing onto the box, Vasily took up the reins and turned into the traffic flowing back towards the West End. There, it would be his mission to relay this "information" directly to Sir Humphrey himself, thus—if possible—exonerating himself in Griff's eyes, and redirecting suspicion against the Indians.

Meanwhile, it was our task to retrieve the decoy. "Do you have the canisters?" Mimi asked as she and I waited for an opening in the traffic. I patted the heavy pocket hanging beneath my skirt and nodded. The two of us stepped into the street and made towards Lascar Sally's.

* * *

While these events were happening in the street, Nijam and Alphonse stood upstairs in the Indians' cramped room, to which their presence had brought more than a little perturbation.

The young lascar had been sitting cross-legged on the iron bedstead to the right of the room, with two older Indians beside him on his right and his left. Both wore white caps and embroidered tunics. A third bent over the small coal-fired stove just within the door, and the fourth, a tall soldierly fellow, had closed the door behind Nijam and now stood against it, breathing down the visitors' necks in a way that was both worrying and overly familiar.

After a moment's hurried conference in his own tongue, the young sitar-player—Nijam had a good view of this instrument as well as some drums and pipes where they lay carefully stowed beneath the bed—addressed her in English.

"How did you find this place?" the sitarist demanded.

"My friend followed you from the coffee house yesterday," Nijam confessed. She had taken the sutras out of her pocket and now held them before her as a shield; she had the distinct feeling that rather than finding herself in the presence of a gang of unemployed sailors, she had stumbled upon a court in exile. "Please excuse my abrupt departure. It shocked me to learn that this was only a treatise on poetry, and I responded hastily. And now I see," she added, making a guess, "that I was speaking to the Mirza Dara himself."

She finished this little speech with an awkward bow. Beside her, Alphonse shifted uneasily as the large Indian crowded a little nearer; and one of the older Indians said something sharply in his own language. The Mirza waved him silent and gave Nijam a flashing smile.

"I told you that if I could not assist you, the Mirza certainly could not."

"But perhaps one of your learned friends would be willing

to do so," Nijam answered, with another bow towards the older gentlemen.

From behind her, the Mirza's bodyguard said something in a warning tone. Again, the Mirza waved him silent.

"If we tell you what you want to know, will you go away and forget my name? I am in your city the way Peter the Great came to Europe: to witness its glory in secret."

It appeared that he suspected her of nothing more sinister than a genuine search for knowledge; and Nijam nodded eagerly. The Mirza then signalled one of his courtiers to take the manuscript; Nijam and Alphonse were directed to take their seats upon a scrupulously clean carpet; and the serving-man brought them tea made with milk and spices, which Alphonse drank happily but Nijam put aside after the first sip, wincing a little at the overpowering flavours.

At length, after some nodding and muttering, the two scholars spoke first to their prince in Hindustani, and then to Nijam in English.

"This manuscript is beyond price," said the sage on the left. "It is a copy of the *Mritasanjivani* by Halayudha, a poetry treatise written five hundred years ago as a commentary on the Pingala Sutras. There is a copy in the Mirza's archives; I thought it was the last."

A poetry treatise! Nijam felt her heart sinking. "I was looking for a different Halayudha manuscript; on mathematics."

"This is the only Halayudha manuscript known to exist," said the second scholar.

"Perhaps we have been mistaken all these years," the first put in, "but I do not think so." He leaned forward, offering the manuscript back to her. "Whatever you choose to do with this, remember that it is a very great treasure, and ought to be preserved."

Nijam accepted the manuscript doubtfully. "Is it valuable, then?" Perhaps, even if it was not the manuscript for which she had a buyer, it could still be of use to her.

"Valuable?" the Mirza put in with a disbelieving laugh.

"Poetry is no use to me," Nijam said honestly. "I'm a scientist. I'll have to sell it. Perhaps you can give me an idea of what it might be worth."

There was a silence. The scholars were shaking their heads and even the Mirza looked slightly disdainful. Then, the second scholar on the right began to speak in soft, mellow tones; after a moment he changed to English:

"The prison of grief and the bondage of life are one and the same. Why should man be relieved of this sorrow before death?"

The other scholar replied, and they took up the couplets like a dialogue:

"I asked my soul, 'What is Delhi?' It replied: 'The world is the body and Delhi its soul.'"

"The road crossings have turned into guillotines. Each house has become a replica of a prison."

"For you this is only a sorrowful story, but the pain is so great that to hear it the stars will weep tears of blood."

They spoke as though of things they had seen; and while they spoke, the Mirza bent his head and put his hand over his eyes. The whole room hushed; and Nijam had the most peculiar sensation, as though her soul had left her body and taken up habitation within the men who spoke; their grief became her grief, their experience hers.

"Thus the poet Ghalib mourned the desolation of his home at the hands of the English, who ravaged the city like mad dogs," ended one of the speakers. Silence fell. Nijam struggled back to her own body; then she glanced at Alphonse, and to her surprise, saw that his face was streaked with tears.

"How much is a tear worth?" asked the Mirza presently, uncovering his eyes. "Answer that, and you will know what price to set upon this manuscript."

Nijam tucked the book into her pocket in silence. If tears were worth anything, she thought, then she ought to have a hundred laboratories by now. *And perhaps,* said another inner voice, which to her surprise sounded something like Alphonse's, *if more people read poetry like this, the tears would indeed be worth something.*

The thought still held her speechless when Alphonse said sharply, "What's that racket? Is something happening down-stairs?"

A commotion had broken out somewhere in the building—running footsteps and, after a moment, a confused shouting which resolved into cries of "Fire! Fire!"

The Indians exchanged startled looks. The bodyguard threw open the door, admitting an unmistakable burning smell. Alphonse leaped to his feet, helping Nijam to hers. "Everyone should evacuate at once," he declared. "If this place catches it will be an inferno."

* * *

A passage pierced the tenement from its front to its back, passing the dark central stairwell to a grimy backyard whose primary feature was a foul-smelling outhouse and the imprint of a vagrant shivering pitifully beside it. It was in the shadows of this hallway that Mimi and I, a minute previously, had set alight the four canisters Nijam had prepared for our use.

At first the fuses only burned meekly, providing little light and no smoke at all. "I still say we ought to have lit a real fire," Mimi said with an air of dissatisfaction, as she pulled her bandana over her nose.

I was once again hidden beneath my mother's veil. "Mimi, we can't very well burn down people's houses over their heads."

"It's a horrible place anyway," she said defensively, "and a real fire would be more convincing"; but then the fuses burned out and the canisters began to give off a horrible stench and smoke that was entirely convincing to both of us, for we were forced to withdraw up the stairs, coughing and weeping.

"Help! Help!" I cried at the top of my lungs. "Fire! Fire! Someone call the fire brigade!"

Nor did my call go unanswered. Pandemonium erupted. Doors slammed open, people shrieked at the thick clouds of smoke rising through the stairwell, and someone started banging what sounded like the bottom of a saucepan with a hammer, by way of makeshift alarm.

"Go on," I told Mimi as people began to descend the stairs in a flood. "I'll be all right," though indeed I could not help but wish Vasily had been able to remain with us.

It was not long before we saw Nijam and Schmidt descending the stairs on the heels of the Indians, one of whom—the big, burly fellow with the night-black beard—I was sure had been the one who caught me on the steps of Sir Humphrey's townhouse. Mimi slipped into the crowd just ahead of them; and so, bracketed (unbeknownst to themselves) by our people, the Indians passed into the street. Concealing myself in the darkness of the stairs that led down to the basement, I waited for the rush to abate as the denizens of the boarding-house quitted the building.

The crowd must have given Mimi every opportunity for her clandestine search: in less time than I thought possible, the transmitter in my ear buzzed and I heard her say, "I've searched their pockets, and the necklace isn't there."

"They brought nothing from the room," Schmidt confirmed, "not even their musical instruments. Miss Dark, I'm afraid the rest is up to you."

My heart fell. With Vasily establishing his alibi in Portland Place, and Mimi required in the street to pick the Indians' pockets, and Schmidt and Nijam continuing their masquerade as a pair of earnest manuscript-hunters, I had volunteered to remain in the tenement to search the emptied room. "Not that it will be necessary," Nijam had said, with her usual confidence. "It would not at all be reasonable to depart a burning building and leave the decoy behind."

Yet this was precisely what they seemed to have done. Nijam's faith in humanity's reason, I thought, was oftener misplaced than otherwise. Still, seeing that the flood of evacuation had ceased, I quit my hiding-place and flew up the stairs towards the room Schmidt had indicated on the third floor.

"Wait," Nijam said suddenly through the transmitter, "where's the Mirza? Schmidt, have *you* seen him?"

But it was too late, for I had reached the Indians' lodging and blundered within; and there stood the young man I had known previously only as a shadow in Portland Place on the night we gained and lost the decoy. He had a stout iron crowbar in his hand, with which he was in the act of levering up the floorboards.

I stopped dead in my tracks. Here, then, was the answer to the location of the decoy! and here, also, was a vigorous-looking young man drawing himself to his full height, with a face that was stern and shuttered and a crowbar clenched in one hand.

Mimi and Schmidt were down in the street and could not help me; but I brought my fluttering hands to my face, switched my transmitter on, and said the first thing I could think of. "Begging your pardon, mister, but this is *my* room!"

"This is Room Eleven," he said coldly. "Shouldn't you be evacuating?"

"It's Room Nine—it says so on the door!" I blundered further in, evading his attempts to bar my way. "I came back for my violin. It's my bread and butter! I can't let it burn."

"I'm coming for you," Schmidt said in my ear. "Keep him talking."

"It's right here, under the bed," I babbled on, reaching in the indicated direction, and drawing out the sitar. "Oh, where is it? What have you done with my violin?"

"This is not your room," the Mirza said coldly. He faced me from the doorway now, and his crowbar was held in both hands across his body, as though to bar me leaving. "Nor is this house the sort of place a well-dressed lady would lodge in."

I stilled. It was true that Mother's mourning-clothes had once been very good, but I *did* think they might have been old and shabby enough to make me a convincing East-Ender. I wrung my black-gloved hands in unfeigned distress. "Oh, governor, don't be angry. Don't hold my fine clothes against me. Blimey, I *do* have the wrong room. I suppose I'll be going, then."

"I remember you from Portland Place," he said, advancing into the room. "Is there even a real fire?"

139

I could have cried with vexation. None of them ought to have remained in the building at all! Where was Schmidt? —but at that moment something struck the house and it trembled as though it was no more than a little tin shack.

Schmidt's voice cracked into my ear. "Good heavens, that's Vandergriff! How did he come here so quickly?"

"What?" cried a voice muffled with distance—Vasily—and "What?" cried I, altogether forgetting the young Indian and his crowbar. *"Griff* is here?"

"You must fly," Vasily ordered.

"Hold your tongue, your grace, and do your part!" Nijam snapped. "Dark, there's no help for it now. Vandergriff must have been nearer than we thought." There was no need to say more. Vasily and I had played our little comedy; and Griff had overheard it, as he had been intended to do; and the risk we had taken, that he would interrupt our task before it was done, had rebounded upon us with a vengeance.

"Schmidt," Vasily was saying. *"Do* something!"

"Out of the question," Nijam panted. "It's too danger-ous—Vandergriff's a prosthete—*Schmidt!"*

"For heaven's sake, Schmidt," I began; but my distraction had proved fatal, for the young Mirza pounced and caught my wrist.

"Who are you?" he demanded. "Who are you speaking to? *Who is here?"*

Again the house shook; it sounded as though something was tearing through the wall. Over the transmitter I heard a battle-cry from Schmidt; followed by the sound of a blow, and a feeble groan.

Oh, heavens!—There was no time to waste, no other choice. Throwing back my veil, I faced the Indian boldly. "The prosthete is here. Quickly: you must save the decoy."

The Mirza stared at me with slightly parted lips—I am afraid that even at that moment, without the veil to impede my vision, I could not help noticing how extremely good-looking he was—but then there was a sound of heavy footsteps upon the stairs below. At that the Mirza recoiled from me, attacking the floorboards with renewed vigour.

"Get out of there, Dark!" Nijam hissed in my ear, as splinters flew and boards cracked.

"I can't," I whispered. "He'll see me."

"Then stand behind the door," Mimi put in; and I saw at a glance that this was the only possible hiding-place. I shrank back against the wall just as the Mirza tore away a floorboard and extracted the jewel-case Mimi and Schmidt had taken from Sir Humphrey's safe. I heard Griff approaching with inexorable footsteps, flinging open the door of each room as he came to it. Just as he reached ours, Mirza Dara dashed for the window and flung it open.

The door burst open, striking me and rebounding. In the same moment I saw the Mirza outlined against the grey April sky, the case poised at his shoulder. Then he threw it with all his might.

And a great, long, jointed, whiplike thing lashed out from the other side of the open door—brushed past the Mirza—reached into the sky, and plucked the jewel-case from the clouds!

I fell to my knees, gasping from the blow dealt me by the door. But I saw the whole thing quite clearly; saw the long whiplike appendage retract as swiftly as it had extended, and as the case whistled back in at the window, saw it strike the poor Mirza on the temple. He staggered to one side, and then the case clattered to the floorboards and Griff himself leapt into the room. The long appendage, which was made of shining brass segments, clattered back into place and proved to be a right arm built of cables and gears, without even a decent covering of imitation flesh.

He leaped upon his stunned prey, seizing him with one hand of flesh and another of brass. The transmitter was a terrific clamour in my ears—Schmidt's groans, Vasily's demands to be told what was happening, Nijam shouting for him to be quiet and let Mimi speak. I remained on my knees, still dizzy with pain. Now was my chance to get up and stagger away, but that would mean leaving the necklace behind…

I pulled my veil over my face, tottered to my feet, and then ventured forward, one silent step at a time, to snatch up the case where it lay on the floor.

Griff, for the moment oblivious to my presence, loomed over his captive. "Who are you working with?" he snarled. When the young Mirza failed to reply, Griff lifted him bodily from the floor and thrust him half out the window, repeating the question in a voice like thunder: "I know you didn't do this alone! *Who are you working for?*"

"Do you think I have a master?" The Mirza's voice was shaken but resolute. "You are mistaken. I *am* the master."

Already the case was in my hand; the door stood open behind me, and Griff's attention was still fixed upon the man at the window. But the prosthete's next words arrested me.

"You are lying," he said in a low, adamant voice. "Someone hired two men and a woman to burgle Sir Humphrey's house in Portland Place. The same person stole the diamonds of the Crown Princess of Roumania twelve months ago from a hotel in Cannes. I know his name. I know his place of residence. The one thing I do not have is *evidence*. Name him before a court and I will see that you go free."

My last hopes crumbled. *Griff knew.* He had indeed spoken to Marie of Roumania—had likely seen the list of guests at the hotel from which her diamonds had been stolen. From the moment Griff appeared on the Orient Express, Vasily had been a marked man.

We had all underestimated him. It was all a fiendish game: a trap—and the Noor-Jahan was the bait.

I must have made some slight sound of distress; perhaps it was only an intake of breath, or the rustle of my black crepe. Be that as it may, Griff heard. Had I cherished any hope of being treated more kindly because of my sex, this was dashed at once. Griff turned towards me, depositing the Mirza safely upon the floorboards. His prosthetic arm unspooled—fastened about my throat—dragged me inexorably nearer.

I beat uselessly at the segmented arm with the little tortoise-shell jewel-case—to no avail. In another moment he would have my veil off, and the whole conspiracy would be laid bare to him!

All seemed lost; until Mimi thrust herself between us and shoved a burning smoke-canister beneath the detective's nose. Griff must have drawn breath and gotten a lungful of the horrible stuff. Releasing me, he recoiled towards the window, coughing and spluttering.

In the same instant, Alphonse Schmidt lunged past us and gave one hearty shove, catching the American absolutely off his guard. Griff disappeared through the window. Even then, he did not entirely lose his advantage. That segmented hand lashed out, scrabbled against the sash, and took hold. A moment later the house shook as the prosthete's body collided with the wall.

"Mimi!" I rasped weakly. "Schmidt!"

Mimi shied the billowing smoke canister out the window at the dangling prosthete, then slammed the casement on the brass knuckles. "Time to go."

"Wait," the Mirza gasped, struggling to his feet. He took first one and then a second look at our rescuers, evidently recognising Schmidt even beneath the latter's mask. "I have an exit prepared. This way."

He darted out at the door and beckoned us to follow him—not down the stairs, but *up*.

"Very sensible," Mimi murmured. "Not only looks, but brains too!"—and with that we all fell into step behind.

Chapter X.

The young Mirza led us to the attic, where at the end of a dark passage cluttered with unused furniture, a small door hidden behind a dusty mattress led directly into the adjoining house.

This second building, like the one we had come from, was hurriedly emptying to the clang of a makeshift fire alarm. None of us spoke as the Mirza led us downstairs amidst the rush of fleeing people. My throat ached from Griff's crushing grasp, but now that we had concealed our escape and lost ourselves within this seething stream of humanity, it seemed unlikely that even the prosthete would be able to find us. Gradually the terror of the past few minutes receded, leaving me faint and dizzy

Presently we emerged into the crowded street to hear the bells of the fire-engine ringing in the distance. The Mirza's attendants were awaiting us near the step. Our guide, having addressed them in a commanding voice, turned to me. "Have you the decoy?"

I hesitated, and Nijam's voice crackled in my ear: "Don't you dare hand it over, Dark. *We* stole that decoy fair and square."

But it hardly seemed right to me: the Mirza had been of great help to us all just now, and a discomfiting suspicion was growing in my mind.

"The diamond belongs to the Nawab of Bihar," I said.

The Mirza chuffed with annoyance. "Why else do you think I am here?"

And there it was. No doubt it was wrong to shut them out of our game, as though they were children and I was their governess, with the privilege of dictating how the wrongs perpetrated against them should be righted. "The decoy is safe in my pocket," I said, "but we ought not to discuss it here."

"Indeed," the Mirza agreed. Just then a tram-bell went. "This way," he called, and we all climbed aboard and were taken up the West India Dock Road towards the City. The Mirza seated me firmly by a window, with himself occupying the aisle-seat. His men took up positions around us both, leaving Schmidt and Mimi sitting watchfully at some distance, where Nijam soon joined them, scowling in my direction.

"Now you've done it," she muttered via the transmitter. "They have you *and* the decoy hostage."

"Bozhe moi," Vasily broke in—his voice was far clearer now, as though upon hearing the commotion he had turned and made his way back towards Limehouse. "Will no one tell me what has happened? Is everyone alive?"

"Why are you speaking aloud? What if Griff hears you?" I protested, abandoning any pretence of my own.

The Mirza glanced at me sharply, but Vasily replied with the same agitation. "Why do you think? I pitched the spider into the street the moment I heard what was going on. Schmidt? Mimi? You are not hurt?"

"No, sir."

"Miss Dark?"

"All's well, and he didn't even see my face," I assured Vasily. "But there is no time to lose: you *must* go to Portland Place and

146

establish your alibi before Griff returns." Naturally I should have preferred not to hold this conversation in the presence of the Indians, but whether because we represented his only allies, or his best means of support, Vasily seemed peculiarly anxious for our safety, and I did not trust him to follow the plan if I did not allay his fears.

"Very well; but I'm coming to Brixton after."

"No!" I said. I didn't want him near my sisters again, and besides, there were the Indians to deal with first. His own quarters at the Savoy were off limits; and once those were ruled out, there was only one other place we might use. "Meet us at Nijam's laboratory."

"You have another confederate," the Mirza observed. "We will accompany you to this laboratory to meet him."

Nijam glared the length of the tram car and protested softly into the transmitter. "I can't have a whole gang of lascars walking into my lab! People will talk!"

"Never fear: Schmidt will charm them," I assured her. The Mirza's demand made sense, after all: he and I evidently needed to negotiate, and to have any guarantee of our holding up our end of the bargain, he had a right to insist upon meeting all our confederates. Nijam's only reply was a low sound of displeasure which, in anyone less spectacularly beautiful, I would have described as a growl. I told the Mirza we were going to the University.

Indeed, the Indians managed to pass pretty well among the many coloured students of the University, and although the informal clothing of the Mirza and his bodyguard drew some censorious looks, I was surprised when one of the sages was greeted by a passing professor, and turned out to be an eminent scholar of languages. "I didn't know you knew

147

Alphonse Schmidt!" the professor said to his Indian colleague. "Is he holding a demonstration of his experiments?" I sent Nijam a very speaking look when this happened, but she pretended not to see it.

The Mirza, unfortunately, was difficult to hoodwink. When we entered the laboratory at last, he looked around the temple of Science in which he found himself and asked, "What are you making here?"

Closing the door, Nijam parried the question. "How do you think we filled that tenement with smoke?"

The furnace in the corner still radiated a little heat. The Mirza prowled over to it. "It is a simple matter to make smoke. You would scarcely need equipment like this."

"Only a box of matches," Mimi agreed plaintively.

"Don't touch those," Nijam snapped, as the Mirza studied the blackened crucibles that stood cooling on the bench.

"Up to five thousand degrees," he observed, with a glance towards the temperature dial on the furnace. "At that temperature you are not cooking bread, I think."

"Very funny," Nijam retorted, licking a finger and touching her crucibles gingerly. They must have been cool, for she touched them more boldly, and then picked one up in her bare hand. "More failures, I'm sure."

"This is why we want the decoy," I told the Mirza, digging the tortoise-shell case from my pocket. "Show them, Nijam. Vasily is some way off yet."

Reluctantly, she broke open each of the crucibles. The first and second both contained a fascinating slag; but the third—

"Oh!" Nijam cried. It almost sounded like a cry of pain, and Schmidt turned from the window, saying, "Are you hurt?"

"No," she answered breathlessly. "Look."

148

She held up a hand heaped with clear, glimmering crystals. Schmidt picked one of them up, sending glitters of light dancing across the ceiling. "It *was* the yttrium," Nijam breathed. "You were *right.*"

"We must test it," Schmidt said, taking out his pocket-knife. The two of them put their heads together as Schmidt scraped at the surface of the crystal again and again.

"It's only blunting the knife," Nijam breathed. She turned abruptly, putting both her hands on the bench, ignoring the ghostly mouse nibbling on a husk of grain there. "I don't believe it."

"You solved it."

"*You* solved it," she said, with the most curiously softened look I had ever seen on her face. "Imagine what wonderful things you could do if you had all your memories."

The back of Schmidt's neck went red—he must have blushed to his toes. The rest of us might have been a hundred miles away—until Mimi cleared her throat. The Mirza turned to me. "You are *making* diamonds?"

Nijam heard him and frowned. "Not diamonds—a real diamond would almost certainly put a scratch in one of these."

"But an imitation good enough to fool the British Museum," I elucidated. "You understand, don't you, Mirza?"

"You are planning to make an exchange?" The Mirza frowned. "We claim the Noor-Jahan on behalf of the young Nawab of Bihar. We will not return to India without it."

"We did not know there *was* a Nawab to claim the stone."

"The former Nawab was killed during the rebellion. Because he left only a daughter, the English claimed Bihar as their own under the Doctrine of Lapse. You understand?"

I shook my head.

"It was a law they made for us," the Mirza explained. "Should any Indian ruler die without a male heir of his body, his realm became the property of your Queen. So the young Begum was swept aside and married off. Her husband lived only long enough to beget a male heir, and so in the eyes of many of us, Bihar has a Nawab again. Perhaps he will never be the Nawab in more than name, but the emblem of his authority was stolen by the man who killed his grandfather, and so I have come to London to retrieve it. I warn you: do not stand in my way."

Of course, it might only be a story—but something told me I could believe him. "I don't mean to," I assured him. "As far as I'm concerned, you may have the diamond and be welcome to it. Our primary concern is to deprive Sir Humphrey of the fruits of his father's crime. Isn't it?" I added, turning upon the others. Schmidt agreed, and Nijam followed suit.

Mimi looked crestfallen. "Are we not to steal the diamond after all? I only wished to touch it, and gaze into its depths."

The Mirza regarded Mimi with fascination. Her pouting disappointment, it seems, did more than my most earnest assurances to persuade him of our sincerity. "What—do you expect me to believe that you are philanthropic thieves?"

"It's not a bad description," I said. "I am a simple woman, and I cannot eat a diamond the size of a hen's egg. Nor is it easy, without very exalted connections, to sell such a famous gem for more than a fraction of what it is worth. My plan to profit from the theft was always quite different. Perhaps we can help one other. You may steal the diamond; we will offer you the services of Miss Laine, who is a very accomplished thief. The thing must be done cleanly, you understand, or all of us are liable to face great embarrassment."

He frowned. "And in return?"

"In return," I said, "you will allow us to make wax casts of the decoy, and you will transform Miss Nijam over there into an Indian Begum."

"What?" Nijam erupted. Until now, she had looked worried, but not terrified. "Me?"

"My dear Nijam, who else is going to do it?"

Before she could demur, a knock sounded at the door, and my heart receded into my boots. No doubt this was Vasily; and I could not imagine that Vasily would be happy with the thought of losing the Noor-Jahan to the Mirza.

Indeed, it was Vasily who now entered—saw the Indians—and blinked once or twice. "My dear," he said very silkily, coming to stand beside me, "forgive my language, but what the devil is this?"

"These gentlemen, your grace, are here on behalf of the Nawab of Bihar."

"Oh! are they!" He raked them with a half-contemptuous look. "And I suppose they want the Noor-Jahan?"

"In their place, wouldn't you feel the same?"

"My dear, I don't *need* to be in their place to sympathise very strongly with that desire." He dragged off his hat and tossed it to Alphonse Schmidt, who meekly took and hung it on the coat-stand by the door. "O very well! I suppose that's fair, so long as they can provide accreditation."

If, dear reader, you find it difficult to believe that Vasily Nikolaevich Romanov would so readily consent to the destruction of all his plans—then I quite sympathise. I felt precisely the same misgivings.

"Dark," Nijam said in the direst tones, "what do you mean, you intend to transform me into an Indian Begum?"

"Well," I said, unconsciously adopting the placating tone I was wont to use with fractious children, "how else are we to parade the false Noor-Jahan before Sir Humphrey? You shall wear it where he can see it, and if he does not rush off to the British Museum at once to test that the real stone is there, my name isn't Mary Angelica Dark."

"Angelica?" I heard Vasily murmur.

"And then," I added, "with Sir Humphrey quite sure that the Noor-Jahan is safe, our opportunity will come. While Griff is investigating the Indians of London, we shall effect our substitution in peace and quiet. But in order for this plan to succeed, Nijam must learn to impersonate the Begum of Bihar."

"My dear Mary Angelica," Vasily said, "don't you think you're being just a little too clever? Surely if we wish to baffle Sir Humphrey with our own decoy—which I take it Nijam has at last produced—the best choice would be to keep our imitation a strict secret."

"But we must distract Griff," I said, with a quiver in my voice. "Do you suppose that I feel *clever*, having seen him on the hunt, and felt his hands about my neck?" So saying, I drew aside the veil, which I had disposed in such a fashion as to reveal my face, but obscure my neck. I bruise easily, and knew that the skin must already be marked by the violent, inhuman hand Griff had laid upon me. The sight must have been far worse than I guessed. Vasily first paled, and then flushed.

"Vandergriff did this to you?" he said thickly. His hands clenched. For a moment I thought he would say something more, but he restrained himself with an effort.

It was Mimi who spoke. "Don't marry him," she said flatly. "Any man who will do that to a woman is bad news."

I shivered. Surely, though, Griff could not have known he was assaulting a *lady.* He had always treated *me* with the utmost respect.

The Mirza said in English—"Your terms are acceptable to us. If Miss Nijam will come to the Hindustani Coffee House she will be taught what she needs to know."

"You'll do it, Nijam?" I begged her, and she threw up her hands in exasperation.

"I don't particularly like the thought of having Vandergriff's hands around my own neck! but I'm clearly the only one to play the part."

With that, the meeting broke up. The Indians went off, and the rest of us climbed into Vasily's brougham to be driven home. Nijam's lodgings were nearby in Bloomsbury, not far from the Museum; Mimi left us a little further south not far from St Giles'; and then Vasily and I were alone in the carriage.

The evening had almost entirely faded to full night, and it had begun to rain, so that the streets were shiny and reflective in the glare of the gaslamps. I found myself letting out a sigh, feeling as though all the excitement and terror and difficulty of that day—the confrontation in Limehouse, and the negotiations at the laboratory—had risen up to overwhelm me.

Vasily watched me from the seat opposite; and suddenly he rapped upon the roof with his walking-stick. Schmidt pulled the carriage to the kerbside, and I looked about, puzzled. "This isn't the Savoy."

"Do you think I would leave before seeing you home? You injure me," Vasily replied with that satirical note in his voice; but I did not know, this time, whether the satire was directed at himself, or at me. He climbed out of the carriage and went in at one of the glowing shop-windows that shone out onto the street. Within a very few minutes he returned, carrying a small paper bag and a little brown-paper parcel. "Saltoun Road," he told Schmidt; and then, to my surprise, he sat beside me and handed me the bag.

"This will make you feel better," he said.

I looked into the bag and found—humbugs and barley-sugar.

"Pax?" he asked, with one eyebrow canted up.

I sighed. Of course there could be no pax. Not if he was still planning to betray me; certainly not now that I had promised the real Noor-Jahan to the Indians, and must therefore find a way of preventing his getting away with it. But no truce is meant to last forever—and the awkwardness that had hung over us since last night's confrontation on the stairs had been a rather unhappy thing. "Pax," I agreed, popping a bit of barley-sugar into my mouth. "Humbug?"

"No humbug," he replied. "Not this time, at any rate. Allow me." Gently, he removed the veil from my bruised neck.

"Does it look so very bad?"

His fingers lifted my jaw. The streetlamps passed the carriage in a rhythmic flare of gaslight that by turns illuminated his face and then slowly faded away, almost to nothing. There was an oddly wistful look in his eyes as they fastened upon the skin of my neck, as his thumbs traced the line of my throat and settled upon the fluttering line of my pulse: and I felt suddenly, horribly conscious of what this man had once been.

Doubtless he was conscious of it too, for he gave half a bitter smile. "I have seen worse. I have *done* worse myself." Abruptly he released me and tore open the brown-paper parcel, which proved to contain a jar of arnica ointment. He used his fingertips, light and impersonal, to work it into the

154

bruised skin. "Well?" he added. "Now that Vandergriff has spoiled this pretty throat, I suppose you will be obliged to marry him, monster that he is?"

"Griff," I repeated hoarsely—for some reason my throat was not working quite the way it should. "Griff is using the Noor-Jahan as bait. He knows you are the one who took Marie of Roumania's diamonds. That's why he's been watching you—he doesn't suspect, he *knows*."

"What?" Vasily's hands slowed to a halt. "What makes you say this?"

"I heard him questioning the Mirza. He believed you had hired him."

Vasily frowned. "Even after our little act for the transmitter? It's an ill omen if we haven't managed to throw him off after all."

He continued to knead the ointment into my skin, and by degrees I found myself calming beneath his ministrations. "That's where the Indians may be useful. Let Griff chase you, if that's what he chooses to do; and Mimi and the Indians may steal the diamond at their leisure. Unless you have some other way to head him off."

"I'm afraid not, my dear. Not if he already knows who I am and what I have done. The lost diamonds are the least of it. The price on—" He caught himself and released me abruptly. "I beg your pardon," he said in quite a different tone, clapping the lip onto the jar of ointment and offering it to me, "that is probably enough for the present."

"But you were saying?" I prompted, intrigued by this sudden retreat.

"Suffice it to say that it would be very much against Vander-griff's interests to let me go. Which means—Miss Dark, you know that I have always warned you against an association with me. Perhaps it is time—"

My mind had leapt to the only possible construction of the sentence he had stopped himself from completing. "You never told me there was a *price* on your head."

He muttered something under his breath in Russian. For a little while there was silence. And then he said bitterly, "How would you like three hundred thousand pounds? All you need do is arrange for me to be delivered in chains to the custody of my cousin Nicky. You'll be a rich woman. Oh, it isn't common knowledge; but all the royal families in Europe will reward you. You'll have the money you always wanted—and you won't need to marry Vandergriff. There's your future, little mouse; and you may take it, with my blessing, if you'll only promise me not to marry that abominable American."

The amount of the sum, tremendous as it was, was not what shocked me. "Do you think so little of me—that I would hand over one of my own confederates to such a fate?"

"Shouldn't I?"

"No," I told him, trying not to feel hurt. "I'd rather marry Griff."

There was a long silence. "You can't mean that," he said at last. "If you won't trust me, trust Mimi, who has known more than her share of monsters."

I could not help putting a hand to my tender throat. Mimi's words echoed in my ears—*Any man who will do that to a woman is bad news.* Still, I could not let Vasily see how shaken the encounter had left me. "You promised you'd help me to secure him," I said. "Are you going back on your word?"

He made a gesture of disgust. "Why not? We both know I am a scoundrel." At that, we lapsed into a profound silence, which lasted all the way to Brixton.

I had more than enough to occupy my mind. Griff and Vasily—Vasily and Griff! What a nerve Vasily had, to warn me away from a respectable man who, after all, was only doing what he thought was his duty! Three hundred thousand pounds' reward, and Vasily had concealed it from me, because he thought I might avail myself of it? What a thought! Had I been capable of such treachery, I would have betrayed him three months ago in Vienna, the moment I learned the Russian secret police were on his trail. It would have been a convenient means of getting him out of my way; and I had chosen not to do so—at least not for any longer than was absolutely necessary! Did that mean nothing to him?

Griff might be a cold, unfeeling creature, and one who was overzealous in the pursuit of justice; but so far as I could see, *he* had not for a moment suspected me of wrong-doing. Griff was a gentleman; and Vasily was a scoundrel. He did not even *pretend* to be otherwise.

Why, therefore, did I feel so uneasy at the thought of marrying Griff?—and why did I so greatly dread Vasily's impending departure? Had I gone mad?

No, the problem was quite a different one. There in the dark carriage, I permitted myself to admit that I had become rather fond of the silky blackguard. It was no more than I had expected, of course. It had always been quite clear to me that if I let my guard down for a moment, Vasily would steal my heart as easily as he had stolen Marie of Roumania's diamonds. Now I was in a pretty pickle, for I had refused to let my guard down, and yet I *was* fond of the blackguard.

When the carriage rolled to a stop, Vasily caught my hand as I went to descend from the carriage. "Once again, I have made a fool of myself for a pair of blue eyes," he observed. "You hold my life in your hands. How you choose to secure your future is entirely your affair, of course. But since neither of us intends this arrangement to continue forever, do not spare a moment's kindness for me. Be sure that you arrange to profit from our parting, for I assuredly do not mean to neglect my own."

With that the carriage rolled away, leaving me on the pavement quite at a loss for words. Could he be serious? Sooner than see me marry Griff, did Vasily really wish me to turn him over to his enemies?

Chapter XI.

Time had run short. Had I any doubts, after Vasily's warnings, that this was the case, they would have been allayed the following morning when a telegram arrived from my mother at Carlsbad.

"It's from Mother?" Lilias asked. "What does she say?"

Katie and I exchanged glances. I saw in a moment that the same horrible thought had occurred to her as it had to me—that the telegram was bad news, that Mother's illness had not responded to treatment, and that she was being sent home to die by inches on mist.gent.alk. and cod-liver oil. My hands shook as they accepted the flimsy blue strip; but when I read the message and sat down very suddenly on one of the kitchen chairs, it was not out of despair. Quite the opposite, in fact:

Course of treatment successful. Coming home Tuesday with clean bill of health as missing you terribly.

"She's coming *home*," Emily said, as though she could scarcely believe it. "She's well and she's coming home!" and then she sat down and burst into tears.

I put a hand over my mouth. With the first shock of relief passed, I could scarcely help the thought that I now had a very few days left in which to steal the Noor-Jahan and placate the demands, not only of the Indians, but of Vasily and Griff as well. And what if things went wrong, and Mother arrived home to find the name of Dark being dragged through the mud by every newspaper in London?

Of course I was wonderfully glad that Mother was well again; for just a moment I had felt as light as air. But with Daddy gone, Mother had always relied upon me to be steady and helpful and *good*. I felt quite secure in my own conscience. I had done only what I believed to be my duty—but how could I look Mother in the face when I felt how horribly disappointed she would be if she *knew*?

I was still mulling this over when a carriage stopped outside the house and a footman in the Seton livery brought a message to the door. The message proved to be from Griff: he begged I would avail myself of Lady Seton's carriage to meet him in Hyde Park to walk; and he invited my sisters to join us.

I found, to my surprise, that I did not like the notion at all. My throat was still very tender; that morning I might have measured the size of Griff's mechanical hand using the bruise that had developed. I believed him to be a gentleman, but what if he decided that I was no lady? I could not help being afraid to meet him again so soon after the scene in the tenement; and I did not at all like introducing him to my sisters.

Still, short of pronouncing a death sentence upon Vasily, how would I secure my future if I did not marry Griff? and in any case, it was of the greatest importance to the Noor-Jahan job that I should remain in his confidence. If I refused to let Griff meet my family, he would certainly smell a fish; quite likely the only safe course of action was to do as he asked. So I bade my sisters fetch their hats, and at eleven o'clock, as he had suggested, we were meeting Griff beneath the Statue of

Achilles.

In spotless flannels and a straw boater, Griff looked utterly unthreatening and even a little boyish. I could not help thinking that my worries had been overblown, as they so often were! Still, the bruises concealed beneath the high neck of my frock served to remind me of the secret he kept hidden beneath the glove on his right hand, and it struck me that this was a signal difference betwixt Vasily and himself: Griff kept his monstrosity hidden away, while Vasily made practically an exhibition of it.

If I allowed myself to dwell too long upon my doubts, I should never secure either the husband, or the jewel. I shook Griff's hand and presented my sisters. Griff said that he was delighted to meet them; and then we moved off along a shady avenue beneath the trees.

"What a charming little place this is," Griff said. I refrained—as did my sisters—from informing him the place was named Lover's Walk. "When the weather is fine, London really isn't so bad… Your sisters seem like nice, ladylike girls, Miss Molly."

I offered a prayer of thanks that the nice, ladylike girls were, at present, behaving themselves. In fact, they had come over rather tongue-tied in the presence of Mr Vandergriff; they did not often meet strange gentlemen, and his was not Vasily's easy manner with them.

"I confess I think the world of them," I said, lowering my voice and hanging back a little to prevent their overhearing. "Have your investigations progressed of late?"

"They've been keeping me busy," he said. "I practically had the malefactors yesterday—indeed I had my hand around the throat of one of them. But they gave me the slip."

"Oh dear," I said faintly. I had not expected him positively to boast of what he had done; not to me. The thrill I had felt evading him one or two days ago at Claridge's had dissipated entirely. "You said that one of them was a woman."

"Yes; but what does that signify? *When lovely woman stoops to folly,* and so on, she must expect what she gets. You don't expect me to go easy on a thief, merely because she is one of Eve's daughters."

This was undeniable—and yet.

"I could never do what you do," I said with a genteel shudder. Griff sent me a smile, as though to say *I should think not!* "I don't mean to set up as a detective," I added. "I know I haven't the brain for *that.* But, to send people to gaol, or the gallows! I don't know how you bear it."

"How I bear what?"

"Well," I said, almost at a loss for words, "it is such a serious thing to take a life. A murderer might kill for selfish reasons, and a hangman might kill for the common good, and because it is his duty. But to hunt down the murderer, and hand him over to the hangman, purely for sport, because it amuses one to do so…" I glanced up at him hopefully. "I suppose that you feel a duty to see justice done."

"Well, naturally," Griff said with a laugh. "But I shouldn't do it at all if it didn't amuse me."

"It doesn't trouble you at all, to hunt men and women for sport?"

"Not in the least. Your kind heart does you credit, Miss Molly, but the law is the law, and those who break it put themselves beyond the pale."

I prided myself on mending broken hearts, and it had occurred to me that Griff's peculiarities might have their

162

origin in some long-concealed wound. Yet this, it seemed, was not the case. Griff was simply deficient in some vital spark of humanity.

Still, how was I to complain? Griff amused himself by hunting criminals, I by pursuing his fortune. Each of us was cold and calculating, single-minded in the pursuit of our prey. Had Griff been capable of deep feeling, I could never have brought myself to trap him into a mercenary marriage. As it was, I could not injure him by doing so: we deserved each other.

We had now walked a short way in silence. At length Griff said, "How serious we have become! Let us speak of something pleasant. Tell me something about yourself, Miss Molly; I feel I know so little."

"I don't know what to tell you! I'm sure I am a very uninteresting person."

"Then tell me this: where would you like to be five years from now?"

It was an odd sort of question, but I considered it anyway, and answered it honestly. "I should like to have a husband, and a home of my own, and a little family."

"You are fond of children, then?"

I still felt a pang of loss when I recalled Steffi and Ada, the little Viennese girls who had been my former charges. In one respect I had liked being a governess very well: I delighted in children, and could think of nothing better than to have some of my own one day. "Extremely. I don't think I could have borne to be a governess, if not for the children."

"I approve," Griff said. "I don't like this Old World custom of handing the children over to nannies and never seeing them. No man can be master in his own home without keeping a close eye on things. And what would you bring to a marriage?"

It was clear where these questions tended, and a certain grim satisfaction warred within my breast with the consciousness that I could say very little to recommend myself. I could hold séances, mend broken hearts, and convince a house full of perfect strangers that I was a melusine and their long-lost cousin; but those were scarcely the sort of dowry that would appeal to Warren Vandergriff. "Nothing, I'm afraid, but a sincere heart and the ability to run a household on tuppence a week."

"Thrift!" he said, smiling. "I approve of that, too. How delightfully old-fashioned!"

On this topic I must be quite honest with him. "It isn't a matter of fashion with me. You must know that I have nothing but what little I can earn myself."

He nodded. "A self-made woman? I can respect that. Say, you didn't call off your work to come walking with me, did you?"

I could scarcely confess that at present my job *was* to fascinate and extract information from him; any more than I could explain that my need to work for a living was a result of necessity, not virtue; that had I the luxury of being born into riches I should have been more than happy to be carried, as the old hymn has it, through the clouds on flow'ry beds of ease. "I assure you that my morning was unspoken-for. My employer spared me a few days to look after my sisters during Mother's absence."

"Well, it is kind of you to spend so much of your time in my company. Sometimes I ask myself what you see in me," Griff responded, with a satisfied smile.

This was an obvious cue for flattery. With my customary self-command I restrained the answer that rose to my lips—that he represented my best chance to die of old age rather than under-nourishment. In any case I was saved from having to answer by the approach of two gentlemen, one of whom, with a fatalistic inner sigh, I recognised.

"Upon my word, what a surprise!" Vasily said, lifting his hat and bowing. "Mr Vandergriff—and the Misses Dark! Frank," he added to the young gentleman at his side, a soldierly-looking young man with a cleft chin and a luxuriant moustache, "will you allow me to present Mr Warren Vandergriff of New York, Miss Mary Dark of Brixton, and her sisters..."

As he listed their names and elicited their curtseys, I was glad to see that the significance of this moment had not been lost upon my sisters: for if even Mr Vandergriff was being presented to Vasily's friend, he must be a very exalted person indeed. In fact, Vasily ended by informing us that his companion was none other than his serene highness, Prince Francis of Teck—that raffish young royalty-about-town whose sister Princess May had so recently been led to the hymeneal altar by none other than the Duke of York himself.

"Please be on your *best* behaviour," I whispered into the twins' ears as Griff made his bow, sensing that this unexpected meeting would go off most smoothly if my sisters were squelched into silence by the presence of royalty. Vasily's appearance had filled me with the liveliest apprehensions. To Griff, the Grand Duke was only a distant acquaintance of mine; and if my sisters treated him with the familiarity he had invited, I was going to have some *awfully* ticklish explanations to make.

"Frank, I know you have some of those French paintings the Americans are so fond of; I'm sure Vandergriff would be interested in them," Vasily said, before singling me out with the practised dexterity of a sheepdog. "Miss Dark, would you do me the honour of walking with me?"

If he was trying to separate me from Griff, he was disappointed, for I did not want him playing sour-grapes-in-a-manger now that he had decided the prosthete was a danger to me. I evaded him with equal dexterity. "My dear Grand Duke, what makes you suppose I'm not interested in French paintings myself?"

"Perhaps Miss Lilias will keep me company, then," Vasily said wickedly; and only the awareness that he was almost certainly doing it to tease prevented me from stepping on his toe.

"I'm sure she will, if you promise to behave like a gentleman."

"Why, Miss Dark, do you care much for art?" Frank of Teck asked with a raised eyebrow.

"To tell the truth I can scarcely tell my Old Masters from my Pre-Raphaelites," I told him, "but I'm sure Griff knows all about it; he's ever so clever."

That made both of them laugh, well pleased with my antics; and after that, the conversation flowed well. Within a very few minutes, I had charmed the Prince and steered the conversation to such purpose that his serene highness had promised to let Griff take his pick of the paintings and name his own price. Meanwhile Griff cast me a sidelong glance or two, which I returned candidly, with the deployment of those same blue eyes that had on more than one occasion brought Vasily to grief. Although I could hardly make an outright boast of my abilities, I did not wish Griff to be in any ignorance of what he stood to gain by me; and I thought I saw the wheels beginning to turn in his head.

Vasily walked ahead of us among my sisters; their own conversation was desultory, as though all his attention was bent upon those behind. "And what were you discussing with the Grand Duke with such animation just now, your highness?" I asked Prince Frank, as we reached the end of the Lover's Walk opposite Grosvenor House and came to a halt in a friendly circle.

Frank laughed; rather knowingly, I thought. "Oh! I was only trying to convince him to hold another of his famous balls."

"The Grand Duke holds balls?" I asked, noticing that my sister's ears had also pricked up. Sir Humphrey had alluded to something similar, that evening at the Museum. "You surprise me!"

"Indeed! they were all the rage in Piccadilly only a year or two back; weren't they, Vasily?"

To my amazement, Vasily looked discomfited; opened his mouth, and then closed it again, as though absolutely lost for words. "They were very good balls," he said at last, "of their sort."

"They were *excellent* balls," said Frank.

"Why, you never said you held balls," Emily said wonderingly.

And Lilias added, "Please don't be content to tell us about them! It is so much better to experience such things in person! *Do* throw us a ball!"

The Prince seemed to think this was very funny. "Yes, Vasily, why not throw them a ball? It isn't as though you've found religion, and given up dancing altogether?"

"Such religion would never find *me*," Vasily said weakly. I didn't have the slightest notion what was going on; but I did gather that Prince Frank was needling Vasily in a very able manner; and that Vasily had little or no defence. I will admit to feeling more than a little secret satisfaction—and an envious sort of admiration for the Prince.

Besides, if Vasily threw a ball it would be highly useful for my own purposes. So I said wistfully, "For five years I've been teaching children to waltz, but I've never *been* to a ball."

I hoped I had not overdone the thing in front of Griff, but Vasily sent me a look only a little less baleful than the one he had sent the Prince; and I knew that he had taken my meaning.

Emily clasped her hands. "Then you'll say yes? *Do* say yes!"

"Miss Dark's wish," Vasily said with an ironic bow, "is my command."

With that he took his leave; and Prince Frank followed suit, appearing to laugh at some secret joke as he strolled away. This left the rest of our party to turn and make its way back to the carriage.

"You and your sisters seem very well acquainted with the Grand Duke," Griff observed in a mild tone in which I nevertheless detected a note of reproach.

I wrung my hands and whispered, unwilling to let my sisters hear. "Oh! yes! He's taken quite an interest in me since he returned to London. My sisters have no notion of such improprieties, and I would not enlighten them—but I cannot believe that he would have any honourable designs upon a mere gentleman's daughter. Still, what can I do? He is royalty, and I have no friends. My only hope is to entertain him where I can, and pray that it goes no further."

"That is not true," Griff assured me, with a little pressure upon the arm that was caught within his own. "I am willing to stand your friend, Miss Molly. But you do right to be wary of that man. I am not surprised he blushed to own those balls in your hearing."

"How so?" I was agog with curiosity; but maddeningly, Griff only shook his head.

"They were affairs of the demimonde. Not for the world would I sully an innocent young girl's ears with the knowledge."

Probably I ought to have been shocked. Reader, I was not. I had already divined that Vasily was in possession of a chequered closet. What surprised me was his palpable embarrassment under Prince Frank's teasing. Just who was Vasily Nikolaevich, that he was able both to exalt in his wickedness and to blush for it?

"I suppose that in the course of your investigations you have looked into him very thoroughly?"

"I have."

"And you have concluded?"

"Nothing, as yet. Some complicating factors have arisen. Seton is more convinced than ever that the culprits are Indians, but I think it's evident they are not the only players in this game. For instance, it's the Grand Duke who implicated the Indians in the first place."

"But if the jewel originated in India, would it not be the likeliest thing in the world that Indians should wish to retrieve it?"

"Likely that they should wish, but not that they should succeed." The end of the Lovers' Walk came in view, and Griff cleared his throat as though to change the subject. "I meant to ask, Miss Dark, whether you might ever be willing to leave London."

"I have been working on the Continent as a governess for some years," I reminded him.

"The Continent is nothing; you might travel home to see your family whenever you like. But would you leave them altogether—say for New York, or San Francisco?"

This was it: the next thing to an offer of marriage. I felt a little dizzy with my own success. All I needed to do was say yes.

But we were speaking at a normal volume, now; and at Griff's question my sister Katie threw a sudden, alarmed glance to me over her shoulder. With that forlorn look the word died upon my lips. He evidently did not envision that he should have anything to do with his wife's family; it was me he wanted, not my sisters.

Here, perhaps, I must make an explanation. I had been born to parents who were very happy in each other's company. For all the guilty secrets I harboured—for all the improper things I had done, or had wanted to do—*one* desire, at least, had always been as constant as it was conventional. I had always wanted a husband, children, and a home of my own; a desire that was as natural as breathing before my father died, but as fierce as an aching wound after he was gone and I was forced out into the world to earn our bread. A part of me would never be happy until I found my way back to the peace and safety and comfort of the home I had lost; until I had provided my children with the same carefree happiness I had once known myself.

Now, even as I congratulated myself that this dream was about to be realised, doubt struck me. Even if I could overlook my own fears and Mimi's warnings, I knew that Griff could never love me as warmly as did my sisters. No house he inhabited would really be a home; and it seemed madness, in that instant, to relinquish the family I loved for such an uncertain future.

But whom, I asked myself sternly, should I marry if not Griff? For some years I had been a governess; I had passed directly from the schoolroom back to the nursery, and apart from Griff the only men of my acquaintance were Vasily and Nijam's Alphonse. Even had he not been spoken for, Schmidt would have felt like a brother to me; and I could not *seriously* think of marrying Vasily!

I had thought myself equal to any sacrifice, so long as it brought me and mine financial stability. But now the thought of all I would give up struck all words from my lips.

"You need not answer me now," Griff said, releasing my arm as once again we reached the statue of Achilles. "I know it is a very great change."

He signalled for Lady Seton's carriage and helped us all in before sending it back to Brixton. Scarcely was Griff out of earshot than my sisters turned upon me with despairing looks.

"Does that man want to marry you, Molly?"

"Don't do it! He'll take you away to America and we'll never see you again!"

"Please say you won't do it, Molly! ...Why won't you say something?"

I passed a hand over my eyes. "Girls, girls. I must support you somehow—and I'd rather do it at ease in a home of my own, rather than slaving away in someone else's!"

"I'd rather go into service," Emily said defiantly.

"If you *must* marry a rich man, why can't you marry Grand Duke Vasily?" Lilias demanded, and *that* suggestion I had to put down as quickly as possible.

"Because, to begin with, Lilias, he *isn't* a rich man. Now for heaven's sake give me a little quiet; I *must* think."

171

But really, the only thing I *could* think chased itself through my mind all the way home—the knowledge that I had been the most colossal idiot not to say yes when I had the chance.

* * *

By that evening I had quite made up my mind.

"Molly, tell me what you think," Lilias demanded, pulling me into Mother's room, where all three of my sisters had assembled with a pile of shoes, stockings, gloves, and afternoon dresses. She was dressed in a pale apricot silk that had been Mother's just before Daddy went away, the colour of which was precisely wrong for her. "Doesn't it fit me well? I can't wear last year's lace, for I spilled ink on it; but Emily still has hers, and I can fit into this dress of Mummy's, and I think Katie will not do too badly if she can borrow your silk blouse and wear it with the striped taffeta skirt Great-Aunt Beryl gave us for theatricals. What do you think? Will it do?"

The three of them watched me hopefully from the dimly-lit bedroom, for they had eschewed lighting the gas in favour of the more economical light of an oil-lamp. My heart sank at the sight of their hopeful faces. They were so very pleased with their scrounged finery, some of which had not been modish for twenty years at least.

"Very pretty," I said, "but what do you mean? Will it do for what?"

"For the *ball,* silly," said Lilias with a laugh.

"My dears," I said as gently as I could, "if the Grand Duke *does* invite us to a ball, it's out of the question that any of you should go in old afternoon dresses."

Their faces fell. "They're not so *very* old," Lilias insisted, and

Emily said, "Mine was new last year!"

"I could remake the skirt," Katie began diffidently, but I shook my head at her.

"It will be a very fashionable affair." I did not know how to tell them how cruel fashionable people could be. The likes of Miss Henry, who had been so unkind to me at the Museum, would not spare my sisters at a ball. "None of my own dresses are suitable, and I am afraid…"

"Then we will stay home, and you must have a new one," said Emily loyally, "so that you can find yourself a husband who will stay with you in London."

I hesitated only a moment before taking the plunge. "Not a bit of it. You shall all have new dresses. I daresay something simple in white satin will do."

Katie blanched. "But, Molly! How can we possibly afford such an extravagance?"

"Without the slightest difficulty," I said. "There ought to be quite enough in what you girls put aside over the past few months. That is, unless the twins have their heart set upon a bicycle." The twins assured me that this was not the case. "Then it is settled. We shall visit a modiste tomorrow."

And then, I vowed, I must give Griff the answer he desired.

I sought refuge in my own room, only to find that once again it was occupied—this time by Vasily, who had the nerve to be stretched out indolently upon the counterpane of my bed, smiling over a book. For a moment I was quite lost for words; and then I fetched the cushion from the armchair that stood by my window, and threw it decisively at his head.

"Oof!" he exclaimed, half sitting up.

"Keep your voice down!"

"Very well, but what was *that* in aid of?"

"Oh, I was merely testing whether you were an imprint. They have a habit, you know, of being summoned by a stray thought, and appearing at the most inconvenient moment imaginable!"

He smiled. "Ah—then you were thinking of me!"

"Not, I assure you, out of any desire to see you *in my room,* reading—is that *my* book?"

He glanced at the spine. *"Can You Forgive Her?* But of course. A favourite of mine."

This distracted me from my outrage: the thought of *Vasily,* of all people, diverting himself with the misadventures in love and politics of the English gentry, was beyond even my powers of imagination. "A favourite? *Anthony Trollope?"*

He shrugged. "Don't look so surprised! I made the gentle-man's acquaintance at a time when I was being held hostage in Coburg; and I've kept up the connection since. Contrary to popular belief, the life of a thief is so infrequently interesting!"

Perhaps he was telling the truth; or perhaps he was simply trying to charm me by claiming to love the book I was reading. I narrowed my eyes. "Well—and *could* you forgive her?"

"Alice Vavasour never did a wrong thing in her life," was the prompt reply. "Breaking off her engagement to John Grey was the best judgement she made in the whole book, and she ought never to have taken him back."

"And now you've given away the ending!"

"Oh! it's quite clear where the story is tending! and it's a poor sort of book that can be spoiled in such a way!"

"How can you say that, in any case? A woman *ought* to marry; John Grey is a decent sort of man, and he would have saved her from falling into the hands of that despicable Cousin George!"

Vasily's eyes danced. "Come, be honest, Miss Dark. You

aren't even the slightest bit fond of that wicked Cousin George?"

He was laughing at me—the wretch! "I can't say that I am *fond* of him," I said in my most cutting tone, "but I do find that his presence makes the story ever so interesting. Indeed I'm sure I keep reading mainly out of eagerness to witness his downfall!"

"Touché," he said. *"You* would not fall into the hands of such a scoundrel, would you? But surely Alice made no mistake in breaking things off with John Grey. *She* wished to lead a useful life in the sphere of politics, while he wished to be a country idler. Naturally she could not—she *ought* not to resign herself to a life so unsuited to her talents, any more than surrender herself to the violence of her cousin."

He spoke with unaccustomed earnestness, and I wondered uncomfortably if he truly meant what it seemed he did. If I married Griff, what sort of life would I lead? In truth I did not know; Griff had asked me what I had to offer him, but had neglected to tell me anything about the life *he* might offer *me.* Of one thing, however, I could be practically certain: I should never make use again of my ability to see the imprints. I should never hold another séance or trick another murderer into confessing their crime. For the first time I found myself wondering if I could really do it. Griff himself was surrounded by grim memories; and I wondered, with a shudder, how many more would join them over the years, and if so, how I would be able to bear the constant reminder of his ghastly pastime.

Above all I resented Vasily for forcing me to acknowledge this, when he was the main reason I found myself obliged to marry Griff. "And did you climb in at my window to discuss a popular novel, or was there some other business you wished

175

to see me about?"

"Naturally there is," he said, tossing the book onto the table beside my bed. "What is your game in getting me to throw a ball?"

This question concealed its own pitfalls; yet I felt on firmer ground now that Vasily was no longer giving me veiled advice. "A society ball would be the perfect opportunity to display our Noor-Jahan decoy to Sir Humphrey. Who better to introduce our imitation Begum to high society than Grand Duke Vasily Nikolaevich?"

His face shuttered. "My dear, you should know that I've never given a society ball in my life."

"But Prince Francis said—"

"Damn Prince Francis!" Vasily spat. "They were demimonde affairs: you understand?"

"No," I said, as guilelessly as possible. "Should I?"

"Absolutely not, and it would be improper of me to enlighten you."

"Would that be more or less improper than climbing in at my window and lolling all over my bed?"

He dragged a hand down his face and gazed at me wrathfully. "You little witch! I don't believe you're half so innocent as you pretend to be!"

At that, I had the grace to blush. "Well: Griff told me they were not respectable gatherings! Only I'm surprised that you should be ashamed of them."

"I'm *not* ashamed of them," he retorted. "It's only that such things are not fit for a lady's ears—and you yourself warned me against corrupting your sisters."

"Not the least bit ashamed!—of a thing too bad for me even to hear of? Then how can it possibly be fit for you to partake in?"

"What an appallingly bourgeois sentiment," he said loftily.

"Why should that matter? What's sauce for the pot is sauce for the kettle."

There was a silence. Vasily appeared to be struggling with some strong emotion, or perhaps a mixture of them. "Very well," he said, "if you wish for your ball you shall have it. When is it to be? and where?"

"Make it where you please," I said with a triumphant smile, "and as for when, the sooner the better. Since the season has not yet begun, and no one has anywhere else to go, I take it no one will object if we make it Monday night."

"No one except Nijam, if she is unable to produce a crystal large enough by then." Vasily stepped to the window and swept me an ironic bow. "But why quibble? Your wish, as I have said, is my command."

Chapter XII.

I pass over the following days—in which the ball was announced, and the invitations sent, and the dresses ordered—to the evening that found us at the University College laboratory eagerly awaiting the result of Nijam's further experiments. Now that her tests had been successful, it was time to attempt the creation of a crystal large enough to substitute for the Noor-Jahan.

"I had the Indians cut the first crystals I made," Nijam announced, dropping three or four large, flashing gemstones into my palm. She then set to work opening the three large crucibles on the bench, while I held the imitation diamonds up to the light of a lamp. Cut and polished, they were now—even to Nijam's more discerning eye—indistinguishable from real diamonds.

"This is remarkable," Alphonse breathed. "You must register this with the Patents Office, Miss Nijam."

"No niin, you'd much better go into the diamond trade," Mimi put in. "Imagine the money you could make passing these off as the real thing!"

"It would work," Vasily said, laughing, "for a while, at least."

"You are both completely shameless," Nijam said, using a small hammer to break open the hard shells of slag that surrounded the crystals. "Schmidt, wouldn't you prefer *not* to be beholden to these people?"

Alphonse looked pained, but did not answer. Almost afraid that his reply would be in the negative, Nijam dared not press him. Instead, she uttered a sound of satisfaction and held up to the light a raw crystal the size of her fist. "We have our decoy," she announced. "I suppose we'd better take it at once to be cut."

She put the raw crystal into a chamois bag, and Alphonse helped her on with her coat. "I also have the things *you* requested, Grand Duke," she added, finding a small box in her coat pocket and handing it over to him.

Vasily glanced within. A mournful look crossed his face. "To think that I should be reduced to this! Thank you, at any rate; this ought to repair the—er—deficiencies of my costume."

Nijam and Alphonse ventured out into the street and hailed a cab to take them to Marylebone. It was a journey they had made several times since the adventure at Lascar Sally's, and Nijam occupied the time in mentally reviewing the phrases of Hindustani, the greetings, and the accents she had been drilled in by the Mirza and his confederates. Arriving at the back door of the Hindustani Coffee House, she and Alphonse were quickly whisked upstairs by Mr Dean—or Din Mahomet, as the establishment's Indian habitués still addressed him.

"The Mirza will come later," Mr Dean informed them as he led Nijam and Alphonse through a lamplit upper corridor decorated with richly-coloured arsenic-green wallpaper. "Tonight is for the things which he cannot teach you."

He opened a door, revealing a small room which had been converted for the occasion into a jeweller's workshop; a short, rotund Indian in a leathern apron and sleeve-garters stood up, wiping his hands, as the door opened. Nijam nodded to the craftsman and handed the chamois bag to Alphonse, who disappeared inside the room.

Mr Dean, meanwhile, ushered her into a snug, warm room at the end of the corridor, where Nijam was confronted with three ladies—two of them young, but one of them old and stately, seated in an armchair. Mr Dean spoke to them in Hindustani before turning to Nijam. "Their English is not good," he apologised, "but they know their task. They will bring you downstairs when you are ready."

With that he went away again before Nijam had had the chance to ask what, precisely, that task might be. As the door closed, she smiled tightly at the three women before her. They were splendidly, even regally dressed in heavily pleated lengths of shimmering silk, and their bare arms and necks, their ears and noses and even the parts in their hair jingled with intricate gilt jewellery. Only the oldest of them, draped in simple white, was almost innocent of jewellery apart from a diamond in her nostril.

Only when the two younger women held up a vivid length of silk did Nijam understand what was about to happen. She would need to peel off her severe and sensible black coat and dress, and her thick black stockings and her plain, serviceable petticoats, and allow these women to drape her in iridescent silk.

She was going to look like a parrot.

Happily, there were several choices of drapery and the women allowed her to select something in black. Consisting of a flimsy, transparent chiffon decorated with golden dots and borders, it was far from Nijam's idea of a respectable garment; but it was better than the crimson or peacock-blue silks. She was hurried behind a screen in the corner and obliged to peel off her clothing; when she emerged in her corset and combinations, she was sent back to remove yet more layers. This done, they laced her into an abbreviated black-and-gold blouse which left her arms and her middle, to say nothing of her back, quite naked; and she was made to supplement this with a plain petticoat, consisting of a narrow tube of black cotton slit to the knee to allow for movement. After this the length of silk—*saree,* they called it—was wound about her, tucked into the drawstring of her petticoat in precise knifelike pleats, drawn up to cover the goosefleshed skin of her middle, draped over her left shoulder and then drawn up around the front and pinned to her right. After this, they began to stack her arms with bangles; they hooked heavy gilt earrings over her ears and added a gold ornament to the part in her hair; and last of all, they took the Noor-Jahan decoy—missing its central glass stone, which must be in the other room acting as a pattern for the zirconia imitation—and hung it around her neck.

The two ladies stood back. The old woman, who had been watching from her throne, occasionally putting in a word of advice, clapped her hands and broke into a delighted smile.

"See," one of the women said, turning her about to face the mirror in the room's corner. Only the younger women had any English, and that only a few words

Nijam could not help a soft "Oh!" of surprise.

The saree was not at all scandalous. So generously was it draped and pleated that it quite satisfied the dictates of modesty, leaving only her arms bare. But the saree was nothing compared to the frightful things it did to its wearer. There, looking back at her from the depths of of the mirror with wide and almost frightened eyes—draped and pinned and decked with jewels—was the Padma Nijam whom she had always tried to keep hidden: the half-caste Indian who had, at long last, *given up*—who no longer tried to disguise her foreignness with whalebone and bombazine, who no longer pursued the approval and acceptance of her peers in the scientific world.

She had always expected this Padma Nijam to be the dirty, lazy, ignorant heathen whom civilised people talked about whenever they mentioned Indians. But she was none of those things.

She was *glorious.*

With a creak, the old lady rose from her armchair. There were actually tears in her eyes as she said something in her own language. With the words, she passed her hand over Nijam's head as though snatching something out of the air and then carrying it back to her own temple. Taking Nijam's hand in hers, she went to lead her from the room. Attempting to stride after her, Nijam was at once restricted by her saree, lost her balance, and very nearly toppled to the floor.

Softly tutting, the two younger women steadied her again. She had to walk more carefully down the hallway and the stairs, and the journey seemed interminable. When at last she reached the restaurant—lighted with lamps and filled with chattering, gorgeously-dressed Indian women in place of its customary clientele—Nijam reached out for Mr Dean and said, "It's no use. I can't move in all this."

Mr Dean said something to the old lady, who made a pithy comment in Hindustani. Mr Dean shook his head. "She says that if she can learn to move gracefully in a saree, so can you." He made a bow, first to the old lady and then to Nijam, before disappearing into the upper room.

The old lady clapped her hands, gaining the attention of everyone in the room—perhaps twenty women, of all ages, in a great many different dresses: long tunics over loose trousers, colourful blouses with filmy skirts, dresses that flared into sparkling, meticulously embroidered skirts from a high fitted waist. At the old lady's summons, they flocked towards her and seated themselves in a ring upon the floor, some of them with musical instruments: a drum, a sitar, a pipe. The music started, and someone began to sing.

It was a slow, wild, bitterly sad music. Nijam did not know what to do with herself. The Coffee Club's cane armchairs had been pushed back, freeing the floor, and a low table had been brought in and spread with aromatic food. Nijam, who had been working all day without respite, felt hungry enough to risk the rich and overwhelming flavours. But she had not been invited to sit, she did not know what the women were singing, and she was half afraid to move in her magnificent draperies for fear something should be torn or untucked. So she was still standing there, stiff as a doll, when there came a movement at the corner of her eye and she turned to find that another lady stood beside her.

This lady also wore a saree, although it was in a crisper, stiffer fabric, a riot of red and gold. Her jewellery was very fine: not gilt, but surely real gold. She greeted Nijam with palms pressed together, and Nijam, recalling her manners, followed suit.

What followed was a silent lesson conducted entirely in dumb-show. As the music went on, the lady in gold showed Nijam how to walk with a little kick of each foot to prevent her treading upon the hem of her gown; how to sit upon the floor and then rise again in a fluid, graceful movement; and even a few steps of a simple dance. In time the movement eased the pleats of the saree and her own nerves, until the draperies were hardly more restrictive than her own full layers of petticoats, and considerably lighter and cooler. At last the music stopped and the guests gathered about the table for their meal. Nijam found herself seated at the right hand of her silent tutor; and one of the younger women, who appeared to do the duties of a maid, hurried forth with a basin of water, which she offered to the lady in gold.

It was then that Nijam, who was grimly determined to watch closely and miss nothing, experienced a shock. The lady dipped her fingers into the perfumed water and out again; but her hands entered and emerged without a ripple, and there was no glistening moisture on the fingers she shook daintily to dry them.

But that was impossible; and since the light in the room was rather dim, an explanation was easily arrived at. When the basin was offered to herself next, Nijam dipped her hands into the water thinking that it was high time she invested in a good pair of spectacles.

The meal began, a convivial affair with much chattering and some attempts on the part of the younger women to translate some of the conversation for Nijam. The lady in gold did not speak and scarcely ate, but she once or twice had her maid transfer choice morsels from her own plate to Nijam's. Nijam was discomfited the first time this happened, but one of the younger women leaned over to explain, in broken English, that this was a sign of honour. At this, Nijam used a clean spoon to pass one of the morsels on to the younger woman; and at once she was surrounded by broad smiles and approving sounds.

The meal went on merrily: and although some of the food was too highly spiced for her sensitive palate, Nijam found herself beginning genuinely to enjoy herself. Nothing in this room—the music, the people, the language, the food—was familiar to her, and much of it was overwhelmingly strange; but she felt curiously at home. She was being taught manners, but no one was trying to *civilise* her, or watching her for some outbreak of savagery. It was like opening a door in a strange house and finding oneself in the half-forgotten cosiness of one's own childhood bedroom.

Perhaps it was this; or perhaps it was the comfortable, melodious ebb and flow around her of the language she did not understand that cast such a dreamlike pall over the large room, with its potted palms, its green wallpaper, and its muted lamplight. The lady on her left did not speak, only presiding over the company in state until the meal finished with soft round curd dumplings soaked in a syrup flavoured with rose and cardamom. Nijam, who harboured a secret sweet tooth, ate them with relish. When she put down her spoon, comfortably full, she found that a hush had descended upon the table as the lady in gold gathered her feet beneath her and gracefully stood.

With the same motion, everyone else followed suit. The lady turned to Nijam. The hush became expectant. Nijam, mellowed with good food, was not entirely sure what was expected of her. She pressed her hands together, bowed, and asked the question teasing at her mind.

"Begum, who are you?"

Few of the other women in the room could have understood the question; but at least one of them did, if her soft intake of breath was any indication. What happened next was like a nightmare. The lady in gold clapped a hand to her heart, as though Nijam's question had pierced her like a bullet. A dark red stain appeared rapidly between her fingers; she shuddered horribly and then fell, vanishing altogether before she reached the floor.

Nijam recoiled with an unscientific shriek; and this time she really did fall. Landing upon the cushions that surrounded the table, she stared at the empty space where the great lady had once been.

"What happened? Where did she go?" she gasped.

The old woman in the white saree began to speak, and one of the younger women haltingly translated.

"She is only our memory of the old Begum, who died years ago when the Noor-Jahan was taken."

Later, when I had Nijam describe to me the lady with whom she had eaten, I recognised her as the poor woman shot by the old Baronet Seton, whose imprint I had seen at the Museum. The case was of considerable interest to me, for in all my previous encounters with memory-imprints, not one of them had deviated from the actions they had taken in life; Nijam's tutor, on the other hand, had interacted with her and with the others at the table. I suppose, therefore, that enough of the older women recalled their dead lady sufficiently to summon up a particularly strong imprint, and even to project what she might have done to instruct Nijam.

Nijam, however, was utterly discomposed. Nothing in her mental landscape had prepared her for such an experience: she had long made up her mind that such phenomena were no more than the ravings of an unhealthy brain. The thought that hers might now be among them was more than she could stand. With a stifled gasp, she gathered her pleated skirts and rushed upstairs.

Her first impulse was to burst in on Alphonse; but she shrank from confronting him in all her heathen glory. Instead, taking refuge in the dressing-room, she unpinned and hurried back into the protective shell of her own garments. Scarcely had she finished buttoning her bodice when a knock came at the door and she heard Alphonse quietly calling her by name.

She wrenched the door open and pulled him inside.

"What has happened?" he asked, beholding her agitation. "Mr Dean said there was a disturbance downstairs—"

"A *disturbance!*" Nijam hissed scornfully, cramming a foot into one of her boots and sitting on the ottoman to tie the laces. "I can't do this, Schmidt!"

"What happened?"

"If I tell you, you'll think I am mad. Perhaps I *am* mad." She looked around wildly. "*Where* is my other boot? I'm sure it was just—"

"Here," Alphonse said, holding out the item. "Try me."

Sooner than confide in him, Nijam would almost rather have been forced to walk down Piccadilly in nothing but her combinations; but she was too agitated to resist. Having related the story, she finished, "It's as I told Dark: I'm not one of these people, and I can't be. I am a *scientist.* I believe in things I can *see*—and *predict*—and *measure.*"

"But you *did* see the Begum," Alphonse said. "So surely it makes sense to believe in her."

"My mother's cousin Harold used to see pink elephants, and all *that* meant was that he had delirium tremens!"

"Why, Miss Nijam, I had no notion you were concealing such a shameful secret!" Alphonse said with mock solemnity. Nijam could not help but smile. "What," he added, "is so very incredible about a shared memory? It's surely no more impossible than a revivified corpse."

He was referring, of course, to the dreadful revenants which until lately had so thickly populated the police forces of Europe. Nijam sucked in a quick breath. "I know nothing about the revenants," she said, "but everyone knew they were created by some measurable and predictable process. That was *science.*"

"Still, not everything *is* measurable or predictable," he said. "One cannot deal out a cupful of hope, or a thimbleful of love."

He had been wont to say such things in the past, and until now Nijam had always found this propensity rather maddening. Tonight, it felt comforting. "Then you *don't* think I'm losing my mind?"

"Miss Nijam, you have recently invented a brilliant chemical process for synthesising an entirely new substance. Of course you are not mad."

How tempting it was to believe him! And yet—"I don't know why I'm asking you," she muttered, tying off the laces on her second boot. "You aren't even a scientist anymore."

"No," he admitted, "but even if I was, why *shouldn't* I believe in things that go beyond what I can see and touch? Science is simply the art of measuring material things materially. Why should it be expected to explain the immaterial?"

Nijam sighed. "That's all very well for a man who looks exactly like Apollo, but what about me? Oh, no! I'm just an ignorant, credulous savage!"

Alphonse's mouth opened, but no sound came out. Too late, Nijam recollected that the Greek god thus evoked was known for his ideal beauty as well as his rationality and learning. The unintended compliment seemed to have quite overwhelmed him. But at length he got his tongue untangled from his tonsils, and said weakly, "Then it's just as well this is all meant to remain the most deadly secret."

She had no argument against that—or perhaps no argument against the kindness of his smile. It was, at that moment, all she could do to restrain herself from throwing her arms about his neck and confessing how desperately she loved him. Instead, hardening her heart, she sniffed loudly and stood up. "It had *better* remain a secret," she declared, "for if you tell this to Molly Dark I shall never hear the end of it. I suppose we'd better be going."

She crossed the passage to the room where the jeweller was at work. Alphonse had left the door ajar when he came to her, and beyond it the sound of the grinding-discs had ceased. Within, a voice spoke in English, scarcely above a whisper:

"Tomorrow night," said the Mirza, "while the Russian prince gives his ball. You will keep the secret?"

Nijam came to a dead halt.

"I'll do anything, so long as you make it worth my while," Mimi responded from within.

"That will present no difficulty. The Noor-Jahan must not be left in the hands of our enemies a moment longer than necessary."

Nijam backed away a step; but Alphonse, who had not overheard the few murmured words and did not notice her alarm, brushed past her, throwing the door open. "How goes the work?" he asked. The jeweller replied that he was still hard at work on the stone; but the Mirza, just inside the door, stepped away from Mimi looking almost guilty.

Nijam gave Mimi one reproachful look; then hurried downstairs, through the restaurant where Mr Dean was clearing away the remains of the feast, and out into the street where she hailed a cab to take her to Brixton.

Chapter XIII.

It was nine o'clock, and I was tucked into bed with a hot-water bottle trying unsuccessfully to read *Can You Forgive Her?* without constantly reverting to Vasily's warnings some evenings ago, when a hansom cab rattled to a stop outside the house. A minute later, a knock came at the door. I knew at once that it must be Nijam. Vasily or Mimi would have knocked at my window; and as for Alphonse Schmidt, he was much too thoughtful a person to intrude upon a lady after she had retired for the night with her hair done up in rags for the following evening's ball.

My guess proved correct, of course: Nijam charged into the sitting-room with a look of grim determination. "Dark," she said, "something has come up."

"Vasily," I guessed, with a thrill. "We are betrayed!"

"What? No," she said, pacing to the hearth and back again. Between her very sensible black coat and hat she was quite incongruously wearing large, intricate bell-shaped earrings. "Not Vasily—not yet, at any rate. But I overheard the Indians telling Mimi that they meant to take the Noor-Jahan tomorrow night during the ball. They are paying her to keep it a secret."

"Oh, no," I gasped. "Not *Mimi*. I *did* think we could depend

191

on *her*."

"Good Lord, why? Mimi's *always* been for sale to the highest bidder," Nijam said with some asperity. "I don't reproach her; she is a known quantity, and that's the main thing. But these Indians are *not*. If I go to the ball wearing the false Noor-Jahan, and word arrives that the real thing has been stolen, *I* shall be taken up for the crime; and where will we be then?"

I clutched at my temples. It was quite necessary—for *us*—that events should occur in a certain order; but of course the Indians had only one objective, and every reason to hasten it. "Oh, Nijam! This is the most frightful mess."

"I won't do it," Nijam said doggedly. "I'll simply stay home tomorrow night."

"But then you should have made that wonderful gem for nothing."

"But Sir Humphrey will still lose the Noor-Jahan, and that is the main thing."

"No," I said, "the main thing is to do some *good* for your people—not simply to hand over this jewel to the young Nawab as a trophy!"

My words were still ringing in the air when the sitting-room door opened. Expecting to see the scandalised countenances of my sisters, I congealed in horror. Instead, Mimi said, "I thought I'd find you here!" and walked in, as cool as you please.

Faint with emotion, I sank onto the sofa. "Mimi! How did you get into this house?"

"Through the upstairs window," she said. "I was coming to see you. Good evening, Nijam. I take it you've already heard the Mirza's plan. What do you propose?"

Nijam opened her mouth and then shut it again. "Mimi!" I said faintly. "You *promised* him you'd keep it from us!"

"Of course I did! Swindling is the art of telling people what they want to hear. Is it not? Had I refused him, he might have said, *Mimi does not understand; better to do it without her, tonight.*"

I did not quite know whether to believe her; but in the end it was true what Nijam had said, that Mimi would do anything for money, and in her place I might well conclude that playing both sides was the most profitable choice.

"You must delay them," Nijam said firmly. "They are relying upon you to gain them admission to the Museum, are they not? Well; then it is very simple. When I have appeared at the ball, Sir Humphrey will run at once to the Museum to test the real Noor-Jahan; and once he has done so, we shall signal you that it is safe to proceed."

Mimi nodded. "Nothing easier. Your transmitters are good for something, after all."

"Of course they are," Nijam said, offended. "It isn't *me* who uses them for teasing Vasily into a ferment." Reader, I have no idea at all why both of them turned to fix censorious eyes upon *me*.

In any case, that brought our little collogue to an end. Nijam and Mimi went off together, and I returned to my hot-water bottle and my book.

I didn't know why Vasily had teased me about Cousin George, who was a perfectly horrible man, constantly bullying the people around him. Vasily, wicked though he was, preferred to get what he wanted by wheedling and manoeuvering.

Griff—how did Griff get what he wanted?

A new jewel-case in morocco leather sat on my dressing-table; another present from Griff, more extravagant even than the flowers. It was a necklace in the *collier de chien* style affected by the Princess of Wales, composed of more than a dozen strands of tiny seed-pearls strung through fine gold bars and terminating at the front in an enamelled motif. He had sent it with his compliments, and begged me to wear it at the ball tomorrow night. The flowers, now distributed around the house in vases—I still had an enormous spray of pink roses on my dressing-table—were bad enough. But I was not sure that I liked the pearls. Still, at this crisis in my affairs, I could scarcely afford *not* to wear them. At least, with the help of a little powder, they would serve to cover up the fading bruises which Griff had imprinted upon my neck.

Shivering, I said my prayers and turned out my lamp.

* * *

The following evening was the night of the ball and the culmination of all our plans. Vasily had hired the ballroom at the Savoy—an eminently respectable establishment, he said mournfully, would be better—and it was a good thing too; for when my sisters and I reached the head of the receiving-line, where beneath the blazing chandeliers Vasily stood to welcome his guests, the short man ahead of us in the line nearly lost his monocle in surprise.

"What the devil!" he expostulated. "Is that Amelia? What is my *wife* doing here, Grand Duke?"

"I invited her, my lord," Vasily said blandly. "What sort of entertainment did you think this *was?*"

"I—oh! *Well.* Seen the error of your ways, have you?"

"It's bold of you, my lord, to suppose that the error of my ways was ever hidden from me. Do enjoy the evening. Ah, Miss Dark."

Vasily smiled at me—but oh, such a terrible smile! His two canines seemed to have grown to needle-sharp points, and his eyes were as red as blood. My sisters gasped; and when I could draw a steady breath, I murmured, "Nijam's work, I presume!"

His smile disappeared. "Really! is it so obvious?"

"Well, *I* know you aren't a monster," I whispered.

This did not put him in a better mood. "Well, I'll thank you to keep it to yourself!" he retorted, taking out a pair of dark-smoked glasses, and putting them on to conceal the redness of his eyes. In a lower voice he added, "I see you're wearing a transmitter! Nijam particularly informed me I ought not to do so!"

I had hoped that he would overlook this little detail: I wanted to remain in communication with Mimi tonight, without Vasily knowing anything about it. "Nijam always has excellent reasons for everything she says," I assured him, and hurried my sisters on into the ballroom.

"What did you mean, Miss Nijam's work?" Katie wanted to know, as I paused to get my bearings in the great gleaming room. "Does she make *dentures?*"

I nearly choked with laughter; for of course it was true. "Miss Nijam makes a lot of different things," I said, "but you can be discreet about it, can't you? Think how embarrassed the poor Grand Duke would be if anyone knew he was getting around in false teeth!"

They all, being very kind-hearted, nodded solemnly and swore they would not tell a soul. Meanwhile, I cast a glance about us. Blazing with light from the electric sconces that lined the walls, the Savoy ballroom was all done up in white and gold, with four square pillars to hold up the roof and

195

a marvellous floor of blue-and-white inlay. A profusion of flowers, colourful paper lanterns and immense potted palms gave the place a festive appeal that was only heightened by the splendid throng—men in tailcoats and orders, ladies in jewels and feathers and the *most* wonderful silk and velvet gowns, fresh from Paris.

"Ohhhh!" Emily breathed. "Oh, if only I had brought my sketchbook!"

Katie paled, looking down at her simple white silk. "Oh, Molly, and at home I felt so splendid!"

"Please tell us you *know* some of these people," Lilias begged, more ill at ease than I had ever seen her. I understood her doubts, for I felt somewhat panic-stricken myself. What if I couldn't remember how to waltz? What if I trod on someone's feet? What if no one asked any of us to dance at all?

"Of course I know some of them," I said doubtfully. "There's Grand Duke Vasily, of course, and I'm sure that Sir Humphrey and Mr Vandergriff are—"

"Oh," Katie said with great relief, "there is Susan Henry! Why, I haven't seen her in *ages!* Do you suppose that Millie is here, too?"

I congealed into a cold pudding. There indeed *was* Miss Henry, whispering to her friend from behind her fan—and now bustling towards us, flanked by her minions! I glanced about for some means of escape, but there was no friendly face within sight.

"Miss Dark," said Miss Henry, far too sweetly. "I didn't expect to see *you* here! And your sisters too! I suppose Mr Vandergriff secured you an invitation tonight, as well?"

"Oh, no," Lilias said innocently. "Grand Duke Vasily invited us! *Ow,*" she added, as I trod heavily on her toe. The last thing

I needed was my sisters boasting that I and the wicked Grand Duke were on terms of familiarity.

Miss Henry gave a catlike smile. "Oh, did he? I thought Mr Vandergriff was your particular friend. Or was I incorrectly informed?"

This time her malice was too plain to overlook. My sisters looked bewildered; and that made me too angry to speak. I was just about to seize their hands and drag them away, when a new voice spoke from behind me.

"Miss Molly!" Griff said. I turned with a start, and he took my hand and bent over it, his lips brushing my glove. "What a vision you are tonight! I see you wore my gift. Don't the pearls suit her well, Miss Henry? I ordered them from Paris, and they cost me every penny of five hundred pounds!"

For a moment Miss Henry positively gaped. Then she said in a rather nasty voice, "I *see*," and turned her back without saying another word.

"There," said Griff with satisfaction. "I fancy I've taken the wind out of *her* sails. Miss Katie, why don't you and your sisters go to my aunt? No one will bother you under Lady Seton's protection. And now, Miss Molly, may I have this dance?"

No doubt he thought he had rescued me. In fact, I had rarely been so humiliated in my life. "It hasn't," I said in a low voice, when my sisters were out of earshot. "Taken the wind out of her sails, I mean."

"What do you mean?" he asked as we moved into the flow of the dance. "It sounded as though she doubted your word."

"She did; but here in England gentlemen do not give ladies costly gifts unless there is some sort of understanding between them."

"Sure, and now she knows I have my eye on you."

"I'm afraid she believes your intentions to be dishonourable," I whispered. "That is why she turned her back on me; not because she was at a loss for words."

"Miss Molly, I protest! My intentions are perfectly honourable, and I will see to it that Miss Henry understands!"

This was gratifying, as far as it went; but Griff went no further. I had hoped to provoke a declaration. Sighing, I changed the subject. "I take it Sir Humphrey is here?"

"Yes. He is over there speaking to that gentleman, whose name has escaped me; but I am told he's a Cabinet minister."

"What a very great number of exalted connections the Grand Duke has!" I said, disingenuously. I caught glimpses of Vasily as we revolved: he was glowering at me from near the door.

"It seems he has cultivated quite an acquaintance among you British," Griff said dryly. "It is said that he gathers a great deal of interesting gossip for his cousin, the Russian Emperor—or did, before their falling-out."

"You don't mean that he was a spy?"

Griff smiled. "That's such an ignoble word for a grand duke, isn't it?"

"I am shocked," I said, trying to look it. Inwardly I was not at all shocked. If Vasily had been reduced to purloining jewels, it stood to reason that he should have begun by purloining whispers and letters—and perhaps even votes in Parliament! It was an uncomfortable thought, but not unexpected. "You must have turned up all sorts of things in the course of your investigations. Are you any closer to finding the burglars?"

Griff shook his head. "The scent has gone cold, I'm afraid—I've been unable to track down either the woman in the tenement, or the lascars themselves. So I have been amusing myself keeping watch on the Grand Duke—and the diamond." But then he smiled. "Slippery customer that he is, I've noticed that our host seems to take a marked interest in *you*, Miss Dark. It seems I can always find him in *your* vicinity."

"Indeed I wish it were otherwise," I said piteously, but this was distinctly worrying! Surely Griff had not begun to suspect *me?*

My fears were not allayed even when he seemed to change the subject: "I believe your mother is a widow, Miss Molly?"

Now, was this a sinister allusion to the fact that the mysterious woman in the tenement was disguised beneath a widow's veil—or simply the sort of question asked by a respectable man to ascertain whence he must seek the bestowal of his beloved's hand?

In any case I must respond as though I believed it to be the latter; and so I said quite candidly, "She has never remarried; it was impossible for her to forget my father."

He said something about it doing her credit. The sweep of the dancing took us past the door. I saw that the receiving-line had come to an end, but Nijam was nowhere in sight. Vasily, meanwhile, watched me with a frown stitched between his brows.

If I meant to secure a rich husband, I must cease to beat about the bush.

"Mr Vandergriff," I began rather nervously—for although my mind was quite made up, it seemed indelicate to take the initiative.

"Griff," he prompted.

"Griff," I said, with a perfectly genuine blush, "I did not give you an answer earlier this week, because I was rather taken by surprise; but I think I would like, very much, to see America one day."

He looked down at me with those pale blue eyes. "As my wife?"

I would *not* make the same mistake twice; I would secure my future. "Yes," I whispered.

My heart was in my throat, but Griff did not miss a step; he only continued to glide steadily across the floor, and said as serenely as ever—"Splendid. You have made me the happiest of men."

Victory was less sweet than I had expected to find it. In fact, as the dance ended, I found myself looking ahead in life with very little sense of relish. I could not help feeling as though a door had closed upon me, locking me into a small room from which I would only watch, and not participate, as life passed by.

Griff asked me if I cared for a glass of punch, and I must have murmured some sort of assent, for I soon found myself alone, a prey to melancholy thoughts. Now that the prize was actually within my grasp, I could not help but think of all the things Mimi and Vasily had said against the match; and I did not like to imagine what Vasily would say when he learned of my engagement.

Like the devil, of whom it is said that he will appear if you think or speak of him, Vasily chose this moment to appear at my elbow. "How very serious you look, Miss Dark! A penny for your thoughts?"

I rallied. "I believe my thoughts are worth a great deal more than a penny, your grace."

"Very well—a pound for your thoughts, but that's my final offer."

His face was inscrutable behind his dark glasses, but the

sharpened smile he gave me made me wonder if he might actually be in earnest. Then he removed doubt altogether by seizing my arm and whisking me through a nearby door into what proved to be a small vestibule, white-and-gold, with a side door that led to the lane outside.

"I beg your pardon!" I protested.

"Your sisters tell me," Vasily said without preamble, "that Vandergriff is asking you to go to America with him."

"And what if he is? You know very well what my errand was in this city!"

He threw a glance about the vestibule and took off his glasses to reveal the reddened pupils of his eyes—I did not know how Nijam had done the trick, but it was entirely convincing. "Don't marry him," he hissed. "You already know that he's the sort of man who will strangle a woman."

"Griff," I whispered faintly, "is a gentleman. He treats me like the lady I am."

"By wringing your neck? *Slava!* As for being a gentleman—! A man is only as good as the way he treats those who *cannot* hold him to account. What happens when he finds out what you really are?"

At that my heart turned over altogether. *"When* he finds out? Why should he? Will *you* tell him?"

Vasily bared his elongated teeth. "Perhaps I will! Do you think I will not? Have I not warned you I would betray you?"

And his crimson gaze burned, as though he meant to overpower me with his mere presence.

But I was armed against him with suspicion and worry—and beyond this, I did not care to let him see me afraid. So I scraped together the shreds of my dignity and said, "No. You'd never dare. You don't wish to turn me against you—and Griff isn't interested in *me* half so much as he'd like to arrest *you.*"

"In other words," he hissed, "you feel quite safe from me! Well, that is pleasant! Meanwhile, here you are fraternising with the enemy. Tell me, my little mouse: when the crisis comes, which will you choose?—the job, or your fine suitor?"

Here was one thing I had overlooked: that Griff was now my betrothed, and had every right to my confidence and loyalties. I felt the blood flee my cheeks; but I held Vasily's gaze steadily enough, and said, "That, your grace, is an outrageous question and I refuse to answer it."

With an exclamation, Vasily flung away from me. "This is impossible," he muttered, pacing angrily. *"Bozhe moi,* if I had my teeth—if I was still myself! What am I now? Not a grand duke—not the master of the demimonde—unable even to mesmerise a chit of a girl!"

"Thank God for *that,*" I could not help saying, startled. I had been unaware that vampires had their own form of mesmerism; this was useful to know. "What does it matter to you, in any case? Anyone would think you were jealous of him!"

"Jealous of whom? of Vandergriff? Ha, ha! No; I'm against the match because I believe it to be dangerous and *know* it to be a shocking waste of your talents!"

"I consider it quite a triumph of my talents," said I. I would have died in that moment, rather than let him see my own qualms. "Don't do that—you'll ruffle your hair."

But it was already too late: with one rake of his fingers, he looked as though he'd been caught in a hurricane. My warning only made him smile, sudden and ominous.

"Ah, Miss Dark, ever the governess! Ever certain that all I need is a wash and a brush and a good night's sleep, and I will be a good little boy in the morning. Well—" he seized me by the arms—"you don't know who I am. I am Vasily Nikolaevich Romanov, and I have drained the blood from more than one woman's veins. I am more than a match for you."

I thought—absurdly, for why should he?—just for a moment, that he meant to kiss me. But he only gazed intently into my eyes, so that I was reminded, a little, of the melusines at the Schloss Frohsdorf. Clearing my throat, I said, "Are you trying to *mesmerise* me, your grace?"

He drew back haughtily. "What? Absolutely not!"

I managed just enough pity not to laugh at him; but I could not help tweaking him just a little. "No, do go on. I think I *did* feel *something.*"

Vasily did not seem to find this at all funny. "One day," he snarled, "you will be eaten alive, and I can only pray it isn't—what *is* it, Schmidt?"

For the door by which we had retired had opened, and Schmidt burst through like a jack-in-a-box. I could not take it upon myself to say with any certainty what his complexion was doing; for he seemed to have both paled and flushed at the same time.

"She's *here,*" he gasped.

"Who, man?"—and then Vasily himself supplied an answer—"Not Missy of Roumania?"

"No," Schmidt stammered.

I dashed into the ballroom to see what he meant; and Vasily, coming up behind me, said in a blank tone, "Why, it's only Miss Nijam."

I came to a speechless halt. It was Nijam; but *what* a Nijam! She was a column of black, diaphanous silk, flecked with gold; more gold decked her head, wrists, and ears. Her night-dark hair, which for as long as I had known her had been pulled severely back from her face, now surrounded her head in a nimbus of modish waves; and I was nearly certain that someone had applied a little discreet powder and rouge in shades that complemented her dark colouring. In short, Nijam, who had always impressed me with her regal beauty, was now transformed into a veritable goddess. One must have been absolutely indifferent to feminine beauty not to be completely overawed by her. Even as Vasily advanced to greet her, I could not help sending Schmidt a sympathetic look. So that was the reason for his agitation!—and what an excellent thing, thought I, for Nijam!

But I could not contemplate Nijam's romance for long: Vasily, having composed himself with an effort, approached her with outstretched arms. "My dear Begum," he said. Nijam turned, and a ripple of astonishment passed around the room as she did so; for the false Noor-Jahan hung on her breast looking, in the blazing electric lights, yet more brilliant than the real thing.

"What the *devil!*" a well-known voice exclaimed, before the general commotion swallowed up whatever else Sir Humphrey had been about to say.

Smiling, I turned away and touched the transmitter in my ear. "Mimi," I murmured, still somewhat short of breath following the altercation in the vestibule, "await my signal; our fish is hooked."

Chapter XIV.

That whole evening, Nijam told me later, it felt as though she had a bull's-eye painted on her bosom. In her view, it was the false Noor-Jahan that drew all eyes—and soon, nearly every soul in the ballroom—towards her. I refrained from opining that the jewel could only have been a pretext for their attention—that it was her own remarkable looks and dignified carriage that made everyone in the room eager to seek her acquaintance. Even I, who knew her so well, felt irresistibly drawn towards this fairy-tale princess. It was no wonder that others should feel the same.

It was Frank of Teck, Vasily's companion that morning in Hyde Park, who first assailed her. "Vasily, won't you introduce me? The Begum of Bihar, wasn't it?"—Nijam pressed her palms together and responded with a stately bow. "Forgive me for asking, but I must know: *is* that in fact, the famous Noor-Jahan?"

"Indeed it is," she replied. "It has been in the possession of my family for many generations."

"Has it, by Jove! *I* thought it was in the British Museum! Or was Seton good enough to fetch it out for you to wear?"

"No, I did not!" said that gentleman, wheezing with emotion as he arrived upon the scene. Nijam recognised him at once: she had spent some weeks painstakingly cultivating an acquaintance with the Seton household servants, during which he had passed her several times in the street without once paying her the slightest heed. Naturally he did not recognise her now. "Madam, that necklace is my property!"

"Demmit, Seton, you can't go up to a lady and ask her to hand over her jewels," Frank said with a grin. It is possible that Vasily had dropped a word in his ear. "I'm sure the Begum has an excellent explanation."

"I'm not sure what there is to explain," Nijam said. "The necklace belonged to my father, the Nawab of Bihar; and when Sir James Seton murdered him, together with my mother, it passed to *me*."

She had the quiet satisfaction of seeing Sir Humphrey turn nearly purple. "Now then," he said, "this is slander! And burglary! That is a bit of glass—a decoy that was recently taken from *my* safe. Young woman, I'll have you summoned!"

"You know yourself that my father had *two* decoys made," Nijam said serenely. She did not enjoy being shouted at, but she was not about to let it daunt her; she had learned some very specific truths from the Mirza Dara, which Vasily and I had mixed gently into a stew of untruths. "It was the decoys, of course, which your father stole that day. The real Noor-Jahan never left India until now. Here," she added, unclasping the stone and offering it to Prince Frank. "See how flawless and brilliant it is? You may test it if you like."

"Oh, no," Frank said, raising his hands with a laugh. "I'll take your word for it, ma'am!"

"Allow me," Sir Humphrey snapped, lunging for the trinket. Nijam relinquished it with a smile. She did not enjoy danger or suspense; but in that moment she felt none. Having created the false jewel herself, she did not for a moment doubt that it would accomplish its purpose.

The baronet squinted at the jewel with suspicion before withdrawing a penknife from his pocket and scraping it across the vast flat surface of the imitation. From the dead silence observed by Sir Humphrey Nijam felt no doubt that the zirconia had stood up to the test. He tried once or twice more before she felt justified in saying, "Well?"

"Give her back her diamond, Seton," Frank of Teck drawled.

Sir Humphrey thrust the necklace at Frank and stalked towards the corner of the ballroom in which Griff and I were drinking punch. In this way I heard Sir Humphrey, still stertorously angry, whisper into Griff's ear: *"That woman has my diamond!"*

Nijam, meanwhile, permitted Prince Frank to fasten the necklace once more about her neck. "How correct Vasily was!" he observed, with a chuckle. "This *has* been a most amusing evening!"

"Strange that there should be *two* Noor-Jahans in existence," said another of the gentlemen who, flocking near, had witnessed the dispute. This was a soldierly-looking man with a long equine face and a magnificent drooping moustache. "I wonder if someone has found a way to stabilise baddeleyite in its crystalline form?"

This gave Nijam a distinct shock. "I *beg* your pardon," she said icily. "I don't believe we've been introduced!"

"Percy MacMahon," the learned gentleman said, bowing. "Forgive me, ma'am—I didn't mean to cast aspersions upon your heirloom! Allow me to congratulate you upon your excellent command of the English language."

"I've spoken it from my cradle," she said, with some of the

testiness that had always accompanied her answer to this naïve observation. "But I beg your pardon—you are not MacMahon the eminent mathematician, who has done such excellent work on symmetric functions?"

Mr MacMahon's eyes, which had until now been rather heavy-lidded and sleepy, now lit up with pleasure. "The same!" he said. "Are you also a mathematician, ma'am?"

"A mere dabbler," Nijam told him, gratified. Why had no one ever told her how much politer people were when you wore two million pounds' worth of dazzling jewels? "I know enough to get by, but numbers are much too theoretical for my taste. Are you not the gentleman seeking to acquire a copy of the Halayudha Sutras on a mathematical topic?"

"Indeed I am; but I had very nearly given up my search. Do you mean to say that you might be able to provide what I seek?"

"I'm not sure I can," Nijam confessed. "I *do* have a copy of some of Halayudha's Sutras; but I fear they are not the ones you want. They deal only with poetry."

"I'll take them," Mr MacMahon blurted. "I mean—forgive me!—if you would be willing to part with them—even if only long enough to permit a translation! Ma'am, you don't know what a boon they might be to the cause of science!"

Nijam felt unsure whether she was asleep and dreaming. "I should be delighted to help you—but you had better have someone look them over first, to ensure they are the sutras you want. I was quite positively told they concern poetry."

"Ah! But of course, to Halayudha, the principles of poetry, and those of mathematics, are one and the same."

"I beg your pardon," Nijam said faintly.

"Are you not familiar with the work of the great Vedic

mathematicians?"

"Not so much." She had, of course, *heard* of the ancient mathematicians of India; but it had hardly occurred to her that they might have been poets, too. She had always imagined quite rational, steely-eyed men in neatly-pressed coats. Could she have been so misled? Why, she might have had her own laboratory, and begun work restoring Alphonse's memories, *days* ago!

"I am staying here, at the Savoy," she added, interrupting Mr MacMahon in the midst of a paean on Vedic mathematics. "Call on me tomorrow and you shall have your sutras; but for now, please excuse me—I must take some air."

With this incoherent excuse, she extricated herself from the crowd and hastened towards the exit. There was surely no reason to stay any longer: Sir Humphrey had been confronted with her decoy, and wonder of wonders, she had sold the sutras. Now she itched to begin compiling a list of everything she would need to set up her laboratory.

Sweeping out at the great doors, she nearly collided with Alphonse Schmidt, who was standing on guard there, evidently fulfilling the role of a detective. But at present the only person he seemed to be watching was herself.

"Miss Nijam!" he stammered. "Are you leaving so soon?"

"The job's done; there's no point in my staying any longer. Give Dark my regards, and tell her I'll write to her at the Schloss Frohsdorf if my address changes."

"But…" He seemed to stop himself in the midst of whatever he had meant to say. After a moment, he said: "Do you not mean to see this business through?"

"Why should I?" She started towards the stair which led upwards to the hotel's great foyer, and thence to the rooms she had engaged on an upper floor. To her great annoyance, Alphonse followed.

"But they're your people," he protested. "And it's only right to see justice done for them, surely."

Once—perhaps only a few short days ago—she might have retorted that on the contrary the Indians were *not* her people, and that she recognised no duty towards a degraded and uncivilised nation. But to speak in such a way now would be wilful ignorance. Nijam sighed.

"I *have* seen justice done for them. My part in the thing is done; and now I have other—more important—work to do." He made no reply; only stood there looking incredulous and a little disappointed. And she did not want to disappoint Alphonse Schmidt. "Look," she said desperately, "that manuscript *was* the one I want, and once I've sold it I'll no longer need to bow and scrape to people who think I'm a savage, just to get a little time in a laboratory. I can set up my own. I can study what I *want* to study—which is memory. Think of it, Schmidt! What if I found a way to restore *your* memory?"

Alphonse's response to this was far from what she had imagined: his face paled, and he gazed at her with every appearance of dismay. *"My* memory?"

"Of course," Nijam faltered. A slow, cold tide of dread seemed to be taking hold of her. "Don't you *want* to be your old self again?"

"My former self was a *criminal.*"

"That doesn't mean anything!"

"It does to me," he protested. "Miss Nijam, if *you* were in my place—if *you* had done something terrible enough to be condemned to a place like the *Akbar*—would you wish to become that person once more?" He looked at her with a mute appeal she could not quite understand. "Would you *wish* to make me unfit for your company?"

Nijam clenched her teeth hard enough to feel the muscle twitch in her jaw. "I *know* you, Alphonse Schmidt, and I don't for a *moment* believe that you were in that place through any fault of your own. You'll see. I'll find a way to restore your memories, and then whoever put you there will have to restore everything they took from you." She raised her voice to override his protests. "Don't you see how they treat you at the University College? You were a prodigy! Now what are you?"

He reddened. "Am I worthless to you, now that I have lost what I used to know?"

For a long moment they only stared at each other, Nijam wretchedly aware that she had allowed her emotions to get the better of her. And she prided herself on always being so clear and objective!

At last, Alphonse cleared his throat. "Miss Nijam, I don't know what I might have done to merit such fervour, but I must insist that you respect my decision in the matter."

It was her turn to flush. "I beg your pardon! I only meant to help you!"

"If you want to help me, then help me to make amends. Help with the task in hand. Or do you think that I am more deserving of justice than the Indians, merely because I am what is called *civilised,* and they are not?"

Nijam bit her lip in vexation. *He* was called civilised? He had just this moment called himself a criminal. He still believed that the monsters who put him in prison were better than himself. Could he not understand that, just as he wished to see justice done for her people, she wished to see justice done for him?

She only said, bitterly: "You cannot be serious!"

"I am *entirely* serious."

Alphonse had always been supremely accommodating—up to a point, beyond which he became as hard as adamant. She had forgotten how hard! Almost, she could have yielded to him. But then she thought what it would mean for her: more of what she had endured these past days, always in the company of the man she loved, feeling that love grow more and more with every passing word and deed, until the burden of keeping silent threatened to crush her. "You do not know what you ask of me," she said in a low voice.

Before he could make any response, a commotion broke out upstairs in the Savoy's entrance foyer. There was a sound like doors bursting open; a medley of shrieks and gasps; and a savage, dog-like growling. Nijam turned—and the blood congealed in her veins as she beheld three enormous, shaggy beasts loping down the stairs towards them. Their blazing eyes, alight with a fiendish intelligence; their long white fangs, bared in challenge; their grey pelts, and the havoc their sharp claws wrought upon the velvety pile of the Savoy carpet, combined to announce the awful truth even before the word broke from Alphonse's bloodless lips—

"Werewolves!"

He seized Nijam's arm and turned her to face him, a globe of salt-water ready in his hand. "Go," he told her. "Hide!"

"And leave *you* to face them?" she panted. "Here's your transmitter: put it on." There was no time to say more: the monsters were upon them.

Chapter XV.

I must retrace my steps a little. "That woman is wearing my necklace!" Sir Humphrey said to Griff, within my hearing; and Griff responded quite calmly.

"Oh, I should think that pretty unlikely, Seton."

"Why should you think any such a thing?" Sir Humphrey shot me a glance and lowered his voice, but I still heard his demand. "Someone had better go to the Museum at once. What if the real Noor-Jahan has been taken? Perhaps *before* it ever went on display?"

"Calm yourself, Seton. Remember that we tested the museum stone following the disappearance of the decoy; and at that point it was indubitably the real thing. I cannot conceive how it might have been tampered with since."

"But what if that Indian hussy has got her hands on it? Once it leaves this hotel, we shall never see it again!"

"I'll not sleep before I've tested the stone at the Museum. On that you have my word."

Sir Humphrey looked relieved. "You're a white man, Griff! Forgive my anxiety, but it would set my mind at rest!"

I did not share his feelings of relief as I slipped into the rear vestibule, switching on my transmitter. "Mimi, are you there? Griff means to test the Noor-Jahan tonight, but not for a few hours longer. You must continue to delay."

"Fine," Mimi replied. "If it comes to the worst, the tide will rise sufficiently to cut off the tunnel altogether, and the Indians will have to wait for tomorrow."

As the reader may recall, Mimi's plan required breaking into the Museum basement via the tunnel which drew cooling water to the plant room; a passage which was blocked by a large iron gate like a medieval portcullis. She had already picked the lock—an exercise which had taken her the best part of the preceding week—but for the purposes of delaying the Mirza, she had told him that there was a little more work to do. Now, of course, she was obliged to hide in that dank passage as the tide rose about her feet, awaiting my signal before returning to tell the Indians that their way was open. I did not envy her.

"You're a brick, Mimi."

"Words are cheap. I want caviare."

"I'll save you some," I promised, and returned to the ball-room. Thus far, the evening was going pretty much according to plan. For better or worse, I had secured Griff's proposal; Mimi and the Indians would shortly secure the Noor-Jahan; and as for Vasily, his antics in the vestibule had convinced me that whatever game he was playing, he held the losing hand. It was evidently time to celebrate my success at the buffet table, where my sisters were still gathered beneath Lady Seton's watchful eye.

I was wholly unprepared, therefore, when Alphonse Schmidt burst through the ballroom doors for all the world like a rag doll tossed by an angry child: he tumbled across the floor in a shower of broken glass and saline drops before sliding to a groaning halt at the centre of the ballroom. I need hardly describe the effect of this upon the assembly: screams, shouts, gasps and a general panicked movement away from the source of the commotion. And then the werewolves entered.

I had never beheld one of these creatures before, yet I had no doubt at all that I was in the presence of German royalty. As all the world knows, the royalties of the Continent are sadly prone to taking on monstrous forms and eating the unwary alive. I daresay it is very dreadful, but there! it is only the way of the world. No doubt most of our astonished guests had contrived not to trouble themselves about this fact, right up to the moment at which three of the ghastly creatures entered the ballroom in a phalanx. Then those who did not at once fall prostrate with terror sank into trembling bows and curtseys. In England it was not, of course, considered *polite* for foreign royalties to display their fangs in society if such a thing could be helped. But different rules prevailed on the Continent, and the werewolves themselves were not embarrassed at all.

Only I could see the shadowy retinue that followed the creatures: the imprints of men and women bloodied and savaged. Violence hung in the air, so thick that I could almost taste metal on my tongue.

In the midst of my horror, Vasily appeared at my elbow. "Vasily," I hissed, plucking at his arm. "These creatures are killers."

"Yes; I know," he said wearily. "Find your sisters and go. Ask Vandergriff to help you if I cannot."

He then advanced into the centre of the suddenly-cleared room where the three werewolves awaited him, and Schmidt was attempting to rise.

His instructions echoed in my ears. Ask *Griff* to help us!?

That, more than anything else, filled me with dread: if Vasily really wished me to seek the protection of the prosthete, things must be very serious indeed! My next thought was for my sisters, who clung together in a little white cloud of satin at the other end of the buffet. I started towards them as Vasily addressed the werewolves with a bow.

"Ah, your highnesses! To what do I owe this very great pleasure?"

"So it is true! Grand Duke Vasily has returned to London," one of the werewolves snapped.

"And thrown us a blood ball! You shouldn't have."

"Bring on the dainties!" the last of them yelped.

I gasped—and I was not the only one. Was that, then, the truth about Vasily's scandalous demimonde balls? Had blood as well as flesh been traded at those entertainments, after which Sir Humphrey and Prince Francis had so eagerly inquired? And was all that horror about to break forth upon us here? I felt almost sick with terror, but there was no time to be lost: I had brought my sisters into this danger with me.

"Girls," I panted, throwing my arms about Lilias and Emily, "come away at once."

We were not far from the rear vestibule; I bundled them into the small room and at once seized the handle of the door opening onto the alleyway. To my horror, it was locked!

"Stay here," I told them, "and for heaven's sake don't stir a foot from here in the company of anyone but myself—or one of my friends."

"Don't go back in there, Molly," Katie begged, seizing my hand as I turned back towards the ballroom. "Stay here with us!"

"Molly, what's a dainty?" Lilias asked. Of *course* she did.

216

"Never you mind," I told her. "Let go of me, Katie; I'm going to find Mr Vandergriff. Remember what I said!"

I shut the door on them firmly. Mind you, I was not entirely certain I *did* want to seek out Griff. He would insist upon escorting me from the scene, and I did not wish to leave—at least, not without seeing that Vasily and Schmidt were safe.

They now stood side by side, Schmidt with his second salt-water bulb poised in his hand. "You are quite mistaken," Vasily was saying coolly. "There are no dainties here, and I cannot think you mean to offer any insult to the ladies present."

"That's a shame," barked the werewolf who evidently acted as the ringleader. "You ought to have arranged the proper entertainment. Suppose we help ourselves to the price on his head, Wolfgang?"

The other werewolves uttered a very unpleasant laugh. I pressed a hand to my heart. Oh, this was just our luck! Was there *no* end to the number of exalted personages who wanted Vasily dead?

As I stole through the nervous crowd towards the buffet table, a crackle in my ear heralded Nijam's low voice. "Pardon the interruption, but perhaps I can be of assistance?"

"Nijam!" I hissed, clutching my ear. "Where are you? What do you know about werewolves?"

"Absolutely nothing, which is why I am asking *you.*"

A new voice spoke. "Silver," Alphonse Schmidt whispered into his own transmitter. "Wolfsbane. Salt-water. Sensory overstim—" He broke off as one of the werewolves snarled at him.

Vasily was saying: "If you'll pardon the observation, your highnesses don't seem quite yourselves tonight. I should advise against making a greater spectacle of yourselves."

"Enough," the werewolf leader growled. "Let's step outside."

Nijam must have heard the creature's suggestion, because she cut in at once. "No. Keep them there, in the ballroom. I have an idea."

"I hope you know what you're doing," I hissed, emptying a pair of salt-shakers into one of the punch-bowls on the supper table.

"Step outside? What, and be taken up for brawling in the street?" Vasily responded, pleasantly, to the werewolves. "What an appalling notion! Why don't you call on me in the morning, and we can talk things over like civilised people."

"At Coburg you forfeited any right to civilised treatment," the werewolf snarled. Suddenly he turned upon the onlookers and barked, "Out! Out!"

The crowd had already dwindled quite significantly as people stole away in the face of the gathering storm. Now the retreat became, not merely general, but precipitous. A stampede occurred; feathers tossed and gowns tore. The wolves did not linger to ensure the room was clear before hurling themselves upon Vasily. Schmidt stepped before him and hurled a glass bulb of salt-water straight down one of those three yawning red gullets. Uttering a ladylike shriek, I snatched up the bowl of salted punch and doused the remaining two werewolves with the contents, even as they snapped at the empty air where Vasily, a moment before, had been standing.

I do not know what use the information may be to my readers in the future, but you may take it from me that salted punch, when deployed against werewolves, is as effective a remedy as Schmidt's salt-water. The creatures yelped, their hair coming off in clumps as the skin below blistered and burned. The third fell over altogether, whining in pain and pawing its muzzle, where Schmidt's saline-laden bulb had shattered.

Vasily, who had somersaulted gracefully away from beneath the attack, rose to his feet at my side. Schmidt, meanwhile, produced two long knives from sheaths at his calf—each of which bore what appeared to be a bright silver inlay running down a groove in the blade—and now took his place before us.

"Sir, you ought to leave," he said.

"Miss Dark ought to have left," Vasily said accusingly.

"Don't change the subject," I retorted, with perhaps a slight return to my days as a governess. "Haven't you any knives—or salt-water, or wolfsbane, or *anything* useful?"

"I do! I have Schmidt."

"Then he's right: you're no use, and you should leave."

But it was already too late: the wolves had taken their own respite and now approached us with hackles up and teeth bared.

"I should be very careful if I were you," Vasily sang out in a clear voice. "Schmidt dips those knives of his daily in wolfsbane. You know that it only takes a scratch, and I should so hate for an accident to happen."

"He's bluffing," snarled one of the wolves; but they hung back all the same, and spread out to encircle us.

The purpose of this was evidently to cut us off from the buffet-table, with what was left of the salt and the punch; and then to attack from all sides at once. This was very bad—let them work up enough rage, and I did not think that even the prospect of a wolfsbane-dipped knife would stop them leaping at our throats. Judging that it was time I made my exit,

I waited until one of them snapped at my heels; let out a quite genuine scream, and fainted not *quite* dead away in a puff of white satin.

"Miss Dark!" Schmidt cried. The chivalrous idiot turned towards me, whereupon the wolves leaped upon him. His shout was swallowed up by a shriek of pain, and I sat up in a horrified shudder to see the blood and the raw flesh blossoming on his left forearm beneath the jaws of one of the wolves. Only for a moment; and then Vasily, to my entire surprise, threw himself upon the creature, locked his long thin fingers about its throat, and with a strength born of desperation throttled it away from Schmidt's arm. That left Schmidt wrestling with a second wolf, which had been received upon the point of his right-hand knife. Rising from the blue-and-white inlaid floor, which was now become daubed with blood and scraps of grey fur, I threw myself towards the table; but the third wolf, which had been snapping at Schmidt from behind, now abandoned its pursuit and got its jaws fixed in the satin of my skirt. Alas! my foot slipped, and I measured my length upon the floor; I turned with nothing but my own teeth and nails with which to meet those of the werewolf—and then all the electric lights in the ballroom dimmed a moment (they had been flickering oddly for some time) and became suddenly very bright, until one by one each of them *exploded*. In quick succession each of them let off a thunderous bang, a searing light, a rain of fine glass shards, and a cloud of smoke; there must have been a dozen of them going off in the sconces along each side of the ballroom, so that it was rather like being caught in a cannonade. The fusillade left me nearly blind, nearly deaf, and choking on the stench of smoke. In the darkness a dead weight fell across my feet.

It was hairy and limp: the wolf, with his more finely-tuned senses, had fallen stunned.

"What—" I gasped; but although I felt the thrum in my throat, I could barely hear the word over the whine in my ears. As the white-hot after-image faded from my eyelids, Vasily came out of the smoke and darkness carrying one of the candelabras from the table. In that light—all too feeble to my ravaged eyes—a pale and staggering Schmidt could be seen grasping at the streams of blood that flowed from his wounded arm. Vasily seized him about the waist to support him.

"Huzzah for Nijam," Schmidt said: I could only hear the words in a muffled way, but I read the movement of his lips.

Nijam, then, had saved us! I touched the transmitter in my ear and panted, "Was—was that the sensory stimulation?"

Her voice was muffled beneath the ringing in my ears. "Just tell me whether it worked, Dark."

"Yes," I panted. "No need for anything more." To Vasily I said, "You take care of Schmidt; I must collect my sisters." Taking another of the buffet-table candelabras, I reeled away from them towards the rear vestibule, treading upon scraps of fur and shreds of silk and feathers as I went. All I was thinking, as I smoothed my hair with a trembling hand and pushed through the doors, was how on God's green earth I should explain the events of the past ten minutes to my sisters.

"Girls," I began; but the remainder of my words died in my throat. In the vestibule, my sisters were no longer waiting for me; but Mr Vandergriff *was*. His arms were folded, and he smiled at me in an odiously triumphant manner.

"Well," he said, "I've got to say, this has been a *very* illuminating evening!"

Chapter XVI.

All my life, in all the little moments of embarrassment that entangle the unwary, feminine distress has served me well. It is very difficult for the average man to keep his head when a fair-haired, blue-eyed, genteel sort of female is losing hers. Tears need not even be employed: there is the widened eye, the wrung hand, the trembling lip; and in moments of the most pressing trouble there is, as the reader has seen, the fainting-fit. The really *useful* thing about all these stratagems, of course, is the fact that if one's cards are played correctly, the distress need not even be counterfeited. The more genuine the emotion, the more salutary the effect.

I ought, therefore, to have been amply prepared for the performance of a lifetime. Alas! one weakness of the strategy had now made itself clear to me. It is very difficult to put on a show of trembling innocence when you have just been flinging basins of salted punch at werewolves. One look at Griff's triumphant face cured me of the instinctive hope that he might not have seen me rush to Vasily's defence. His next words removed all doubt:

"The burglarious widow, I presume!"

"I don't know what you mean," I gasped, putting a hand to the collar of pearls about my neck, which almost seemed to be choking me. "Where are my sisters?"

"I sent them home with my aunt," Griff said, advancing. "I guess I have the right to take you home myself, since I am your affianced husband."

His tone made it clear that he would brook no denial, but I held up both my hands to fend him off. I was aware that Vasily and Schmidt could not possibly have yet secured their escape; and neither of them were in any shape to confront a prosthete. "Wait!"

"For what?" he demanded inexorably. "Don't fear; I'm not going to confront your confederates. In fact, I'd like it best if this little conversation remained between ourselves."

Before I quite knew what he was about, he plucked Nijam's transmitter from my ear, disconnected it from the heavy battery which I had hidden within my coiffure, switched it off and tucked it into his pocket.

Somewhere in the ballroom behind me, a door banged shut. Vasily and Schmidt had departed, wholly unaware of my own predicament; and I was alone in the metallic hand of my enemy.

With the coast clear, Griff hurried me through the ballroom and up the stairs to the hotel foyer, my arm tucked firmly within his own. I had half a hope that we would be stopped and questioned on the way out; and indeed as Griff drew me through the foyer I caught a glimpse of a plain-clothes detective and a sleepy-looking sergeant chatting with a gentleman in evening-dress whom I took to be the hotel manager. Griff raised his hat to them as we went past. The manager cleared his throat, but only to say:

"I do hope you weren't inconvenienced, Mr Vandergriff?"

"Not at all," Griff told them. "I thought it was a pretty good show, myself. You shouldn't visit the Old World without seeing the royalties in their full glory."

The detective chuckled. "That's the spirit, sir. Have a good night."

And Nijam's Alphonse had nearly been *killed!*

Only when we were both ensconced within Griff's carriage did he address me again. "You are curiously silent, Miss Molly."

I do believe he was genuinely surprised by this. "I have nothing to say to you," I said in a rather shaken voice. All he knew for certain, after all, was what he had witnessed himself this night. "I gather that I have been accused of burglary."

"Don't play the innocent," Griff said. "Burglary is hardly the worst of it. A word from me, and that detective would have arrested you for assault and battery."

"I beg your pardon! When am I supposed to have assaulted anybody?"

"Why, just now in the Savoy ballroom. Committed upon royalties, no less!"

I had told Griff, and had meant to stick to it, that I had nothing to say to him. But this was ridiculous. "That was self-defence! Every Englishman has the right to that!"

"I believe the child's in earnest," he said after a moment, with a laugh. "Miss Molly, do you really think this is a free and equal country? If it was, you wouldn't have titles and royalties at all; and what is royalty, but the right to be treated better than any other white man? There isn't a judge in England who will find in your favour; you'd be fortunate not to be condemned for attempted murder. In any case it looks particularly bad for a woman to engage in violence, and your name would be bandied about by the common press. I wonder how your sisters would feel about that."

It was pretty rich, of course, to be lectured by an *American* upon the meaning of freedom and equality, as though a number of their states had not quite recently fought a costly war to keep a large part of their population in chains! Yet evidently, Griff's idea of freedom and equality only applied to those like himself; and by the end of his speech, I was no longer inclined to protest. Whether I was charged with burglary, or with assault; whether I was found guilty or exonerated, it would all be over with me. The scandal would attach to my reputation forever after. My connection with Vasily, and our plots to steal the Noor-Jahan, would be exposed to the world's scorn. Above all, my mother and sisters would know; and shame would henceforth be my lot forever.

I could bear any disgrace with fortitude so long as my family still believed in me; but to lose their good opinion I could not bear. "If that is so, why didn't you turn me in?"

"Because *you* are not the quarry I seek," he said with quite brutal honesty. "I want the Grand Duke, and he's a far more challenging proposition. Tussles between royalties aren't unknown, and are too politically delicate to prosecute, so it's no use getting him that way. No: if I'm to convince an English policeman to arrest Vasily Romanov, there has got to be hard proof that he's stolen something, and something big, from an Englishman. That's where you can help me."

I had thought my heart was already in my dancing-slippers, but it proved capable of sinking further still. "What do you mean?"

"You're going to help him steal the Noor-Jahan," Griff said, "and you'll do it wearing one of my little bugs, so that I can catch him red-handed." In the semi-darkness of the carriage, his eyes glowed with a faint cold light as he looked me over.

"Be a good girl, and there's no reason you shouldn't soon be ruling the roost as Mrs Vandergriff. Try to hoodwink me again, and I guess I'll have to turn you in."

This revelation left me torn with conflicting emotions. What—having accused me of every sort of infamy, did he now expect me to marry him? But then, was I entitled to my indignation at all? I *was* a thief and a liar, and my salted punch had done horrible damage to three eminent personages!

"You—you don't wish to break off the engagement?" I stammered hopefully. It was degrading, but the alliance was now my last best hope of salvaging something from the wreck of my life. I could not help feeling a pathetic sort of gratitude.

He smiled, pleased with this sign of capitulation. "That's your prerogative, not mine. Vandergriffs don't welch, and you're a taking little thing, with a deal more wits than I gave you credit for, though you do seem to have been hoodwinked by a scoundrel. Catch me a grand duke, and I'll be as good as my word."

"But I don't know if he *will* want the Noor-Jahan, now that another version of it has turned up in the possession of somebody else," I pointed out.

"Oh, I don't for a moment believe *that* will stop him." Griff's smile became somewhat mirthless. "Let me be very clear with you, Miss Molly: if the Grand Duke fails to rob the British Museum, our deal is off." Reaching into his pocket, he drew out one of his wicked little clockwork spiders, with a transmitter hidden within its elegant body. "Carry this with you at all times, and remember what I said: be a good girl, and things will go well for you. Oh—and you had better take back your old transmitter as well; let us not raise suspicion!"

My cheeks must have been scarlet with mingled shame and

fear, but I took the transmitter without demur and dropped it into my reticule. The short remainder of the journey to Saltoun Road passed with little other conversation. I had never been so humiliated in my life; and I surprised myself with the strength of my indignation. This man meant to frighten me into doing his bidding and then reward me for it after—and what was that bidding, but to seduce my friend into evil-doing should he give ear—for once in his chequered life—to a qualm of conscience!

Still, what choice had Griff left me, but to do his bidding?

Griff saw me to my door; but before I could go inside, he said, "We are engaged now; won't you kiss me good-night?" With an heroic effort, I did not blacken my record by attempting a second assault. Quite likely he said it only to test my submission; and as at so many other moments of my life I was obliged to submit. I put up a dutiful mouth and allowed myself to be kissed; and then went inside.

I closed the door wanting to wash my face in the hottest water I could find, but was besieged at once by my sisters. "Molly, Molly! Where have you been? Why didn't you come away with us? What were those awful creatures? Lady Seton says they are German princes, but what did they want with Vasily?"

I found myself choking back a sob. "I can't talk to you now, girls. I am much too tired."

"Are you hurt?" Katie asked, putting an arm about my waist. "Is something the matter?"

I took a deep, slow breath to calm myself. "Nothing at all is the matter."

"Mr Vandergriff told us you were engaged to him," Emily said, very solemnly. "Is it true?"

"Yes," I said, aware of the listening spider in my reticule.

"Do you *want* to marry him?" Lilias asked.

Not even to keep Griff happy could I tell the comforting lie. "Don't ask impertinent questions," I said; and extracting myself from Katie's support, I fled upstairs.

I half expected to find Vasily lounging on my bed again, but the room was drearily empty. I peered out at the window, seeing that the street, too, was empty; Griff had left me alone, but not at peace. I pulled the curtains shut and began to pace, then arrested myself upon remembering the transmitter in my reticule. I did not want Griff to overhear my agitated footsteps. The thought occurred to me that after all, I would rather face all the wrath of the English law than marry Griff; and that thought shook me a little. Then I thought that I should wish to marry Griff sooner than let my mother and sisters know the truth of my doings. I *should,* and yet—Nay: I did. My sisters were asking questions. My mother was coming home. If all this got into the papers, none of them would ever hold up their heads again. Society had punished them harshly enough for my father's poor judgement, but his had been honest failings, and mine were wilful. My entire family would be outcasts—unable to marry, unable to earn their bread, except perhaps as laundresses, or worse!

I had ruined everything; and why? All this could have been so easily avoided! Sooner than leap to Vasily's defence, I might simply have hidden with my sisters in the vestibule before allowing Griff to escort me home. Why had I not done so? *Why* had I sprung to Vasily's side?—to *Vasily,* whom I *knew* not to trust?

—And now what should I do? I could not risk my sisters' future. But neither was I capable of submitting tamely to Griff.

All my deepest being now recoiled from him—nor was this all. What was it Vasily had said? *A man is only as good as the way he treats those who cannot hold him to account.* I was now one of those people who could not hold Griff to account—quite likely I never had been—and he would deal very harshly with me in consequence, because after all I was not one of those whom he considered to be *free and equal,* so that it was right and good to keep me in my place. Then, too, I remembered the parson's text from the Sunday before last: *inasmuch as ye have done it unto one of the least of these My brethren, ye have done it unto Me.*

Some months ago, when I had had the freedom to choose, I had chosen to accept Franz Haber's mission—to undo those who, like Griff, made earthly might the measure of their actions: who believed that it was the powerful, and not the humble, with whom the Deity dwelt. I was therefore, in a sense, pledged not merely to defy Griff, but to punish him.

It was then, as Providence would have it, that I saw the error in my thinking. Ever since I had stumbled into his trap tonight, I had been thinking of Griff as the hunter, and myself as some helpless prey. How could I have forgotten that I had been hunting Griff from the moment of our very first meeting? I had got him into *my* trap before ever he got me into his. Even now he thought me some childish innocent, moulded to Vasily's will and pliable enough to be bent to his own. It likely did not occur to him to think that I had been coolly baiting traps for him all this time—and it was for this reason that he would fall into another.

At this, I recollected how swiftly the time must be passing. My fob-watch informed me that it was yet half an hour from midnight. I touched my transmitter.

"Mimi?"

"Dark! Where have you been? Vasily has been trying to raise you this past hour, and no one else is answering."

"All right, Mimi. I'll speak to him soon. What about your lot?"

"Tired of waiting," she said. "I hope your American is on his way."

"So do I," I said unhappily. Knowing that Vasily could almost certainly hear us, I made no allusions to the fact that this was a change of plans: "Let me be very clear: no one must reach the diamond before Vasily and myself. Can you manage it?"

"I'll try," she told me, "but don't dawdle. The Mirza wants to lift the cat onto the table."

She switched off her transmitter, and I plucked up my courage. "Vasily? Can you hear me?"

"It would be strange if I could not, my dear, since I am at present approaching your window in the manner of the lover in one of your English tragedies." A faint tap sounded on the glass. I threw open the curtains to see the pale face of Grand Duke Vasily pressed against it. He appeared to have found a foothold upon the bay window which marked my mother's room, beneath my own. "Good heavens!" I said, whipping the curtains shut again. Griff's transmitter was in my reticule still; and I did not doubt that he was using it to listen to every word I said. What was I to do? I must carry it with me; but then, there was Vasily! Coming to a sudden decision, I removed the spider from my reticule and pinned it securely into the hem of my satin skirt. Then, so nervous that it felt as though snakes were writhing in my stomach, I opened the window to admit my guest.

Slipping through the window with the lissom ease of a man

who does it often, Vasily said, "My dear, can you ever forgive me?"

"Why! what have you done?" I cried, fearing I knew not what.

He blinked in surprise—I noticed that he was still all fitted out in the fangs, and the red eyes, which he had worn to the ball. "I exposed you to danger. I was so certain that I should be safe in England! It never crossed my mind that the Germans would be so bold—"

"Oh!" I had not thought to blame Vasily for the presence of the werewolves at the ball. "I ought to have thought of that myself, before demanding you host the occasion—"

"No," he said, clearing away my remonstrances with a sweep of his hand. "*I* knew the danger; *I* ought to have foreseen it. The fault is mine entirely."

Since Vasily had never once before made me an apology, I was more than a little surprised by this; although it amused me to see that he found a way to make this, like everything else, about himself.

"And Schmidt?" I asked, for not all of my anxiety was for the spider hidden within the folds of my skirt. "Has he seen a doctor?"

"No; but I patched him up myself. The wound looked worse than it really was, although he may be out of commission for a day or two. I take it you were quite satisfied with the evening's events? Nijam made quite a stir, and Sir Humphrey seems quite convinced—"

"I'm perfectly satisfied," I said, cutting him off before he could betray the existence of Nijam's wonderful invention to Griff. How could I safely redirect the conversation? "All's well that ends well, despite the werewolves. One of these days, you must tell me what it was you did in Coburg to make so many people so very angry with you!"

Vasily shrugged. "The truth is, that a cure was found for monstrosity, and a number of the exalted monsters were all defanged at a stroke."

"Not truly?" This was not so far off what I had already conjectured, but I had never expected him to answer me. "Strange that they should blame *you* for it; but really, you and I must—"

"That's what I should have thought," Vasily said, injured. "I took the cure only under protest, and because I had no other choice! And as for Missy of Roumania, and the others—why, *they* would have been tricked into taking the cure whether I had helped or not; and now they wish to make me their scapegoat."

I was speechless with horror. On and on he went, making the most damning confessions, and I was incapable of stopping him. I could not even sign to him to be silent, for fear that his response would alert Griff; and I was far more frightened of Griff than I was of Vasily.

"You could not help acting as you did," I said hurriedly, "but really I'm shocked that Princess Marie should have needed defanging! An English princess, becoming a monster merely because she has happened to marry the Crown Prince of Roumania! Why, I wonder what her grandmother thought of *that!*"

"On the contrary," Vasily said gloomily, but he did not answer my question, instead choosing to incriminate himself still further. "It may not have been a part of my plan to defang myself; but I meant from the beginning to bring down the monsters, and quite creditably I managed it, too. As for Missy,

232

she is the one who sent Griff after me, to recover her diamonds. Let us hope that she did not tell him about Coburg. I doubt she would, for none of them imagine that they can continue to rule without their monstrous powers, and the truth of the matter is still the most deadly secret."

Not any more, I thought helplessly. What next? How, now, could I possibly confess to what I had done?

"I flattered myself Missy never knew it was I who took her diamonds," he went on in a low voice, as though speaking to himself. "Was I wrong? Can I not show my face *anywhere* without being hunted, and putting my friends in danger?"

"Vasily," I said desperately, "you know that I *am* your friend, do you not?"

He shook off his mood and positively laughed at me. "Absolutely not! Men of my sort do *not* befriend respectable young women; I was referring to Schmidt. Miss Dark, tonight has made one fact incontrovertibly clear. The longer this association goes on, the greater your danger. I think it is time we went our separate ways."

This was the very last thing I expected to hear him say; and I felt as though the trap in which I was caught had sprung. If Vasily went away, I could not even please Griff, much less support my sisters. "No!" I cried.

"And why not?"

I closed my eyes. I felt weary, and bewildered, and sick to my stomach. But there was one thing I knew about Vasily, and that was that he would stick by my side as long as it was worth his while. So I made it worth his while.

"We have a diamond to steal," I said faintly. "You *must* have overheard Mimi telling me to make haste, for the Indians have taken it into their heads to try for the diamond tonight!"

233

This, at last, produced the desired result. "The Indians!—tonight!" Vasily exclaimed, digging into his pocket for his transmitter. "Why did you not say it before? Come down at once; I'll bring a cab to the door."

Chapter XVII.

Having engineered the dramatic fusillade in the ballroom, Nijam took herself wearily upstairs to her own suite. She had arrived at the hotel with some pomp earlier that day, attended by one of the young women who had dressed her on the previous evening. This young person had now returned home, leaving Nijam in what would under ordinary circumstances have been conditions of the most blissful solitude. The room's furnishings were as splendid as those she had experienced at the Schloss Frohsdorf, yet what could such surroundings do for her now, when all her hopes were dashed? The bed was the softest she had yet lain upon; but she sprawled across it uncaring. Upon the Louis Quinze walnut buffet at the side of the room was French brandy, English gin, and a little box of peppermints which she had already proven to be particularly good. But not even a peppermint, Nijam found, could refresh a broken heart.

For two years all her powers had been bent upon a single problem: the discovery of Alphonse Schmidt, and the restoration of everything he had once possessed: his good name, his remarkable work, and above all the bond they had once shared, nearer than mere friendship. Now, in a few short words, he himself had dashed it all to nothing, and Nijam found herself utterly bereft. She had known Alphonse but a very short time before determining him to be the only man on earth who was capable of making her happy. Even when she had lost him at first—even when she had found him again, only to discover that he had no recollection of her—she had not felt his loss so keenly. Then, at least, there was work to be done. Now, all of that was over. He did not wish to remember whom he had once been; he did not wish to remember *her*. And there was nothing to be done about it.

So she lay on the bed and wondered, if she choked to death on this peppermint, whether it would not be easier in the end than trying to find some other way of going on. There were lines of scientific inquiry which had once interested her; they now filled her with no more enthusiasm than did the thought of the little boy in the sailor suit, with whom she had fallen in love one sunny afternoon at the Royal Botanical Gardens, aged six. The thought that this was a remarkably foolish position in which to find herself—a young woman of undeniable intelligence and capability at the outset of her career—did nothing to lighten her mood. She really ought to behave more rationally. She *ought* to; but she did not.

A knock came at the door. Recognising it, Nijam did not move. No one else knocked in that hesitant, deeply apologetic sort of way; and Alphonse Schmidt was now the very last person she wished to see.

There was an attentive silence on both sides of the door; and then he knocked again. "Miss Nijam? It's me, Alphonse Schmidt."

Nijam neither moved nor spoke. Perhaps, if she was quiet enough, he would go away.

After a moment, she heard him speak again, but not to her.

"I'm sorry, sir, she isn't answering."

Nijam had switched off her own transmitter some time ago. Now, after a moment, and only because she had just now remembered that some of her acquaintances were presently engaged in the jewel theft of the century, she switched it back on.

The first thing she heard was Vasily's voice—from the cab in which he and I were speeding towards the hotel, although of course Nijam could not be expected to know this. "You had better find her at once, Schmidt! If she isn't in her room, then where can she have got to? It's absolutely necessary to have that necklace!"

The false Noor-Jahan lay on her breast like a millstone. Nijam said wearily, "I don't have it. I gave it to the Indians. Won't you tell Schmidt to stop hammering on my door? I want to sleep."

The fib was one she and I had concocted between us, to keep the decoy out of Vasily's hands lest he be tempted to use it for his own purposes. Griff's intervention had changed all that. "There's been a change of plans, Nijam," I told her. "Just hand it over to Schmidt, will you? Then you can go back to sleep."

Sleep, Nijam knew, would evade her tonight. She might, once she handed over the necklace, return to her cloud of melancholy; or she might get up and drown her sorrows in some present exertion. With a sigh, she peeled herself from the bed, opened the door some twelve inches to hand Alphonse the decoy necklace, and then closed the door in his face. "You'll need someone to keep an eye on Vandergriff," she said via the transmitter. "I'll do it."

* * *

It seemed that Mr Vandergriff was at present also lodging at the Savoy: a consideration that had no doubt played into Vasily's decision to join him there. Nijam, who had already planted a transmitter of her own in the prosthete's room that afternoon, assured us that he was still there; he had not emerged since she had heard him direct his valet to dress him in something other than his best evening clothes some time previously. Schmidt having promised to meet us at the Savoy with the Grand Duke's own hired chaise and the decoy necklace in his pocket, Vasily switched off his transmitter and regarded me thoughtfully.

"A *change of plans!*" he said. "Now, I wonder what on earth *that* could signify!"

I managed a sickly smile, but I could not now explain in full. "How shall we find a way into the Museum?" I asked instead. "We cannot take the way Mimi found."

"No; we cannot run the risk of meeting them. We shall improvise. Schmidt assures me that he is well enough to act as our driver, and you must be my helper in Mimi's place. You are not afraid, are you?"

With each passing moment I implicated more of my confederates and gave away more of our plans to Griff; with each passing moment I felt fresh doubt that the path I had chosen was the right one, and yet there was no going back now. "Oh, no," I said, "although I hope you do not want me to climb anything. I'm not an acrobat like Mimi."

"Nothing of the sort," he assured me, but I could feel his eyes upon me, narrowed and calculating. Doubtless he saw my perturbation; doubtless he was asking himself why, if my former plan had merely been to assist the Indians in stealing the Noor-Jahan, I was now assisting *him* to cut in. Well: at least he was not demanding explanations.

Presently we reached the Savoy, where in a shadowed alleyway a bandaged Schmidt awaited us with the chaise and a small black bag, which I knew must contain the false Noor-Jahan. The moment had come to rid myself of Griff's transmitter, in such a way that it should appear like an accident. But at what price? I entered the carriage with my heart in my mouth, seating myself so near the door that my skirts trailed out into the night. Vasily, either from gallantry or from haste, was compelled to help me tuck them around my feet; and that did the trick. He let out a hiss as his hand closed around the pin in my hem, and Griff's "bug" within.

"Hullo! what's this?"

"I'm sure I don't know," said I with such calculated innocence that Vasily's eyes narrowed. He plucked out the pin and held up the little, squirming, shining brass spider.

"Well," he said almost blankly.

"Oh!" I said, doing my best to sound surprised. "Oh—is that—one of Griff's spiders?"

I was not prepared for the look that came over Vasily's face then: he went absolutely white. For an unbearably long time he stood staring at the thing, absolutely thunderstruck, before raising his eyes to mine. I know that my face must have betrayed my guilt, but I dared say nothing.

When at last he spoke his voice was very light, like a man treading over thin ice on a swiftly-flowing river. "I take it I have no secrets from Mr Vandergriff. That's unfortunate! But of course you had no notion how the thing came to be pinned within your skirts!" Then, suddenly, the façade cracked; his face was a mask of fury. "You'll pay for this, Vandergriff," he snarled at the gleaming transmitter, "and so will *she!*"

With that, he dropped the thing upon the cobblestones and crushed it with his heel. Schmidt, from the box, had heard what transpired; dimly through my terror I heard him ask if something was wrong, and I heard Vasily tell him to hold his peace and drive to the Museum. The next moment Vasily settled upon the seat beside me, and closed the door so firmly that it made me flinch.

"Vasily, please," I begged him as the chaise got underway. "You cannot believe I would do such a thing of my own free will?"

He did not answer, instead touching his transmitter. "Nijam," he said, "is Vandergriff still in his room?"

"Yes, and there's no sound of movement."

"I suppose I shall have to believe you," he said, still in that light, terrible voice. He switched off the transmitter before Nijam could ask what the dickens he was getting at, and as the gaslamps passed outside, flicker-flicker, he sat back and watched me with lips pressed tightly together. For an agonisingly long time I waited for him to speak. I had thought he would demand explanations; instead, there was only this seething silence.

"Griff will not follow us at once," I whispered.

"Naturally not," Vasily agreed. "He will not wish to risk alerting me, or the Museum guards, before I have wholly incriminated myself."

I bit my lip. He had evidently guessed a great deal; but why was he still so terribly angry? "I wished to warn you," I told him, "but—"

"Pray don't distress yourself. I'm perfectly well aware that the blackguard must have threatened you in some way. I don't blame you for seeing to your own interests. Had I kept my wits about me, I should not have made an exhibition of myself just now in your bedchamber."

I bit my tongue, not knowing what else to say. Only I could not forget that it had scarcely been three hours since I refused to tell him whether my loyalties lay with him or with Griff; and I felt sure that he had not forgotten it, either.

As the reader may imagine, there was little conversation between us until Schmidt drew up the carriage in Great Russell Street, not far from the intersection with Charlotte Street which ran north towards the University College. "Come," Vasily said, alighting from the carriage and offering me his hand.

I hesitated. "Wouldn't you rather I stayed with Schmidt?"

He gave me the blandest of looks. "Why should I prefer that, my little mouse? Is there something else you aren't telling me?"

I wanted to scream, for his anger was like lightning without thunder or rain. All I could do was shake my head.

"Then if it's all the same, we have a plan, and I'd like to stick to it." With that, he seized my hand without waiting for me to give it to him, and I found myself running breathlessly after him to the Museum gate. At that hour, of course, it was locked.

"Hullo there!" Vasily called, rattling the bars.

Footsteps came towards us, and a light shone out as a shuttered lantern was opened. "Now then," said a loud and rather beery voice, "what's the emergency?"

"I am Grand Duke Vasily Nikolaevich," Vasily said crisply, "and my very good friend Sir Humphrey Seton has sent this young person on an urgent errand to the Seton Collection. I think you had better let us in at once."

"Grand duke, my foot," the beery voice grumbled; but Vasily

reached a long arm through the bars, grasped the man by his necktie, and hauled him forward until they were practically nose to nose.

"Look into my eyes," he hissed. "Do you accuse me of lying?"

"N-no, your grace! I'll let you in at once, your grace!" the guard stuttered, for in the light of the lamp he must have had a very good view of the prosthetic teeth and the crimson eyes. A moment later we were inside the Museum grounds and making our hasty way towards the great portico.

* * *

At that moment, Mimi and her Indian friends were climbing the small iron ladder that led from the flooded tunnel through a small hatch into the Museum plant room. Emerging quietly in the heat and fumes of the great boiler, they replaced the grille in the hatch and wrung out their damp clothes preparatory to going on. To give the men a little privacy, Mimi, who herself was clad in the dark red bodice and knickers of a circus acrobat, ventured a short way into the echoing darkness of the museum basement.

As she had expected, her dark-lantern revealed a veritable labyrinth of tiny rooms, quite easy to get lost in. Having committed an old blueprint, which Vasily had found in the Reading Room, to her memory, Mimi had no fear of getting lost herself; but the rambling warren of storerooms in which she now found herself meant that she would have no trouble leading her Indian friends in circles until such time as Vasily and myself declared that the coast was clear.

Returning to the boiler room, she desired the Mirza, to-gether with his bodyguard and manservant, to follow her through an endless succession of dark crowded rooms: some with shelves for larger artefacts, others stocked with huge chests of drawers for smaller items. Everywhere their lanterns revealed gleams of marble and glints of gold. One room was full of great marble tombs, some of them in pieces. Another (marked *Spirit Room)* held jars of fuming, jewel-coloured liquids, some of them containing what Mimi, with a thrill of horror, identified as human remains—a severed hand, a shrunken head.

"Do you know where you are going?" the Mirza whispered after they had been travelling through the labyrinth for some time. "I am sure we passed this room with the wooden spearmen some minutes ago!"

"Yes, because I thought there was a way through, but there wasn't," Mimi hissed, clandestinely switching on her transmitter so that Nijam and I could overhear her difficulties. "We shall have to go through here instead."

"Here" was a door marked SKELETON ROOM—STRICTLY NO UNAUTHORISED ENTRY—CORRECT PROTOCOL MUST BE OBSERVED.

The Mirza's bodyguard beheld this legend with doubt. "This does not seem advisable. Perhaps we should find another way."

"All right," said Mimi readily, "but we shall need to retrace our steps some distance."

The Mirza, however, shook his head. "Time is running out. I say we take this way."

Mimi shrugged. The door ought perhaps to have been locked, but was not. She pushed it open and entered.

* * *

Meanwhile, Vasily and I followed our guide into the Museum, where a second night-watchman, who seemed less suspicious than the first, led us up the main stair towards the room where old Sir James' treasure was on display. There were, as usual, thickly clustered imprints, not all of them in ancient garb, thronging the steps; but this was not what caused me to clutch Vasily's arm with a hiss of alarm.

Mimi's transmitter was still open: it was this that suddenly gave voice in a shriek of terror: *"They're alive!"* I stifled a cry of surprise. "And they're not happy," Mimi added, the last word coinciding with a grunt of exertion, and the sound of something breakable smashing to splinters.

"Ha! You dare?" the Mirza panted in the background.

"Miss Dark," Vasily said with a warning in his low voice. When I looked up, I found that we had come to a halt at the top of the stairs, and he had moved to shield me from the guard's view. Evidently he also could hear the chaos unfolding downstairs; but I did not think his solicitude was for my peace of mind. He only did not wish me to give him away.

Forcing a smile, I moved on, distracted by Nijam's agitated questioning—

"Where are you, Mimi? *What* is happening? *Who* is angry?"

"The *skeletons*," Mimi gasped. "I don't think they wanted to be taken from their graves!"

Since I could offer no assistance, I switched off my transmitter, silently commending Mimi to Nijam and Providence. It was all no doubt very interesting; for in all my encounters with the dead I had never come across what might be described as animated skeletons—although I had of course been familiar with the revenant gendarmes once employed by some continental states, such as France and Germany.

And what were those, except animated corpses?—I had no time to contemplate the question, however, as the guard now preceded us into the room where the Seton Bequest was kept.

The Noor-Jahan lay, as before, upon its red velvet bed within the cage built to protect it. For days now I had thought of little else but the marvellous stone. I had wondered at the clarity and brilliance of Nijam's decoy; yet still the real diamond held its own enchantment. Beneath the illumination of the electric light set over it, which never ceased to shine night or day, the great jewel blazed like a star—the only illuminated point in that darkened room. About it the shadows themselves were laden with dark memories. I fortified myself with a deep breath, for all about the Noor-Jahan there stood a great crowd of those who had died for its sake.

Neither Vasily, nor the guard, of course, saw anything but the gem. But they, too, paused a moment in silent homage. They might not have seen the ghostly witnesses, but no doubt they felt them.

A moment sufficed; and then Vasily was himself again. "We have been sent," he announced with consummate sang-froid, "to test the Noor-Jahan and ensure its authenticity. Be so good as to unlock the cage, my good man; Sir Humphrey was kind enough to give me the combination of the safe."

And this, of course, was absolutely true; for on that memorable evening when we had first made the acquaintance of the famous gem, Vasily had been watching through his hand-mirror as Sir Humphrey opened the safe! Tonight, he moved with perfect self-assurance—removing the panel at the side of the plinth, revolving the tumblers, opening the safe and activating the trapdoor. A moment later the Noor-Jahan itself was in his hand; and all that time the night-watchman did

245

not protest, but stood impassively looking on with his dark-lantern!

"Now," Vasily went on, extracting a pocket-knife from his coat, "we shall need a little light. If you will give this lady your lantern, my good fellow?"

He sent me a narrowed look, but whether it was my ability he doubted, or my loyalty, I could not have guessed. In either case, I was about to prove myself. "Allow me," I said prettily to the night-watchman, reaching out for the lantern. But I fumbled it as he reluctantly surrendered it to my hands; and the next moment it had rolled to the floor, plunging almost the entire room in darkness and splashing droplets of burning paraffin across the parquetry. The night-watchman swore; I apologised; Vasily tutted; and a moment later, when the lamp had been righted, still with its glass and much of its fuel intact, I knew that the necklace swinging from the Grand Duke's gloved fingers was now the decoy, and that the very slight bulge in his breast-pocket was the real thing.

After that there was only the pretence of testing the stone to be carried out, and Nijam's decoy to be placed within the cage. As Vasily went through these motions, he stiffened and raised a hand to the transmitter he wore in his ear. I followed suit; and what I heard filled me with alarm.

"Dark! Dark!" Nijam was saying in a voice of concentrated urgency. "Do you hear me? I repeat: Vandergriff has already left the hotel. He went ten minutes ago when you and Vasily first entered the Museum—I didn't hear, because he timed his departure during a rain-shower. You must get away from the Museum at once! I repeat, you must leave at once!"

Vasily was no longer looking at me, but at the night-watchman. His pale lips pressed together with sudden resolve—and then he moved. With one tigerish leap, he caught the man in both hands, plucking at the buttons on his tunic and then hurling him away with almost contemptuous force. I did not understand until Vasily turned to me holding up what I had taken to be a brass button, but which now unfolded a number of gleaming legs and struggled to get away.

"A bug!" I choked, and Vasily, with a snarl, crushed the spider beneath his heel.

"No doubt the whole museum is watching us," he said. "Quickly!"

Had Vasily flown at once, it is possible that he may have secured his own escape and evaded the trap which was even then closing about us. But he paused to catch my hand; and that moment doomed us both. There was a strange, grinding, creaking sound all about us; and then first one, and then the other of the great panelled wooden doors at either end of the chamber slammed shut with a great booming echo—sealing us within.

Chapter XVIII.

Vasily hurled himself bodily against the door as it closed; but so heavy and solid was the structure that it swallowed his repeated blows with barely a sound. With a few snarling words, which I did not understand—although it was easy enough to guess their purport—he stepped back and touched the transmitter in his ear. "Mimi! I need you! *Mimi!*" and then to me, "What the blazes have you had Mimi doing all evening, and why did you keep it from me?"

I very much wished to speak to Mimi myself; it had sounded, a moment ago, like she was having a pretty lively time of it, and I could not help worrying that her luck, like ours, had run out. "Nijam," I faltered, "is Mimi all right?"

"I have no idea," she snapped at me in return. "The door was *marked* SKELETON ROOM DO NOT ENTER—why the dickens didn't they go around? The map shows at least a dozen—"

"My dear Miss Nijam," Vasily said with viciously sweetened politeness, "I shall not descend—" here he pounced upon the night-watchman, who after lying stunned for a moment against the wall where Vasily had thrown him, now groaned and began to move—"I shall *not* descend to scoldings, however richly deserved, for the secrets you have all evidently been keeping from me; but *if* you have a map will you perhaps employ it to suggest some means of egress from this *damned booby-trap?"*

And, with a dark look in my direction, he whipped off the night-watchman's necktie and began to truss him like a Sunday fowl.

"Why should a map render it possible to spirit the two of you past locked doors?" Nijam demanded, nothing daunted. "Do you think I am a miracle worker? You are neatly trapped, and I'm sure there's nothing *I* can do about it." I am fairly certain that at this juncture she added something under her breath, scarcely complimentary to our intellects.

I stared about us. With the doors closed, there was no exit from the room; not even a window. The walls were quite thick and built of solid stone, with heating vents large enough for nothing bigger than a mouse. But set in the roof was a set of glass panels, which must admit light during the daylight hours. At night, their black depths only reflected the glow of the Noor-Jahan's illuminated cage.

"A sky-light," I said, shuddering at the thought. "That might be a way out?"

Vasily rose, leaving the guard immobile at his feet. "For me, perhaps," he said with brutal honesty, "but not for you; not unless Mimi has been teaching you some tricks after all!"

I heard what he left unsaid; I read it in the silence after his words, and in the slight narrowing of his eyes. I put a hand to my heart. For months I had known that this moment would come, to no avail; I felt utterly desolate. Vasily put his hand into his pocket and took out the Noor-Jahan so that the jewel flashed between his fingers in the half-light. For a moment he looked at it; and then he looked at the sky-light.

I switched off my transmitter, unwilling to let Nijam hear—whatever was about to happen. "Vasily," I whispered. I was not sure when I had begun to call him that to his face. "Vasily, please—"

"If Vandergriff catches me," he said softly, "it won't just be gaol for me. Cousin Nicky won't have me killed, but he won't need to. The Kaiser will see to it. Or my cousin Sergei; he's the worst beast of us all."

All I had done to prepare for or circumvent his betrayal had failed, and now I ought to yield with grace. "You should leave," I whispered through numb lips. "Take the jewel and go before Griff arrives."

"I should," he snarled. And then he gave a brittle laugh. "It wouldn't be the worst thing I've ever done to a woman I was trapped with. What have I said about my family? We aren't men; we're beasts. And your fate is in my hands…"

Unable to bear his scorching gaze, I covered my face with my hands. I could well imagine what would happen when Griff caught me here, without Vasily and without the incriminating evidence he wanted. He had been very clear about my choices; either I succeeded and he would marry me, or I failed and he would expose me. If there was any other choice he would not allow *me* to make it.

All was lost. In resignation I lifted my eyes, only to recoil. Vasily must have moved in absolute silence; he now stood before me. He caught my wrist—pulled me close—and pressed the Noor-Jahan into my slack hand.

The second time was not like the first. I saw the imprints again, and gasped as their fear and pain flashed through me—but rather than re-enact their terrible deaths, they gathered about Vasily and me in a tight circle: intent and motionless, almost expectant, as though they expected quickly to welcome a new memory of blood and terror to their number.

If so, they waited in vain. "For God's sake, don't look at me like a stricken lamb," Vasily hissed. "I can't leave you here to face that monster alone."

I regret to say that I dissolved into tears.

* * *

I had, as I have said, switched off my transmitter to avoid Nijam's hearing anything; but Nijam meanwhile had at last succeeded in speaking to Mimi.

"Don't tell me you're still in the Skeleton Room," Nijam said when the uproar of battle reached her. "You're needed upstairs at once!"

"Nijam," Mimi panted, "this museum is *haunted.* I am *busy.* The Mirza—"

"Deface their sigil," Nijam directed.

"What?"

"The skeletons are clearly a sort of revenant," she said with exaggerated patience. "Revenants are created through the marking of a sigil upon their bodies, generally over the heart, although I suppose that in this case some large bone, such as the skull, might have been used to—"

"They don't have a sigil," Mimi growled, before I could ask how it was that Nijam knew such a very great deal about the creation of revenants.

"I beg your pardon, but—"

"Nijam, one of them is looking me in the eye, and it *does not have a sigil!*" To all audible seeming, Mimi punctuated the last words of this sentence with a series of heavy blows. "I do not think they are possessed! I think they are just *very unhappy!*"

"Miss Nijam!" A new voice which had for some time been trying to make itself heard broke in on her incoherent thoughts. "It's me, Schmidt! I can help; tell me where to go!"

"You'll never get past the guards," Nijam snapped at him. "For heaven's sake stay put; you're needed where you are."

"Vandergriff has arrived at the Museum," he said. "They're letting him in at the gate. I'm going to intervene."

"Listen to your mother and stay put, Schmidt," Vasily interrupted. It was at about this juncture that he and I returned to the conversation. "You can't fight guards with a mangled arm. Is Vandergriff alone?"

"Sir! Please—"

"Answer the question, Schmidt," Vasily said. On the transmitter, Nijam dimly heard a sound like glass breaking. *"Is he alone?"*

"Yes, but—"

"Good. Now," Vasily added thoughtfully, "if there was only a way to find all of the transmitters with which Vandergriff has undoubtedly filled this room!"

"You needn't find them," Nijam said promptly. "I knew Vandergriff would keep trying to listen in on us, so I built a wireless jammer into the new transmitter I gave Dark to wear to the ball. Trip the red switch on the battery-box, Dark. If there's anything that emits a signal within that room, you'll obliterate it."

"Oh, Nijam," I said admiringly. "I knew you'd save us."

"Your optimism is marvellous," Nijam said dryly. "What's your secret?"

"Our secret is that Griff is alone," I told her, "but *we are not.*"

With that I tripped the red switch, removing Vasily and myself from the conversation. Meanwhile, Nijam scowled at her rapidly-emptying peppermint-bowl, wishing that she had taken a better look at Alphonse when he came to her door for the Noor-Jahan. "What's this about your arm, Schmidt? It's hurt?"

"It's not as bad as it looks," he said. But then he murmured, plaintively: "I did wonder when you'd notice."

* * *

Feminine helplessness, I had begun to discover, is a strategy with certain shortcomings. It may, for instance, be quite simple to formulate a very good scheme for getting oneself clear of a predicament involving a locked room, a stolen diamond, several dozen ghosts, and a rapidly approaching prosthete. But it is another thing entirely to persuade someone else, who is inclined to think of one as a beautiful and helpless child, to put his life in your hands.

During our conversation with Nijam, Vasily had broken into one of the glass display cases and seized—aptly enough—upon the tiger claws Griff had once derided as a weapon fit only for savages. These he now fitted to his hands in a purposeful way that made me shudder to imagine how he meant to use them.

"Oh, please don't fight Griff in that manner!" I begged. "Not even Alphonse Schmidt could do that! He has made himself so dreadfully strong!"

"Well, how else do you intend to—" Vasily cut himself off and darted me a keen glance. "Ah, I see how it is! You think that Vandergriff will be as great a fool as myself? Or do you have some understanding with him, that I don't know about?"

253

"Well," I said tremulously, "he *did* ask me to marry him at the ball tonight; so the answer is both, really."

Vasily bared his false teeth. "I ought to have guessed!" he said. "And having made this little confidence, do you expect me to put my life in your hands?"

I flushed, but stood my ground. He was still angry; but not, I thought, with me. "I believe you *are* jealous of him," said I.

"You have a very high opinion of yourself!" he said, crushingly. "If you imagine that I mean anything by flirting with you—"

"You *are* jealous," I repeated, meaning to be as provoking as possible, "and you mean to relieve your feelings in this suicidal manner! I think it is too bad, for if you do so, then you will be badly hurt and certainly captured, and I shall be obliged to go on and marry Griff after all."

Vasily clenched his fists around the tiger claws and looked so fierce that for a moment I thought he might take off my head. But then, mastering himself, he said in a voice full of suppressed emotion: "And I suppose you have a better idea? Very well, I accept! But on one condition only, my dear: you are to call off your engagement to that creature."

This was no more than I had already planned upon. So I said, "Yes, your grace."

"And don't speak so meekly!" he said, tearing the tiger claws from his hands and tossing them aside. "I can't possibly trust you under such circumstances!"

"No, your grace." I cast a glance about the room. "We haven't much time. If you will be good enough to take up a position *there—*"

But I will not strain my audience's patience with a description of my battle dispositions. We had barely enough time to complete our few preparations before the rattle of a key interrupted us. The doors flew open; the electric lights blared, banishing every shadow; and Griff strode into the room. For a moment I thought he was carrying a short sword or sabre in his left hand; and then with a horrible shock I observed that it was, in fact, a sharp extension of his arm, built of gleaming steel for heavy slashing blows.

Seeing it, I uttered a gasp of not-at-all counterfeit horror.

"Miss Molly," Griff demanded, advancing upon me, where I stood beside the Noor-Jahan's cage. "Where is the Grand Duke?"

"He—he went," I breathed, pointing towards the opened sky-light. "I *am* so sorry! I *tried* to stop him, but he was too strong for me! And—and he found your transmitter; and…"

"And he's somehow jammed the others," Griff added. Blade at the ready, he made a quick circuit about the illuminated room. He did not find Vasily; and when I made a movement towards the door, his telescopic right hand shot out and fastened itself about my throat just as it had done at Lascar Sally's.

"Where's he got to?" Griff demanded. "Out with it, Miss Molly! Don't pretend you can't tell me!"

I was fast conceiving a great antipathy towards my fiancé, who now proved himself capable of treating a lady every bit as badly as he had treated the burglarious widow some days previously.

"The Noor-Jahan is safe," I sobbed. "Isn't that enough?"

"I don't give a damn for the diamond. I want the Grand Duke."

"I've never been treated so brutally in my life," I whimpered. This was true. "I'll show you, but you must unhand me! and

255

put away that sword!"

I half expected him not to indulge me. Perhaps, had he had Vasily's experience of my ways, he would *not* have indulged me. But it did not for a moment occur to him that I was capable of getting the better of him: I was weaker than he, and after all had failed to conceal from him my association with Vasily. The sword retracted into his forearm and he released his hold on my throat.

"Give me your hand," I said shakily. He hesitated, but then decided to humour me. I caught his wrist, brought the Noor-Jahan out of my pocket, and clapped it into his palm.

The effect was stupendous—all I could have asked for. Griff's hand shut convulsively upon the great gem, and he made an inarticulate sound of surprise. His eyes rolled back into his head, and he staggered first to one knee, and then another. The visions which were so daunting to one like me, who was inured to them, must be absolutely overwhelming to him—but I could not linger to observe the aftermath. Who could say how long this brief moment of respite might last?

"I regret to say that the honour of your hand is one to which I no longer aspire," I told him as he keeled over gently to lie upon the floor. It was only proper, after all, to inform him of the alteration in my sentiments. "Vasily, are you there?"

At once the Grand Duke dropped from the sky-light, having concealed himself in the ceiling cavity just beyond the glass. "Ha! ha!" he cried, upon seeing Griff's condition. "We'll take that, if you please." And he reached for the Noor-Jahan.

I stayed his hand with a shriek of alarm. "No, Vasily! It's the only thing keeping him down!"

He looked at me disbelievingly; then back at the convulsing Griff, and he ground his teeth together. "I must leave him with a whole skin, *and* with the jewel?"

My desperation must have been answer enough. Vasily straightened, shot his cuffs, and with the point of his toe swiftly proved—lest I had ever doubted it—that he was indeed the sort of man to kick an enemy when he was down. "This isn't the end, Vandergriff," he cried. "We shall meet again, I swear it! Ha! ha! ha!" and I dragged him, still laughing, from the room.

There was no night-watchman in the antechamber; and in the downstairs vestibule we found Alphonse Schmidt, who, contrary to orders, and despite his arm, was just tidying up the remains of the guard who had been on duty there. Following Schmidt into the outer courtyard—which was just becoming illuminated with the first light of dawn—I flipped the little red switch on my transmitter and said, "Nijam! We've escaped!"

"Then for heaven's sake don't linger in the environs," she greeted me. I don't know what else I expected. Certainly not *oh, Miss Dark! what an unexpected pleasure!*

"Where's Mimi?" I put in, suddenly realising the danger if she and the Indians should attempt to complete their own mission. "Mimi, if you hear me, retreat at once. Leave the Indians, if necessary; but don't for anything go to the Seton Room! Griff is still there!"

"Go back?" Mimi protested breathlessly. (Meanwhile, Schmidt led us past another unconscious guard and opened the gate with a flourish, waving us into the street.) "Go *back?*—Not you, Dara, I'm speaking to the others. I suppose *you* would like to battle your way back through the Skeleton Room, after having barely survived the first attempt!"

"Oh!" I said, intrigued, "it's *Dara* now, is it?"

"Not the time, Dark!" Nijam snapped. "Mimi, I have your

map! There's any number of ways to circumvent the Skeleton Room! If you'll just tell me where you are—"

I switched off the transmitter, for we had now reached our carriage. We got underway in great haste: Schmidt whipped the horses to a brisk trot even before I could close the door, and when Vasily managed to lean out and wrestle it shut, he trapped a good two feet of my skirts, this time not at all by my own design.

Opposite me, Vasily fell into his seat. "Safe and sound!" he said, "but without the diamond! Oh, what cursed luck!"

"It's all right," I told him, "we still have the—"

And I pulled myself up short, for we did *not* still have the decoy! In our haste, Nijam's wonderful creation had been left behind in the illuminated cage; and with Griff having convulsions on the floor we could scarcely have risked staying to retrieve it.

"Mimi," I cried into my transmitter.

"It's no use!" Nijam said peevishly. "She's gone! I was just telling her where to go, and she switched me off."

"Nijam, we left the Noor-Jahan in Griff's hand—and the decoy is still in the display cage!"

Nijam gave one of her long, eloquent silences. "How *ever*," she said at last, "did you all survive the Jerusalem job without me?"

"Well, that's the thing," I said hopefully. "We barely did. And I did think that if you had been with us—"

"Mary Angelica Dark, if you think I have nothing better to do with my life than to prevent you people from running yourselves into one trap after another—"

She stopped.

"Yes?" I said hopefully. She had not finished the sentence.

Perhaps this was a promising sign.

"I don't wish to talk about it," she said—rather sulkily, I thought. "It's like trying to do business with a gang of orangutans. We have been to all this effort, and created an entirely new sort of gemstone, for absolutely nothing. I shall probably lose my invention to some rival, who will take all the credit for it. I hope you are proud of yourselves."

Chapter XIX.

The transmitter went quiet after that, and presently I ventured to ask Vasily, "What are we going to do now?"

He sent me a weary smile; his anger seemed to have ebbed, leaving him bloodless and silent. "We shall of course do the customary thing in such an instance."

"And that is?"

"Leave the country until it is safe to return. Take us to Brixton, Schmidt; Miss Dark will desire to collect her things."

Miss Dark didn't particularly desire to do any such thing; but had made such a hash of her affairs that she could hardly protest. Necessity is the mother of the devil, as they say. We did not hear again from Nijam, nor from Mimi; and not even Vasily spoke again until we had reached Saltoun Road. It now wanted perhaps half an hour of sunrise, and the street was beginning to be full of clerks in shabby suits carrying their umbrellas in the direction of the train station. Ordinarily at this hour, the Dark household would be assembling sleepily for breakfast; but lights already glowed in the front sitting-room, the twins could be heard talking excitedly, and when I tried the front-door knob, it turned quite easily without needing to be unlocked. I had not a thought in my mind beyond the necessity of gathering my things and bidding my sisters a hurried goodbye; but when the door swung wide, all that was banished from my mind. There in the sitting-room, the twins were talking nineteen to the dozen, and my mother was just taking off her hat!

Wednesday! Mother had been coming home on Wednesday—and it was now Wednesday morning!

"There's Molly now!" Lilias shouted joyfully. "Look, Molly! Mother's come home!" Behind me, Vasily helpfully added to my predicament by tripping over one of the bandboxes somebody had littered across the hallway floor and saying something unutterably rude in French.

Perhaps it was this that made my mother's smile falter, or perhaps my utter panic showed upon my face. "Molly," she said doubtfully, "is something the matter? Where have you been at this hour?"

I did not know what to say; I did not know where to look. I could only say, in a voice rather like that of Griff's automaton, "Nothing is the matter, Mother. I'm so pleased to see you home again, and so well! This gentleman is an acquaintance of mine, Vasily Nikolaevich."

"He's a grand duke!" Emily squeaked.—"From Russia!" Lilias added. Their eyes were puffy from lack of sleep, but of course there was no point in hoping that my sisters would *not* volunteer this information with relish.

It was no doubt the best that could be hoped for, that Mother did *not* absolutely draw herself up to her full height and order the unfortunate Vasily from the house. Instead she said a rather frosty "How do you do?"

"I must just run upstairs; I shall leave you all to get better acquainted," I blurted out, fleeing from the room.

To my great horror, Vasily followed me. "Miss Dark," he

261

called, and halfway up the stairs I was forced to turn on him, with a furious gesture directing him to remain behind. It was bad enough that my mother should identify him so readily with the monstrous autocracy of Russia, which ruled its scarcely-emancipated peasantry with bared fang and bloody terror, without her finding out that he was the sort of person who thought nothing of intruding in young ladies' bedrooms!

Vasily was not to be dissuaded. "Miss Dark," he repeated, taking the stairs two at a time, "what is happening? Do you fear something?"

I sank my voice to a furious whisper. "Yes, I do! I'm afraid of my mother finding out that I'm a thief and you're a—a—"

"That I am what I am," he said ruefully. "Very well! You gather your things, and leave your mother to me."

This was not at all reassuring. "What are you going to do to her? Whatever you're thinking of, I absolutely forbid it!"

He half wanted to laugh, I could tell. "What do you think I am? I'm not—" Then he stopped, passing a hand over his face. "I envy you, Molly Dark," he said gently. "Your mother is alive. Mine is dead. My father drained her blood."

I shuddered. "Don't say such things!"

His hand touched mine where it rested upon the bannister. "I beg your pardon. I only meant to say that I am very bad, but I am not my father."

I could not look away from him; not though I was aware that the sitting-room door was open, and no sound came from within. Likely my mother was watching us—likely my sisters were straining their ears to hear what Vasily and I whispered on the stairs. But in that moment what I truly wanted, more than anything in the world, was to believe him. I still felt tears at the back of my throat, where they had been lurking ever since he chose not to take the Noor-Jahan, abandon me to Griff, and fulfil all my fears. Not though he had been so angry with me over Griff's little bug; not though he had been obliged to give up the diamond and any hope of settling the score between us.

"Forgive me," I whispered. There was nothing else I was able to say just then, but his hand tightened briefly upon mine before I stole it away again. "I won't be a moment," I added.

In my room, I began to stuff blouses and skirts and dresses, washcloths and hair-oils and ribbons into my carpet-bag. I had travelled so much that the operation took scarcely any thought. Instead, I brooded over my predicament. How was I to explain my precipitous departure? I could scarcely stay; the moment Griff awoke from his visions he would be on my doorstep with the police. It was true that I had not in fact succeeded in stealing the Noor-Jahan, but I did not think this would dissuade Griff from putting me in gaol on any pretext he could find. Perhaps he was already on his way!

Oh, how neatly he had trapped me! How sure I had been that I had found a way to escape his trap—and how useless had been my struggles! In that moment of weakness I regretted everything, even my faith in Providence. I ought never to have agreed to steal the Noor-Jahan. I ought never to have thought I could fascinate a prosthete—a man who meant to rid himself of humanity, to become a creature of iron and sleepless vigilance.

—No. In truth, the mistake went further back still. I ought never to have kept secrets from my family. I ought to have been blameless and modest and ladylike. I ought never to have been anything more than what I appeared to be on the outside.

I had begun to live a double life; and how could I go on with it?

It was then that the solution occurred to me (though I dare say the reader has seen it all quite plainly for some time). Griff may or may not be on his way here to expose me. In a few hours, if I was not locked up in the Old Bailey, I should certainly be fleeing to a Continental exile. In either case my family must assuredly come to know the truth. I could allow them to learn it from Griff, in which case they would certainly think the worst of me; or I could make the confession myself; after which no one—neither Griff nor any other person—would ever be able to gain such a degree of ascendancy over me again.

It is a grim business, making up one's mind to banish oneself from one's own home. As I took myself and my carpet-bag reluctantly down the stairs, I was half persuaded my mother would cast me off with all my ill-gotten gains, resolving to live in blameless penury henceforth. In that case I must comfort myself with the knowledge that she had benefited from my misdeeds just this far: that she was no longer to die of consumption.

In the sitting-room only peace and harmony reigned. Hannah and Katie were serving tea. Vasily was speaking smoothly and charmingly about a special hospital he meant to endow in India. My mother was asking questions with every appearance of cordiality. Lingering in the doorway, I had a quiet moment in which to look at her. Despite the differences in our respective dispositions (for unlike myself, my mother had always been consummately self-assured and impervious to the opinions of others), in looks I had always taken after her; she too was tall, fair-haired and blue-eyed, although I had once or twice heard people say that while I was handsome enough, it was a shame I would never be a beauty like my mother. All that was past now. Since I last saw her, three years ago, she had become thinner, and there was now more grey in her hair than gold. That day, I felt for the first time that my mother was not an untouchable goddess, but only a frail and ageing mortal.

I felt horribly tempted, just for a moment, to leave well alone. But what would I do then? Slip away and leave them all with no notion of where I had gone? Then she would learn the truth from Griff—and that would be far worse.

Katie saw me first; me and my carpet bag. Her face fell, for she knew at once that I was going away again as unexpectedly as I had come. It was this that gave me the strength to go on.

"Mother," I said.

Everyone looked at me. "Where are you going, Molly?" Lilias asked. Vasily, perhaps seeing the look on my face, got up and said, "I'll wait in the carriage."

All the worry flooded back to my mother's face. Perhaps my own expression gave me away; or perhaps her brief toleration of Vasily did not extend as far as standing by with equanimity as he drove away with her unaccompanied daughter.

"Mother," I said nervously, "I have a great many things to tell you, but not much time. A man is coming here soon with the police. You must tell them that I have gone off with the Grand Duke, and—"

"The *police?*" she gasped, and after that almost all of it came flowing out. Whatever she might think of me, I knew that I was firm in my own conscience about what I had done, and I needed her to know that I had behaved only as I thought I should:

265

"Ever since Daddy died," I said almost defiantly, "I've been able to see memories of dead people, and sometimes I learn things. I learn about crimes that have been committed, and then I must set them right, because there is no one else to do it. That is how I came to know that Sir Humphrey's father was a thief, and that he stole the Noor-Jahan diamond from an Indian Nawab whom he murdered. And that is why I have done…all the things that I have done. It was foolish of me, because I knew that if anything went wrong, you and the girls would suffer for it. But if you tell the police quite honestly everything you know, and don't try to protect me, then perhaps you will not suffer too greatly on my account."

Absolute silence reigned. My sisters looked utterly incredulous; but there was a look of shocked understanding dawning in my mother's face.

"Molly," she whispered, *"what* have you done, that the police should want you?"

I swallowed hard, dreading how the words would sound when spoken aloud. "I—I've tried to steal the Noor-Jahan!"

"From Sir Humphrey Seton?"

"Yes!"

My mother sat down in a heap. *"Molly!* I hardly know what to say!"

"Please don't think too harshly of me," I begged. "I began to do this because I had no other way of sending you to Carlsbad; but I went on doing it because I was convinced it was right! If I do not redress the injustices done to the dead, then who will?"

My sisters stared at me with huge eyes, scarcely understanding what I *did* say. But my mother said faintly, "My mother always warned me that the gift was in our family, but I never wanted to believe it."

I could scarcely believe my ears. "You *knew?*" I whispered. "You *knew* I might have these visions?" And she had never prepared me for the eventuality!

"I did, but I thought you had escaped untouched; I didn't wish to provoke the very visions I should be warning you about! Trudi Haber told that you had restored her son to an inheritance that had belonged to his dead wife. Is that the sort of thing you mean?"

"Yes," I said feebly, "but I didn't set out to do that! I set out to be a thief, Mother!"

"Why—because you wanted to send me to Carlsbad?"

The horror on her face struck me to the heart. "I am sorry," I said. "I knew how much you would hate to be saved on such terms!—but truly, in the end it was all Herr Haber's generosity that made you well, and not any ill-gotten gains at all!"

But she shook her head, and now there were tears in her eyes. "Oh, Molly!" she cried. "Is this what I've done to you? Put so much responsibility on your shoulders, that I've driven you to crime? Oh, my darling, I know you haven't done anything wrong; Trudi told me all about it! But won't you forgive me? It was wrong of me to lean so much upon you!"

"It wasn't!" I cried hotly. There were tears on my face—just such tears as there had been a few short hours since, when Vasily—in the face of everything he had been telling me, in the face of everything I had been telling myself—had refused to betray me. "What else could you have done? Hidden your condition from me? I should have found out only when it was too late to save you!"

"No: I should not have singled you out," she said, taking firm hold of both my hands. "I should never have made you feel, so young, that it was your sole task to provide for us. Molly, Molly! You've been carrying too much of the burden of this family. And if, after all this, you think that I mean to hand you over to the police—well, you are quite mistaken! But why am I keeping you? You must go at once!"

She began to draw me towards the door; and because I knew I must make haste, I did not resist. But I could not quite credit what was happening, either.

"But they'll arrest you for helping me!"

"They'll do no such thing: your sisters are minors, and I have returned from the Continent only this morning, and can have had nothing to do with your deeds."

"But I've been trying to *steal* Sir Humphrey's diamond!" I wailed. "Doesn't that bother you even a little?"

"Not in the least," she said stoutly, "and I'll tell you why, but not now. I'll write to you; care of Franz Haber, I suppose? Now kiss me and *go.* I trust that you will conduct yourself with the utmost propriety in the company of that Grand Duke!"

She embraced me; my sisters, who had listened to all this in utter confusion, rallied sufficiently to follow suit; old Hannah told me gruffly to be good; and then I followed Vasily into the carriage and rolled away in a state of complete mental uproar.

I had confessed everything to my mother—or nearly everything—but instead of turning from me in horror, she had begged me to pardon her. I did not quite know what to make of this; but in that moment I felt as though an inexpressibly great burden, like Christian's in *The Pilgrim's Progress,* had loosened from my shoulders and rolled away.

Chapter XXX.

Nijam was still trying doggedly to elicit a response from Mimi when Vasily, Schmidt, and I returned to the Savoy and assembled in the luxurious rooms which had been engaged for the putative Begum.

"Mimi hasn't spoken in at least an hour," Nijam greeted us fretfully. "There's no possibility at all they haven't caught her. I suppose they've been interrogating *her* instead of running after *you*."

No one said anything, but I sensed the natural conclusion hanging in the air. Nijam's suite at the Savoy had been fixed for our *rendez-vous* with Mimi; but if she had been captured, it would no longer be safe or sensible for us to remain.

"Absolutely not," I said. "No one must think of leaving one of ours in the hands of the enemy."

"My dear," Vasily objected, "I think that Mimi herself would tell us—"

"Dark is right," Nijam interrupted. I had only a moment to be surprised by this before she added: "I refuse to leave my artificial diamond in the hands of those people."

"I was referring to Mimi!" I protested. "You'll make another gemstone; what does the decoy matter as long as we have each other?"

"It matters that no one else should take the credit for my invention!"

"How can you be so cold and unfeeling when Mimi is in danger?"

"How can you presume I don't care for Mimi, only because I can think of other things? Don't you see that every small invention laid to my credit will reflect, not merely upon my own abilities, but those of my entire nation?"

"Ladies, ladies!" Vasily objected. "I beg you to give Mimi a little more credit! Take my word for it; she will very soon come through that door without a care in the world. Why—" he added, as a knock sounded at the door in question, "ten to one that is Mimi now."

"I hope so," Nijam said darkly, "but you had better allow me to answer it, in case it is the police after all."

It seemed that Vasily was not so very confident in Mimi's evasive powers, for he retired with the rest of us out of view of the door, allowing Nijam to answer the knock herself. It was not Mimi: it was a page, who informed Nijam that a gentleman was downstairs asking to see the Begum. He had not sent a card, but Nijam was in no doubt of her caller's identity. "Here's a bit of luck," she said, crossing to the room's safe and extracting the by-now familiar Halayudha Sutras. "Mr MacMahon has called for his manuscript, as he promised. We shall have a *little* money, at least."

She paused only to drape a bit of black muslin over her hair, which at once transformed her from a demure Englishwoman into an arresting pagan beauty. Having slipped the Sutras into a carryall, she ventured into the downstairs foyer and was directed to a quiet corner where not one, but two gentlemen sat awaiting her. One of them rose when she approached;

and Nijam stopped dead in her tracks, experiencing a single moment of perfect horror. It was Sir Humphrey Seton.

The awful moment passed quickly as he bowed, addressing her as the Begum of Bihar. Nijam sank nervelessly into an armchair opposite the second gentleman. Rather than an officer of the law, as she had presumed at first, this proved to be my former betrothed, Mr Vandergriff. Griff drew a second shock from her, for he seemed to be caught in a fit of the horrors. When she greeted him, it took him a moment to withdraw his wide and staring gaze from the far distance and bow in response. Nor did he speak at all. There was a Gladstone bag beside his foot, and he seemed to be rather anxious about it, because several disjointed segments of his right arm crept all the way out of his sleeve and fidgeted with the handle.

"Sir Humphrey Seton! and Mr Vandergriff!" Nijam exclaimed, having taken care to switch on her transmitter so that the words would be conveyed to her confederates upstairs. A nasty moment they gave us, too, before we—like Nijam—perceived that Sir Humphrey had no idea of her being in league with ourselves. "What a surprise!"

"My dear lady, I've come on a matter of private business," Sir Humphrey said apologetically. "Can't we retire to some more discreet apartment?"

This was the furthest thing from Nijam's mind. "No, I think this is sufficiently private."

"Hem! Well, then, I shall be brief. I wish to buy your diamond. I shall give you ten thousand pounds for it."

"I beg your pardon!" Nijam said, startled beyond words.

(Upstairs, I heard Sir Humphrey's request and nearly boxed my own ears in my haste to switch on my transmitter. *"Don't sell it for a penny under a million!"* I hissed.)

Nijam resisted the urge to switch me off, instead tucking her own bag, with the Halayudha Sutras, discreetly behind her skirts. What was she to say? Was this some sinister test? If Griff had been left at the Museum clutching the real Noor-Jahan in his fist, why in the name of all sense was Sir Humphrey now begging to purchase her decoy—which she did not have, as it had also been left at the Museum?

Not for the first time, Nijam reflected bitterly how little she cared for surprises. There was no time to reflect; only to act. Discarding the temptation to ask outright what had happened to the real Noor-Jahan and its decoy, and praying that an explanation for Sir Humphrey's visit would shortly reveal itself, she said instead, "Ten thousand pounds? Excuse me, Sir Humphrey, but do you expect me to part with the emblem of my people for a mere fraction of its worth?"

"Money is no object with us," Sir Humphrey said, casting a severe look in Griff's direction. "I do not believe your diamond could possibly be so fine as the real Noor-Jahan, but if you insist, we are willing to pay whatever you ask."

"Within reason," Griff put in, rather sulkily, Nijam thought.

"Indeed?" Nijam asked. "Why?"

"Why?" Sir Humphrey echoed, managing to sound distinctly offended. "Dear lady, I've made you an offer—and a very good one, too! It is unlikely you will receive such another! Why, you ought to count yourself fortunate you are able to dispose of the diamond as you please. The Maharaja of Punjab, Duleep Singh, was not able to do so much!"

This sounded to Nijam suspiciously like a threat; and of course it made her blazingly angry.

"The Noor-Jahan," she said icily, "is not mine to sell. It

272

belongs to Bihar and the people of Bihar; and is considered by them the emblem of Bihar's sovereignty. That is why you want it, evidently. Not because it is famous; not because it is rich; but because it made a Seton the conqueror of Bihar, and because you believe that the people there are ignorant savages who ought not to be entrusted with such a precious thing, any more than they ought to be entrusted with their own liberty." Sir Humphrey and Griff stared at her in amazement, but Nijam was not to be stopped or interrupted. "Do you believe yourself worth so very much more than my people? Do you believe that it is so very civilised to shoot people in cold blood? And *you*," she went on, turning upon Griff, who startled, "you who pride yourself upon solving crimes, why do you solve only the crimes committed against people of your own sort? It is not justice you want; not really. It is power. Well: I have found that my people are no less savage or ignorant than any of the English. Our history is as rich; our learning is as profound; if you oppress us we suffer, if you shoot us we bleed, if you burn our cities we revolt. You have taken freedom, dignity, and wealth from us; I will not sell you the one thing we have left."

Upstairs, all was in uproar. Schmidt listened to Nijam's speech with an expression of rapt attention; but Vasily paced the floor with inarticulate sounds of protest, and I had begun short-sheeting the bed purely to distract myself from the unfolding disaster.

"What the devil does she suppose she's doing?" Vasily demanded of no one in particular.

"She was supposed to say *yes!*" I wailed.

It was too much, even in that moment of panic, to hope that he would overlook this revelation. "What! you *spoke* to her

273

about this?"

But I was saved from replying. A tap came at the window, and I turned to see a small hand, equipped with tiger claws, clinging to the window-sill. The next moment Mimi's flushed face appeared; before I could recover from my surprise, she had dragged open the window and stepped inside. She was a little cobwebby and dishevelled, and cut an odd figure in her stained circus knickers and tiger claws, but otherwise she looked extremely well.

It was not her costume, however, nor even the tiger claws, with which she had evidently been scaling the building, that claimed my attention. The Noor-Jahan hung about her neck, glowing like a star in the golden morning light and sending iridescent glitters of light dancing across the ceiling.

"Mimi!" I gasped. "You're all right! We had practically given you up for lost! Is that the diamond?"

"No," Mimi said with her customary brevity. "It's the decoy. You left it behind in the cage, you know."

Almost sobbing with relief, I touched the transmitter. "Mimi's turned up with the decoy, Nijam! For heaven's sake stop jawing and let Sir Humphrey buy it!"

This recalled Nijam to her senses—though she insists, with some justice, that there was no point in closing the sale until there was something to sell.

"I have never been so insulted in my life," Sir Humphrey was saying in reply to her speech. "If that is how you feel, madam, then there is nothing left to say!"

"I'll accept not a single penny beneath two million pounds," Nijam said, speaking the words with exactly the same measured, passionless deliberation as her previous speech. "Bihar needs schools, hospitals, wells, and railways more than it needs the Noor-Jahan, and if this is the only way to get them, then I will submit."

Griff startled. "Two *million—*"

"That is what you yourselves boasted it was worth," Nijam said inexorably.

"I only brought fifty thousand pounds," Griff protested, indicating the Gladstone bag. "How can I possibly find *two million?*"

"You had no trouble finding that much when you were shopping for castles in Roumania," Sir Humphrey pointed out unsympathetically. *"You* lost me the Noor-Jahan; it's *your* duty to get it back before the whole world knows these savages stole it right out of the British Museum!"

There was a silence. Griff's lips thinned. Then he reached into his breast-pocket, drew out an envelope, and tossed it onto the small table that stood between them. Opening it, Nijam found that it was none other than the title deed to a Roumanian castle. "There's your two million pounds," Griff said, "and I wish you joy of it."

Later, she said that the old saying had come to her mind, about a bird in the frying-pan being worth two in the fire. "I accept," she said. "Shall we find a lawyer to formalise the transfer?"

* * *

"But *how?*" Nijam demanded some two hours later. The interim had been spent profitably in quiet diligence: Schmidt and Mimi, dressed as respectably as they could manage under the circumstances, had escorted the false Begum and her guests to a lawyer in the City who found himself hurriedly drawing up the necessary deeds of conveyance. This done, Nijam retired to her quarters, where we conducted a hasty council of war.

"Indeed," I said, marvelling at the documents she had displayed for our approval, "something tells me that Mimi holds the key to this mystery if anyone does!"

"Oh, it is very simple," Mimi said with a shrug. "When Dara and I had found our way through the skeleton room, we switched off Nijam, because we do not need to be *worried* at. Then we went upstairs to the Seton Collection and found the decoy in the cage and the Noor-Jahan in the hand of Vandergriff, who had fainted dead away. Dara took the real diamond, and I opened the safe to take the decoy. Then Dara gave me a *real* ruby and took himself and his people off to Limehouse. I suppose they have set sail to India by now!"

"He gave you a ruby?" I gasped. With satisfaction, Mimi held up a glowing red stone the colour of pigeon's blood and about the size of her thumbnail.

"Hum!" said Vasily. "I wonder if that's all he gave you!"

Mimi shrugged, no less satisfied. "We fought skeletons together and retrieved his Nawab's diamond, and now if I am ever in trouble I am to call upon him from the ends of the earth. It is a good thing I switched off Nijam, eh? The instant I saw that the decoy was still in the cage, I knew something had gone wrong."

"Did you indeed!" said Vasily. There was a shard of ice in his soft voice. "I begin to think there has been a conspiracy going on behind my back! Am I to understand that the plan was *not* to exchange the real Noor-Jahan for the decoy?"

Nijam and Mimi both had the nerve to look at *me*. I mean to say, it had of course been *my* plan; but I didn't see why that meant I should be the one to explain it. Nijam, with her utter disregard for what people thought of her, was far better suited to such a task!

There was no help for it: I cleared my throat delicately. "The truth is, Vasily, you must admit that you warned me quite often of your sinister intentions."

His face was a study. *"Gospodin!* So I did!"

"Your plan was to steal the diamond," I said. "Ours—mine and Nijam's, I mean—was simply to let you run off with the real Noor-Jahan, as you evidently meant to do; and then we would sell the decoy to Sir Humphrey much as we have done now."

"What! you would have allowed me to walk off with a king's ransom in my pocket, and never lifted a finger to stop me?"

I felt my cheeks warming. "Why not? What use is a great trinket like the Noor-Jahan to the people of Bihar, except to give their Nawab a very fine opinion of himself? Far better to invest the gold in a trust for the people, for education and medicine and whatever else is needed. And in any case," I added wickedly, "it was a *cursed* jewel. You would have suffered quite enough without my help!"

"Heartless!" he said, shaking his head; but his laughter was a little strained, I thought.

"Of course," I went on—and perhaps I was enjoying myself a little—"then the Indians appeared, but that made no change in my plans; I would allow you and the Mirza to outwit each other to your hearts' content. The important thing was that the diamond should disappear, and that Nijam and I should retain the decoy in order to sell it to Sir Humphrey. That was the real reason Nijam had to display it at the ball. I thought it far more likely that Sir Humphrey would try quietly to replace the diamond, than that he would make a public fuss over having lost it. It was Griff's discovering that you and I were in league, last night at the ball, which really complicated matters." I paused, scarcely knowing how to go on.

"He threatened you," Vasily said in a low growl.

I nodded, unable to look him in the eye. But it was evidently a day for making confessions. "Griff told me that I must help him to catch you in the act of stealing the diamond, or he would have me arrested. I did not mind for myself; but my family would have been condemned to still greater poverty and disgrace."

"You might have signalled me," he said, injured. "I would have understood."

"I know that *now*," I said. I still did not quite know what to think of the wicked Grand Duke; but I was beginning to feel that he might be trusted, after all. "You were very angry with me, I know."

"I was a brute," he said, scowling. "Of course it was at the ball that he caught you! Good God, and you rushed into that battle with only a pair of salt-shakers to defend yourself."

Mimi shook her head in disgust. *"I* would not have done so. Not for you, Vasya."

"I know that I ought to have stayed out of it," I said, feeling myself blush. Vasily made a rather overwrought gesture, but said nothing. "In any case, we were compelled to walk directly into Griff's trap, and I had to give up the Noor-Jahan in order to escape."

"I don't understand how you *did* escape," Nijam said with a frown. "What did you do? Vandergriff looked as though he'd just seen—"

She cut herself off, and I nodded soberly. "As though he'd

just seen a ghost? Indeed. When I put the diamond into his hand, he must have been assailed with visions and sensations such as he had never before experienced in his life. One hopes he is not permanently shattered."

Mimi scowled. "Why?"

"Because, Mimi," Vasily said with a sigh, "our Miss Dark, despite her present company, has been nicely brought-up. My dear, I am speechless." And—suiting the action to the word, like the fellow in Shakespeare—he proceeded to say nothing more at all.

Nijam clapped her hands briskly. "In the meanwhile, it's high time we left the country. We ought to take this title deed to Herr Haber at once, before Vandergriff decides he's been hard done by. If we set out at once, we might be in time to take the twelve o'clock to Dover."

Schmidt stared at her; I did the same. My voice shook with emotion. "*We*, Nijam? You're coming with us?"

Nijam's face shuttered a little. "Have you any objections?"

"Of course not; only you always said…"

My voice trailed away. Nijam said, "Well, that settles it. I'm coming." But then she looked away and went on less stubbornly, "The truth is, I always thought there was something to your ghosts; you *knew* things you could not have known otherwise. Only I couldn't afford to believe in spirits if I was to be taken seriously in my profession. Werewolves, yes; revenants, yes; but not ghosts. But I begin to think I will *never* be taken seriously; not while I am a woman and an Indian. I might as well give up trying."

"Don't give up!" someone said impulsively. To my surprise, it was Alphonse Schmidt. He reddened when Nijam levelled a rather haughty look at him, and stammered, "I mean, you

279

were so very anxious that I should not do the same; I know you will regret it if *you* do."

Nijam stared at him a moment too long; and I, who was near her, thought that her face flushed a little. She turned away from Schmidt abruptly and said to me, "I will always be a scientist, but I am obliged to be without the recognition, or the support, of my peers. In that case, it is my intention to use my gifts for the good of those who *will* accept me. At present, that means you—and people like the Mirza and Mr Dean Mahomet."

"Oh, Nijam," I said, throwing my arms eagerly about her. "Don't worry! You will be able to fund your own researches in time."

"I hope so," she said, scowling, "and I still mean to find out how to treat siren amnesia! Just in case it may someday be useful!"

"Of course you will," I told her, and then, because I couldn't help myself, I added: "You're a white man, Nijam!"

"Oh, lor'!" she said, laughing in spite of herself. *"Please* don't!"

Chapter XXXI.

Evening found us aboard the ship to France. The cliffs of
Dover were painted golden by the sunset as, once again, I left
the land of my birth behind. My emotions, as I leaned against
the gunwale watching England recede, were as starkly mixed
as the sunlight and shadow that played across the waves. Relief
that we had all made our escape from among the dangers that
beset us; a perplexed happiness that I had at last found the
courage to reveal some of my secrets to my mother, with
such a result as I could never have predicted; but above all,
uncertainty and a little homesickness. I had escaped Griff's
trap, but at what cost? When would I see my home and family
again? Perhaps the police might not have been alerted to my
misdeeds; perhaps even Sir Humphrey was ignorant of the
role I had played in the disappearance of the Noor-Jahan;
but I did not for a moment imagine that Griff would give up
his pursuit of Vasily. If his mind survived the shock it had
sustained, he must inevitably come in search of the Grand
Duke; and perhaps, also, of me.

It was now the time of my nightly visitation. I stiffened a
little as my father's imprint approached out of the sunset as
serenely as though he walked upon a Brixton carpet rather
than being apparently suspended in midair above a choppy

sea. An ominous sign, I thought; most imprints faded over time and did not appear in the company of other people, nor in such an extremely unlikely setting. Surely only an infirm mind would imagine gentlemen in quiet business attire flitting about through the sky. It was proof of what I already feared: that my father's imprint was only becoming stronger.

He stopped in front of me, his feet at a level with my own despite having nothing solid upon which to stand. I almost felt the soft brush of his lips upon my forehead; I almost heard the whisper of his voice, *"Be good."* My blood ran cold. One day I *would* hear it, and what then?—farewell sanity?

Just then, despite everything, I could not find it in myself to be resentful. It was true that my father had died tragically early; but I had never blamed him for that. I had blamed him for leaving us poor and disgraced; but even that thought now seemed unworthy. It was as Nijam had said to Sir Humphrey: surely poverty in itself ought not to be any disgrace. Why should I not hold up my head as high as anyone else, simply because I was poor? Why should I not ask to be treated with as much dignity as the most bejewelled lady in St James'? This was a novel thought. Perhaps Nijam was beginning to affect me as much as I, evidently, had affected her.

As the sun went down, the deck began to empty as the other passengers made their way below decks. I heard two of them discussing, as they went, an item of news which had made its way into the evening papers—that Sir Humphrey Seton had decided upon an early withdrawal of his fabulous jewel, the Noor-Jahan diamond, from the British Museum. He would now be returning to Hong Kong sooner than expected, and speculation was rife as to the meaning of this sudden retreat. I did not volunteer my own conjectures; but I smiled. Perhaps

Sir Humphrey at last was about to experience some of the social difficulties so familiar to my own family.

There were certain other dispositions that had *not* made it into the papers. Nijam's last act before taking ship that evening had been to mail the Halayudha Sutras to Mr MacMahon, asking only that he would have them returned with care to India when he was done with them. As for Griff's pearls, I had them concealed in my baggage. I had briefly considered returning them to my former fiancé, but on the whole I thought the trinket might be disposed of more advantageously elsewhere—Antwerp, for instance.

Beneath the sound of wind and waves I did not hear Vasily approach, but tonight his silent appearance beside me at the rail was less troubling than it might once have been.

"I suppose," he said mournfully, "that now I'll never have the chance to sell Vandergriff that French painting."

"Perhaps some other rich American will buy it," I suggested. He bestowed upon me a smile of gentle and ineffable melancholy, which of course I distrusted at once. "Tell me about this painting," I added after a moment: "is it really yours, or is that a—a—shall we say, a *premature* truth?"

"You injure me!" he said. "I assure you, the painting is as much my own as anything ever has been!"

This was somehow not reassuring, although I forbore to say so. Vasily leaned against the rail, but instead of watching the fading light, he fixed his gaze upon me.

"What's the matter?" I asked, discomfited.

"Oh! nothing," he said; but after a moment he went on, with a laugh that was perhaps a little sheepish. "I am only thinking that once again I underestimated you. I warned you not to trust me, and all the time you were coolly planning to profit

283

from my inevitable betrayal. To think how easily I might have spoiled your plans, had I only made up my mind *not* to do so!"

I felt myself blushing. "But you *did* make up your mind not to do so," I told him in a voice a little too soft and tender. "You stayed with me in danger, when you might have escaped and saved yourself; and taken the diamond with you."

"Don't thank me," he said. "The man I once was—the monster—*would* have betrayed you; would have drained your blood to do so, even as you begged him to stop."

"But you couldn't do that now," I said. "Your tastes have changed. And don't tell me they haven't; don't tell me you didn't need to wear dentures and red lenses last night, just to keep up appearances."

He looked away from me then, towards the sea where it melted into the twilight on the world's rim. I had the sense that he was struggling with something; and then he sighed and said in a low voice, "You are right."

I bit my lip but could not repress my smile. "Speak clearly when you address me, young man!" I ordered suddenly. "And look me in the eye!"

He must once have had an English nanny of his own, because he straightened reflexively; but the look he cast me was half-wrathful, half-laughing. "How do you *do* that?" he demanded. "Very well: if I am to be honest with myself, yes! My tastes have changed, so that I could not drink your blood now if I wished to, which I do not. But I consider it a very great shame!"

Perhaps he meant it, or perhaps he did not. But the admission I had wrung from him made me smile with satisfaction. "There," I said, "was that so very difficult?"

"Minx!" he said. But after a moment his look softened

oddly. I had not thought that Vasily could look softly upon a woman. With calculation, yes; with desire, certainly; with raillery, always. But not with softness. "I didn't mean that," he said caressingly, raising my hand from the rail to his lips. "One of your poets spoke complacently of a poor Indian who threw away a jewel richer than all his tribe, but that man was a sage compared to Warren Henry Vandergriff. In his place I would never have let you go."

I was not quite sure why this should have brought a hot tide of blood to my cheeks. But I did not like Vasily's softness, which seemed to go beyond what was necessary for mere professional relations. In some things the wicked Grand Duke might, perhaps, be trusted; but I was not such a fool as to consider him safe: or, heaven forbid, *eligible.*

Touching the tip of my tongue to my lips, I said with an attempt at his own light raillery: "Don't you know me by now, Vasily Nikolaevich? Haven't I outwitted you often enough to prove how far I am from honesty—or disinterest—or modesty?"

A smile seemed to be lurking in the corners of his mouth. "No," he said.

"Well," I answered—and I think it was the most honest thing I had ever said in my entire life, so that the moment the words were out of my mouth I was almost dizzy with terror at my own audacity—"well, you *ought* to. You *ought* to know that you are not the only one with ambitions; with desires; who can play upon the hearts of others like a stringed instrument, and sleep soundly afterwards without a single pang of conscience."

I might have done anything then. I might have gone on to tell him about the girl whose nerves I had shattered at school, or how much I had wanted to kiss Blanca de Borbon when she had me half-mesmerised in her room.

But Vasily waved a dismissive hand and said "Oh, that! I know all about that. I know you're manipulative and unscrupulous; and libidinous too, if that's what you're trying to tell me in that prudish English way of yours. *That* I've known ever since I kissed you in the gold sitting-room at Schloss Frohsdorf, and the rest of it I worked out at about the time you handed me over to the secret police for safekeeping while you passed the Bourbon inheritance to Franz Haber."

"Then," I said feebly—hoping that in the half-light the violence of my embarrassment would be obscured—"then when you speak of me, you should not speak flippantly of jewels worth all one's tribe."

"But that's precisely why I do," he said gently. "It isn't that I think you invulnerable to the ordinary temptations of mortals, Miss Dark; it is that although you feel them, you find the strength to resist them. It is more praiseworthy, surely, to do right when it is hard, than when it is easy."

I can scarcely describe the feelings that this speech provoked in me. At the time all I could think was that I had expected none of this. It had only been my intention to warn Vasily against treating me with too great familiarity; and instead, quite casually, as though it was no great matter at all, he had up-ended all my conception of myself. Was it possible? Seen through Vasily's eyes—seen so clearly, with all my faults so ruthlessly indexed—was I really a light of virtue; and not a scheming, cold-hearted female little better than she should be?

"Do you really mean it?" I could not help blurting out.—"Yes," he said, and for one short moment I abandoned myself to the hope that he did.

"I don't know whether to believe you," I said recklessly, "but I could kiss you, just for saying it."

"Oh, no," he said, laughing. "I can't afford to kiss you." Perhaps the words stung, just a little; but on the whole it was a relief to discover that Vasily, too, felt that it was best we should remain mere professional associates.

Since it was growing cold, Vasily escorted me to the cabin I shared with Mimi. (Nijam, who was a sensitive sleeper, was resting in solitary splendour in a cabin of her own.) Given the eventful nature of the past twenty-four hours, I expected to find my cabin-mate fast asleep in bed; but when I opened the door I found her sitting bolt upright in her berth with a face as pale as paper.

"What's the matter, Mimi?" Vasily asked jovially. "Don't tell me you accidentally gave the decoy to the Indians, and we've sold the real gemstone to Sir Humphrey."

"Hush," I told him; for upon that pale, elfin face was the look of someone who had received a mortal blow and had gone perfectly numb because of it. "What is it, Mimi?"

"Dark!" She seized my hands, staring about the cramped cabin so that I almost expected to see someone lurking in the shadows. "Dark, *do you see anything?*"

"I…" I began, and then broke off, for in the grey light that struggled in at the door I *did* see a pale shape at the end of Mimi's berth. A moment later I was able to make out the forlorn shape of a young girl in white tulle and ballet-slippers, her thin arms wrapped about her graceful legs in a posture of utter despair.

"It's a dancer," I said. "A ballerina…"

"I knew it," Mimi said in a voice that had gone deathly calm. "I saw her in my dream. My little Annushka is

287

dead—murdered." Her hands tightened upon mine. "We must go to Saint Petersburg at once."

"Of course we must," I said. What else could I say? Once we had deposited the title deed with Franz Haber, it would be no trouble at all to make our way directly to the imperial Russian capital. "Although—" I added, and sent Vasily an inquiring glance. For who could forget that he was wanted by the tsar's police?

But the Grand Duke only gave a slow, ruthless smile. "Oh, yes," he purred. *"Do* let us go to Russia."

S. D. G.
Miss Dark will return in
Dark & Stormy

Unhistorical Note

Ordinarily I try not to allow the slightest bit of *real* history to taint these stories, but this one got away from me.

This book owes something to my own family history. Born in Shoreditch in 1924, my grandpa was still a young boy when his Indian father, a travelling fur salesman, was arrested and deported to America where, as it turned out, he already had a legal wife and family. This wasn't the only case of bigamy in my family tree—on the other side, a Scottish merchant's daughter fled to New Zealand with her children in the mid-1800s after she found that due to her husband's previous marriage she had never been legally married at all. Those being Victorian times, flight to the ends of the earth was the only way for a gentleman's daughter to escape such a scandal. But for Grandpa, losing his father meant not so much scandal as living in poverty in London's East End with his mother and sisters, relying on sweatshop labour and the Salvation Army to make ends meet. After a stint in the Royal Air Force during World War II, Grandpa moved to Australia, where he hoped to find better job opportunities and less prejudice against Indians.

Grandpa died when I was very young, or I might have managed to ask him more about his time in London, his experience in Australia, and our relatives in northeastern India. I hope he doesn't mind that I borrowed from his experience for Miss Nijam.

Of course, there were many other Indians in London long before my shady great-grandfather. One of them was Sake Din Mahomet, a Bengali who in 1810 opened London's first Indian restaurant, the Hindustani Coffee House in Marylebone (and thus the London curry predates fish and chips by about fifty years). In reality, the Hindustani Coffee House was a fairly short-lived venture and the place had been closed for decades by the time Miss Dark and her confederates were flourishing, though his descendants still lived in London under the name of Dean.

Other Indians in London during this period included many shiphands, or lascars, who were paid very little and often horribly mistreated; a large number of university students at the University College London; Cornelia Sorabji, who was not only the first female Indian lawyer but the first woman of any colour to graduate from Oxford with a law degree and practice law in England; Dadabhai Naoroji, who in 1892 became the first Indian elected to the British House of Commons as a full-fledged Member of Parliament, representing Finsbury Central; and Princess Sophia Duleep Singh, the suffragette and activist from whose father the British had stolen the Sikh empire of the Punjab and the Koh-I-Noor diamond itself. I wish I'd had the opportunity to include more of these illustrious Indians in my story, but instead I'll just hope that if *you* ever write historical fiction, you'll remember that nineteenth century England included people of colour at *every* level of society.

There is, of course, no such jewel as the Noor-Jahan. Its name is a tribute to the chief wife of the Mughal emperor Jahangir: a remarkable Persian noblewoman who, for more than a decade, virtually ruled the Mughal empire from the zenana. The history of my fictional jewel is more or less stolen from that of the Koh-I-Noor; you can read this remarkable story in *Koh-I-Noor: The Story of the World's Most Infamous Diamond*, by William Dalrymple and Anita Anand. I've also taken liberties with the history of Bihar. As far as I can tell, Bihar didn't have its own Nawab; it was ruled by the Nawab of Bengal until 1793, when Robert Clive, acting on behalf of the British East India Company, abolished local rule—a whole century before the events of this story. The Doctrine of Lapse, however, was a very real instrument used by the East India Company in the mid-nineteenth century to annex more than thirty Indian princely states.

The Halayudha Sutras are real. They're a tenth century commentary upon an earlier work by the ancient Indian poet and mathematician Pingala. In discussing poetic metre, Pingala described the world's first binary numeral system, is credited with the first known use of zero, and also referred to Fibonacci numbers. To all this, Halayudha added a description of Pascal's triangle, seven centuries or so before Pascal. (Please don't quiz me on any of this. I had most of it off Wikipedia, and I am *very, very bad* at maths.)

As always, I am grateful from the bottom of my heart to my wonderful beta and sensitivity readers: Christina Baehr, W.R. Gingell, and Sahrish Nadim. I also want to thank my fellow gaslamp fantasy author Jacquelyn Benson for sending me all her maps of the British Museum, together with detailed instructions on how to break in. It is entirely thanks to Jackie that I found out about the "Skeleton Room" in the Museum's basement, with what irresponsible results, the reader knows!

Suzannah Rowntree
February 2023

About the Author

Suzannah Rowntree lives in a big house in rural Australia with her awesome parents and siblings, drinking fancy tea and writing historical fantasy fiction that blends real-world history with legend, adventure, and a dash of romance.

You can connect with me on:
🌐 https://suzannahrowntree.site

Subscribe to my newsletter:
✉ https://www.subscribepage.com/srauthor

Also by Suzannah Rowntree

The Miss Sharp's Monsters Series
The Werewolf of Whitechapel
Anarchist on the Orient Express
A Vampire in Bavaria

The Miss Dark's Apparitions Series
Tall & Dark
Dark Clouds
Dark & Stormy

The Watchers of Outremer Series
A Wind from the Wilderness
The Lady of Kingdoms
Children of the Desolate
A Day of Darkness
A Conspiracy of Prophets
The House of Mourning

The Pendragon's Heir Trilogy
The Door to Camelot
The Quest for Carbonek
The Heir of Logres

The Fairy Tale Retold Series
The Rakshasa's Bride
The Prince of Fishes
The Bells of Paradise
Death Be Not Proud

Ten Thousand Thorns
The City Beyond the Glass